HEROES ON QUADS

By E.J. Duck

TRAFFORD

National Library of Canada Cataloguing in Publication

Duck; E. J., 1955-
Heroes on quads / E.J. Duck.

ISBN 1-55395-313-4

I. Title.

PS3604.U344H47 2002   813'.6   C2002-905381-1

TRAFFORD

This book was published *on-demand* in cooperation with Trafford Publishing. On-demand publishing is a unique process and service of making a book available for retail sale to the public taking advantage of on-demand manufacturing and Internet marketing.
On-demand publishing includes promotions, retail sales, manufacturing, order fulfilment, accounting and collecting royalties on behalf of the author.

Suite 6E, 2333 Government St., Victoria, B.C. V8T 4P4, CANADA
Phone   250-383-6864   Toll-free   1-888-232-4444 (Canada & US)
Fax   250-383-6804   E-mail   sales@trafford.com
Web site   www.trafford.com   TRAFFORD PUBLISHING IS A DIVISION OF TRAFFORD HOLDINGS LTD.
Trafford Catalogue #02-1028   www.trafford.com/robots/02-1028.html

10   9   8   7   6   5   4   3   2

Forward

On September 11, 2001, terrorists tried to destroy the American way of life. All they really did is just piss us off. We are a strong country. We have shown in the past we will do anything to preserve our rights and freedom and will not cower down to terrorists that threaten us. In fact, when push comes to shove they picked on wrong people. We will hunt you down and destroy you like the rabid dogs that you are. Freedom though comes with a high price bought and paid for by those before us, those of us now and unfortunately, those after us. However, it is a fight worth fighting and as a veteran, I'm proud of those willing to stand up to protect us—to preserve our freedoms and pursue our dreams. In this book, I hope to show how ingenuity helps accomplish our goals. I'm going to incorporate the bravery of our soldiers with vehicles that up until now have been mostly used for sport, the ATV or as some call them quads or four wheelers. I will try to show how some talented and brave individuals work with the ATVs to fight terrorism across the world. It won't be an easy fight, but things worth fighting for seldom ever are.

I would like to take this time to thank all of those involved in protecting this country. A monumental task confronts them. We owe you so much.

Thank you
Eddy Duck

PART I

Chapter 1

It's Sunday afternoon, it's cloudy cool and a light rain has begun to fall—typical weather for late February in South Texas. General Robert Johnson has just returned home with his family after attending church. His wife Jean, glad that her husband is home for a change, is busy fixing dinner for the family. General Johnson had a lot on his mind. Johnson is in charge of unconventional warfare tactics and special operations. With the war on terrorism in full-blown operations, he was really working hard to stay on top of things. He was just heading to office to catch up on some paperwork. He walked past the den where his two teenage sons were watching sports on TV when he realized he hadn't spent much time lately with his boys, Jason fifteen and Jack thirteen. Therefore, he stopped to watch TV with them. They were watching ATV cross country racing. The boys started in on their father to purchase a couple of sport ATVs for them to ride. He started remembering when he was younger and the fun he had riding dirt bikes back in the hills of eastern Oklahoma. He told the boys that they could begin looking and to get him some prices. Jason, the older boy, said he was partial to the two-stroke Yamaha Banshee and Jack said he liked the four-stroke Honda. As the boys and their father talked and watched the race on TV the general began wondering if these fast nimble ATVs would be an asset to his Special Forces operations.

Soon his wife Jean announced that dinner was ready. The general and his boys joined Jean in the dining room. Talk continued about the ATV race and ATVs in general. The boys' mother seemed receptive to the idea but like all mothers, showed concern for the safety of her sons. Soon the topic of conversation drifted away from ATVs to other subjects. The general just couldn't get it out of mind how these ATVs could aid in the war on terrorism.

The following Monday morning the general is in his office holding his usual Monday morning staff meeting. They go through the usual stuff. Training schedules, they talk about any ongoing operations. Anyway, it was a typical business meeting. After awhile it came to new business. The general opened by saying "I would like to propose a brand new unit within the special operations units and I would like to have input from all of you. I would like to start a small unit that utilizes ATV (all terrain vehicles) in their operations. I know you are asking yourselves why do we need ATVs. As you know, we are in a very different war. Our enemies are well trained and have high tech defense systems that can shoot down our helicopters. Their camps are strategically located with limited conventional vehicle access often heavily defended that leaves bombers, missiles and artillery. Well too often, these camps are located in or near areas with innocent civilian populations. That leaves too often assaults by troops on foot. These are slow operations affording the bad people time to escape. What ATVs give us is speed, mobility and versatility. They would allow us a way of attacking from several locations closing exit avenues and allow our soldiers to carry extra arms and fire power to the battles. I know we currently use motorcycles in limited operations but they aren't as stable as ATVs and can't carry the firepower that an ATV can carry. I also know that these ATVs could not and would not be the vehicle of choice in all or even in most operations, but I feel there is a need for ATVs on a limited basis. That's why I propose we create a small but very specialized unit that is adequately trained in specially equipped ATVs. I propose we have very high tech ATVs developed and built for us and then train men to operate these machines proficiently. This would give us another layer in our armor to protect us from terrorism, allowing us to stop potential attacks before they can bring it to our cities." The general looked around the room and he could tell by the way he presented the idea he had removed many doubts. He knew he would have to have the full support of his men to make this work. He ended his speech by opening up to the floor any questions or comments. Colonel Don Hill was the first to speak up. "Sir, exactly how big a force are we talking about here and what would be the prequalification?" The general told him that he wanted an all-volunteer force comprised solely of special operations trained men. Colonel Hill then asked just one more question. "Where do we get qualified people to train our men?" The answer the general gave left some doubt in Colonel Hill's mind as to success of the project. The general told him they would solicit volunteers from the civilians. They would recruit Professional ATV racers. He explained that he had gotten the idea for the ATV unit after watching ATV races on TV with his sons. The general then asked if Colonel Hill had any more questions. Colonel Hill spoke up and said "No sir." The general knew Colonel Hill had many questions for him but knew the colonel would hold those questions for a later time. The general then asked if there were any more questions. Lieutenant Colonel Mike Purcell spoke up. "Sir, what kind of ATV are we talking about here? You know, we already use ATVs on a limited basis in Bosnia." "Good question" said the general. "The ATVs I have in mind are high speed and highly manoeuvrable machines specially built to withstand rugged terrain but yet carry maximum fire power to the enemy." The general then asked if there were any more questions. The room was silent. He then asked if the there was any new business left that needed to be discussed. Again, the room was silent. The general then called the meeting to a close. He asked that Colonel Hill and Lieutenant Colonel Purcell to stay behind. The rest of the staff officers were excused. The three men sat back down but before anything was said, the general's aid, Staff Sergeant Chuck King came in with a pot of fresh coffee and three cups. He asked the general if he needed anything else. The general told him no and for him to hold all calls. Staff Sergeant King said "Yes sir," saluted and left the room.

General Johnson started by saying to his two staff officers, "Don, Mike, I need your help. I really want to see this project work. With your support it will work. I have known you two a long time. I have seen the work you have done and I know you can do it. What do you say; will you work on this project for me?" Both, without hesitation said, "Yes sir." Colonel Hill asked, "What do you want from us?" "Well" said the general, "I want you Don to get out the word that we are forming this unit and ask for volunteers." "That's easy enough" said Colonel Hill. The general continued "Oh, that's not all; I also want you to get me some good instructors. I do not care where you get them but I suggest you try getting pro racers. I know that might not be easy. Offer to work them on their race schedules. Get them under contract. I know you will know the right things to say and do to get these men. I also want you to take charge of this outfit. You will take care of housing, training facilities and schedules. You know all the logistics involved in running a unit. You will report directly to me any problems and progress you are making. Will that work for you Don?" "Yes sir" said Don. "I appreciate the opportunity. I will make it work and when we are through, we will be the envy of all the units. Colonel Hill asked the general about the size of the unit. The general said he would like to start out small. Platoon size and they would go from there. He left to the colonel's discretion how many instructors they would need. He said he wanted to start small as a test and because the ATVs he wanted would have to be specially built and that there may need to be changes made to the ATVs to get what they needed. The general told him that he could get funding for a small unit no problem. After that, he would have to go up the chain. This first unit would make or break the entire concept. He said "I would like to have this unit combat ready within four months, so you've got your work cut out for you. With threats of terrorism on the rise we don't have time as a luxury." The colonel said he would get right on it. The general then said to Lieutenant Colonel Purcell "Mike that brings me to you. I'm putting you in charge of the supply end. I need you and your staff to come up with a workable design on the ATVs. We need well-built machines capable of carrying men and equipment through very rough terrain. I would like to see two basic models—one with light armament, very fast and highly mobile and a little bigger design able to carry a heavier load but not so large as to hinder operations. The larger bikes would be used for supplies and support of the smaller bikes mainly used as assault vehicles. All of these bikes need to be rugged and able to sustain hits from small arms. Mike, I've seen your work on other vehicles and you have had many proven designs. I'm confident that you will be able to work with manufactured basic designs and improve on them. I suggest you visit with established ATV manufacturers to see who can accommodate our needs. I don't need to remind you speed is of the essence. I would like to have our men training on these new machines in ninety days or less. That's why we need to go with the basic designs and not start from scratch. Maybe in the future we can improve and modify the ATVs to fit us better. Also Mike, I need you to get us some ATVs to train on, preferably something close as possible to the combat versions." "Lieutenant Colonel Purcell said with a positive attitude "we'll be ready sir. We'll get right on it." The general told both men again to keep him informed and expected weekly progress reports. He also told them they were relieved of all other duties. He said "If you need anything, get with me and let's make this happen."

Both men stood to attention, saluted the general and left, eager to begin their new assignments.

Immediately Staff Sergeant King came in, saluted and gave the general a handful of messages. He could tell from the messages that the war on terrorism was really heating up. He told Staff Sergeant King to get him on a flight to DC and to grab his ditty bag; he would probably be gone a few days. Staff Sergeant King said "Already done sir. The car's waiting out front and your wife is coming with you so she can visit your sister Sandy." "Great" said the general. "Let's go." Out the door they went.

CHAPTER 2

Colonel Hill's task with recruiting instructors for the special operations team is sitting at his computer researching racers and race locations. He has compiled a list of fifteen to twenty riders that are nationally rated riders. These riders are mostly corporate sponsored riders that race cross-country and motocross. Their ages range from twenty to thirty years old. He turns the list over to the FBI for background checks. He soon discovers that he must himself go visit these young men at the racetrack and decide for himself if they would be the kind of men to perform the task that lay ahead of them. His computer shows him that there is a national motocross race in nearby Dallas that weekend. He also notices a cross-country race near Ardmore, Oklahoma that same weekend and while there were no nationally rated riders at that race, it would give him a look at what the riders face in these races.

Friday morning Colonel Hill his aid, captain Mike Davis and Staff Sergeant Larry Ketcher load up and head to Dallas for the first visit to the potential instructors for his team.

That afternoon the three men dressed in civilian clothes start talking to several young men. Colonel Hill finds talking to these people a very pleasant experience. While some showed signs of cocky attitudes similar to that of fighter pilots, most are genuinely down to earth people doing what they like to do, which is ride to compete. They talked about their machines like they were their girlfriends, but when they ride them it's like the two of them are Siamese twins joined together at birth. Colonel Hill concentrates his efforts on the single guys. He knows if he picks married riders with kids things could get very complicated. The pit area where all the riders and machines are is a beehive of activity. Riders and crew are busy making adjustments to their ATVs. These are not stock machines. They are high performance, high maintenance machines and are set up special for the kind of racing they do. One young man that impressed the colonel was Johnny Hale, about twenty years old, very easy going, polite and very knowledgeable about ATVs. While the colonel met and talked with many fine individuals, Johnny was placed on the list of possibilities. Colonel Hill told Captain Davis to ask Johnny to join them for dinner after the races. Johnny agreed. Well the three soldiers watched the races and they were exciting. Johnny took second in the heat race only to break a tie rod in the final after being tangled up with another rider. After the races, Johnny and his father met with Colonel Hill and the other two soldiers in a steakhouse near the track. Colonel Hill started by telling Johnny what General Johnson's plan of forming a Special Forces unit utilizing ATVs. "What we need from you, Johnny and others like you, is to train our troops to ride." Johnny showed interest in the plan and asked the colonel to continue. "Well" said the colonel, "we will pay you contract wages, supply you with housing and food. We also will allow you time to do your racing." All of this convinced Johnny to do it. With his father's blessings, Johnny agreed. He also gave Colonel Hill the names of a couple of others that may be willing to help. Colonel Hill told Johnny that they would contact him soon. Johnny asked where the training would be conducted. Colonel Hill told him the majority of the training at Fort Hood, Texas and possibly some at Fort Irwin, California. The men finished their meal and said goodbye. The three soldiers spent the night at a local motel.

Early the next morning they traveled to nearby Ardmore, Oklahoma. There a cross-country race was taking place near Lake Murray just outside of Ardmore. OCCRA, Oklahoma Cross Country Racing Association, was kicking off their race season. Colonel Hill was surprised to see hundreds of people gathered to race and watch. Entire families get involved in the racing. It was a well-organized event. The colonel and his men strolled through camp and talked to many real nice people. There were a lot of motorcycles and surprising number of ATVs entered to race. The men were impressed with the ATV riders. They were a close-knit group helping each other and having a good time. There were all kinds of ATVs from sport quads to utility quads as they called them. There was also a large variety of riders, from teenagers to men in their fifties. There's fathers and sons, brothers, cousins, even a pair of brother and sister. Wives and kids were also on hand. Colonel Hill concentrated on the expert class quad riders. For the most part these riders have no sponsors but they have managed to get the most out of their quads. These guys will spend hundreds even thousands of dollars to win on a good day a hundred dollars—often much less. These guys are true competitors. However, if one of them needs a part or a tire they will gladly help them out along with lots of free advice. Colonel Hill really didn't expect to find anyone there qualified to be an instructor. He came to check out the kind of terrain these guys ride over, which, by the way, was extremely challenging. These guys were flying over ruts through creeks, up and down steep hills, bumpy straights, rock logs, just about anything you can imagine. There was one individual that caught the colonel's attention—the winner of that day's event—Bobby Duck. He is twenty-one years old, single, tall, six foot four inches, slim, with a winning smile at all times. He was very friendly and knowledgeable about quads. He told the colonel that he did all kinds of quad racing, cross-country, motocross and flat track. Colonel Hill decided to ask Bobby to join his team. Bobby said he would be glad to help out. He told Colonel Hill his father and sister had both served in the Army during Desert Storm in 1991. He was concerned about school. He was learning to be an airline mechanic. Colonel Hill told him he would make sure the school would hold a slot open for Bobby when he returned. Bobby talked with his father, who also was a racer. His father told him to go for it and said he would help him any way he could. Well, Bobby joined the team. The colonel said he would be in touch.

The colonel and his men returned to Fort Hood. During the next few days, the colonel spent his time on the phone talking to some other possible instructors. His list lengthened after picking up a couple of west coast riders, one from Michigan and one from Louisiana. He convinced these guys to fly to Texas for interviews.

All four men arrived at Kileen, Texas on Wednesday afternoon. Captain Davis and Staff Sergeant Ketcher met the men and took them to Colonel Hill's office. Introductions were made. First was Buddy Bishop from Salem, Oregon, a twenty-three year old farmer, average height and build. He did a lot of riding in motocross, cross-country and beach racing. Then, there was twenty-six year old Chad Duncan from Eureka, California. He was a large

14

framed man and stood about six foot two inches, nothing like the other thinner riders. The third man was Chad Hubanks from Saqinan, Michigan. A twenty-one year old with medium build, about five feet eleven inches. He rides cross-country and motocross, not only on quads but he also races snowmobiles. The fourth man was a Cajun from Shreveport, Louisiana. His name is Harvey Light, a thin, wiry man and the oldest of the bunch at twenty-nine years old, an aircraft mechanic by trade, but his passion is racing and he loves getting muddy. He races motocross on a sport quad and mud bogging on utility quad. All four men were single but Harvey had been married and has two kids. Colonel Hill, having not seen these guys ride, had requested the four men to bring videos in of them riding and racing. He asked Captain Davis to take the men on a tour of the facilities while he viewed the videos. The captain first took the men to the training area. Engineers were busy designing and building a track. During training, they would utilize the track for initial training. They would also use thousands of acres of natural terrain to fine tune skills. After they viewed the training facility, they were taken to the BOQ (Basic Officers Quarters). The rooms were nice. Only one problem, the men would have to double-up. After the tour, they all met with Colonel Hill in one of the mess halls they would be using. Colonel Hill told all four men he was impressed with their skills and their attitudes toward helping to fight terrorism. He had contracts for all of them to sign and issued orders for them to report in thirty days. They all shook hands, and then Captain Davis took them back to the airport in Kileen. Colonel Hill felt good about his team of instructors so far, but he still had his eye on a couple guys from Kentucky.

The next morning found the colonel, Captain Davis and Staff Sergeant Ketcher airport bound for Nashville, Tennessee. After arriving in Nashville, they rented a car and drove to Hurricane Mills, Tennessee, home of Loretta Lynn's Dude Ranch and the site of a GNCC race (Grand National Cross Country). They got a room at a nearby motel. The next day they drove over to the race area. What they found totally shocked them. They found a very well organized event. GNCC is AMA sanctioned. That was almost expected, but what surprised them was the sheer numbers of quad riders. There were literally hundreds of them, five hundred fifty-two to be exact. It was an awe-inspiring sight, so many people located in this beautiful but rugged ranch in Central Tennessee. There was a large pro rider class and almost all of them were corporate sponsored. He thought it might be hard to get some of these guys away from this, but was pleasantly surprised by the positive attitude of a couple of young men. Will Valance and Mick Smalley, two of the best riders in the country, were approached by Colonel Hill and his team. These guys were very friendly and down to earth. The colonel was impressed by the physical condition of these young men. Valance, short, about five foot seven inches, was like a bulldog. Smalley, about six foot one inch, was also well conditioned. There was not an ounce of excess fat on these guys. Colonel Hill introduced himself and his men to the two young riders. He continued by telling them of his mission to find qualified instructors and how they would be doing a great service to their country if they would join his team. He starts to give specifics when the two interrupted him. Valance said "Sir, if you need us, just tell us where to report. We can work out the details." Colonel Hill was floored. He never expected it would be so easy to recruit instructors, especially quality instructors. He told the two men he would leave a contract with them and would pick it up the next morning before the race. They said "fine" and excused themselves saying, "We need to walk this track and check it out." Colonel Hill said "OK" and the two men bounded off. The three soldiers spent the rest of the day and into the night talking to people in the camp. People were relaxed having a good time. Kids were down at the creek throwing rocks and some were fishing and others were swimming. Toward evening grills, started firing up and campfires came to life. As the soldiers started for their car to go back to the motel, Captain Davis turned to Colonel Hill and said "Sir, this is what it's all about" and left it at that. Colonel Hill didn't respond but thought to himself, he's right, God Bless America. It's Saturday morning. The soldiers go back to the track. They go directly to Valance and Smalley. The two men are busy preparing for the race. They stop and greet the soldiers. They shoot the bull for a few minutes and hand to the colonel the contracts, all signed and everything. They invite the soldiers to stick around for the race. The men said they wouldn't miss it. There were so many riders they had two races. Each one had over two hundred fifty riders in them. Before each race, they had a prayer and then sang the National Anthem. At the end of the Anthem, all the riders started up their quads. It was an awesome sight.

Valance and Smalley raced the second race. These guys were good. It was like the quads were part of their bodies. They both finished first and second. After the celebration, the colonel went up and congratulated both men and told them he would see them in about a month. The colonel and his men headed back to Nashville and then on to Fort Hood. They felt very satisfied with the instructors they had gotten.

It's Monday morning. The colonel was in his office. The word of a special ATV unit had already been spread around in the Special Forces units. Staff Sergeant Ketcher walks in the office and hands Colonel Hill a list of volunteers. There were forty-five names on the list, including officers and enlisted personnel. His plan was to give all applicants a chance and then form a review board with himself and the instructors to pick out the best of them. Limiting applicants to only Special Forces, he knew these men were already highly trained for special operation and that alone would allow them to concentrate more on their riding skills. He began issuing transfer orders to all the applicants. He spent the next month preparing the facilities for the training and making workable schedules.

CHAPTER 3

Lieutenant Colonel Purcell, being a design engineer and Special Forces soldier, had a pretty good idea what General Johnson wanted for an ATV force. He knew time wasn't on his side so he knew he would have to depend on the ATV manufacturers to supply him with the specifications on their existing ATVs so that he could determine if they could handle any modifications that they would need to do to them to make them a combat assist vehicle. First of all, he thought modifying two different ATVs would involve a lot of footwork. Instead of bringing in a bunch of men and have them traipsing all over the country, he would enlist the help of one man in contacting and soliciting help of the manufacturers. That man would be Major Gene Dobson, an engineer himself and a highly motivated individual. The two would split up the responsibilities. The Colonel would concentrate his efforts on the support ATV because it would need the most modifications. He would have Major Dobson concentrate and focus on the speedy attack ATVs. They would both have teams ready to do modifications to the ATVs and would be aided by computers and other aids at their disposal. Lieutenant Colonel Purcell got on the phone to Major Dobson and asked him to join him for lunch and that he had a special project for him to work. He said he would give him the details over lunch. He set a time and place and hung up.

The two men met at the Burger King located on base. Not the most formal of settings for something important, but both were busy men and fast food lunches were the norm for them. Lieutenant Colonel Purcell asked the major what he was working on. The major told him he had just finished a mod to Hummers attached to the Special Forces brigade. He didn't offer any details and none were asked for. He then asked if he would be interested in joining him on the ATV project for General Johnson. He said sure, what could he do? Lieutenant Colonel Purcell broke down the project for him and what he wanted him to do. The major agreed to join the team and said he would get right on it. He also told Lieutenant Colonel Purcell that he had some experience with ATVs. He said his son was an amateur moto-cross racer and that he helped him with repairs. Lieutenant Colonel Purcell saw this as a major plus. He suggested that he call and set up appointments within the next few days. "Fine" said Lieutenant Colonel Purcell, "the sooner the better. We are on a tight timetable here." The men finished their lunch and talked about the major's sons' racing adventures.

The rest of the week was spent setting appointments with design engineers for the ATV's manufacturers. In addition, Lieutenant Colonel Purcell developed a list of modifications essential to the machines and some they would like to do: twin 9mm machine guns (bolt fed three hundred round magazines, remote electric solenoid operated swivel mounted for a wider field of fire), two mini rocket launchers on the front and two on rear, Kevlar reinforced tires, Kevlar body parts instead of plastic, a dual muffler system (one stealth mode allows quads to run silent and two, a system would utilize maximum horsepower), a quick attach snorkel system that is collapsible for easy storage, and a bigger battery to operate guns and rocket launchers. These modifications would make significant weight changes so different configurations would have to be tried to balance out the machines. Perhaps specially made suspension could make the difference. The larger support bike would also have twin 9mm machine guns and rocket launchers, but also carry extra ammo fuel cells and capable of carrying two people if needed. They also would need the dual exhaust system, but their weight carrying capacity would have to be increased as much as three hundred pounds. That would mean a larger frame, which would make them less maneuverable. They decided these modifications would be a good start and they would make changes as needed.

That following Monday morning Lieutenant Colonel Purcell and Major Dobson headed for the airport. The men had decided to visit all the major manufacturers, give them their specifications and allow the manufacturers to come up with a workable ATV for them. They planned to visit Honda, Yamaha, Suzuki, Polaris, Arctic Cat and a relatively new manufacturer, Cannondale.

They arrived at the Honda USA headquarters and were greeted by a team of design engineers eager to show what they could do. The soldiers laid out the specifications for their ATVs. The Honda engineers felt confident that they could supply them with a superior assault ATV. In fact, they had been working on a new design for an ATV with a bigger motor that could easily handle the extra load of the armaments. They assured the soldiers they would have a design ready within a week and if the Army approved, they could have two dozen ATVs combat ready in sixty days. They said however, the larger support vehicle would be a problem. While Honda has a large frame bike, they were utility models and might not be what the Army was looking for. They said, given enough time, they felt they could develop a workable model. They suggested we try Yamaha or Polaris. The soldiers said that they appreciated their candor and honesty and looked forward to seeing their design. They also told us that they could have a similar model that could be used for training in thirty days or less. That was a definite positive.

After leaving the Honda factory, Lieutenant Colonel Purcell headed for the Polaris headquarters and sent Major Dobson to the Cannondale plant.

Early the next morning, Major Dobson arrived at the Cannondale plant to meet with design and manufacturing officials. He laid out the Army's plans. Unfortunately, Cannondale, which makes a quality vehicle, said they could not design and produce the quads the military wanted in the time allotted. They did say however, that they could build a superior product and would like the opportunity in the future to present their designs. They also said they would build a prototype for the Army to test. Major Dobson agreed and left for his next stop.

Meanwhile, Lieutenant Colonel Purcell was visiting the Polaris plant. He was impressed with the stability of Polaris quads. They have a good foundation under them—a heavy frame and suspension system. He was shown a new developmental model quad that had increased horsepower. The engineers showed Lieutenant Colonel Purcell, through the use of computers, how they could incorporate the Army's modifications to the newly designed quad. Lieutenant Colonel Purcell was very impressed. In addition, they could have the finished product ready in the time schedule that was required by the Army. Lieutenant Colonel Purcell checked out the manufacturer's facilities. He liked what he saw. They had high standards in workmanship and the workers took great pride in their work. Later he headed for a motel near the airport and got in touch with Major Dobson to see how he fared at the Cannondale plant. The major reported to him, while impressed with Cannondale's product line, he said they couldn't meet the deadline. Lieutenant Colonel Purcell told him about the meeting at Polaris and how well it went. The men agreed to meet the next day at the Yamaha headquarters.

The next morning the men got on planes and headed for Yamaha. Their planes landed within minutes of each other so they met at the airport and drove to the plant together. Once at the plant they were met by engineers and other officials. They tried to sell the Army on their existing product line and were reluctant to make any major changes to their product. They really pushed the big-motored 660 raptor. While the soldiers liked the horsepower of the raptor, they quickly discovered the overall design wouldn't work for them. The raptor, a quality sport bike, wouldn't work because they already seemed top heavy and would have serious problems with the weapons systems required. The soldiers politely listened to the Yamaha officials talk up their product line and its popularity. It was a basic public relations promotion, not what the soldiers wanted to hear. The men left and checked into a motel and later met for dinner. Lieutenant Colonel Purcell told the major that he had basically decided to go with the Honda as an attack vehicle and the Polaris as a support vehicle. He knew there were other quality manufacturers out there but he was so impressed with the two he had chosen, he decided to contact the remaining manufacturers by phone and if they were interested in the project, he would fax the Army's requirements to them and they could contact him at Fort Hood with their proposals and designs.

The next morning the soldiers headed back to Fort Hood, but not before he contacted both Honda and Polaris to start producing their quads. They both said that they had already started. Lieutenant Colonel Purcell told them that their JAG people would contact them with the contracts.

Back at Fort Hood Lieutenant Colonel Purcell reported to General Johnson. He told him of the progress he had made. General Johnson was pleased with his progress. He told the lieutenant colonel of Colonel Hill's progress on the other end. He told him it looked like everything was running right on schedule. He also said he looked forward to seeing a demonstration of the new quads. Lieutenant Colonel Purcell left the general's office and headed straight to the weapons development lab where he met Major Dobson already hard at work. The team had already erected mock up quads to test the weapons and mountings that would be needed. Within a week they felt that they had a workable solution to the weapons mounts. Of course they would have to be tested by riders on actual quads. He then heard from Honda and they told him that they had come up with a company that would build the Kevlar body parts for the quads. It was Boeing Aerospace. They also said the tires needed would be by ITP and they already had a workable composite wheel. This was good news to Lieutenant Colonel Purcell. He asked the Honda people to contact the Polaris people and asked if they would work together on the project. They agreed and said that Polaris had already contacted them about a small yet powerful battery that would not only power the quads but the electronics involved.

Speaking of electronics, this quad set up was going to use a lot of electronic gear, from the control and fire of the machine guns to the target acquisition for the rockets. Power would be needed for communications, navigation, infrared and night vision. All of these systems would be incorporated into the helmets. These helmets would be similar to pilots' helmets. The targeting system was state of the art. You can see a target and lock it in and fire on the move. You didn't have to maintain visual on the target. Once locked in G.P.M. readings guide it to the target. All of this is figured out by a small onboard computer and the information is transmitted to the rockets. The only drawback is the rockets' size so it has a limited range of only a thousand meters, which is perfect for the quads.

The uniforms the men would wear would be designed to completely cover the men utilizing a material that would foil attempts to be picked up by infrared. Also flexible body armor would be used. When it came to boots they would use motocross style riding boots but with a twist they would provide maximum protection but would be flexible enough to walk or even run in if need be. There would be three different color combinations—green camo, desert camo, and black—depending on when and where they would be used. Lieutenant Colonel Purcell, along with Major Dobson and the rest of their team, had worked long and hard on the project. Still there would be more work to come. Lieutenant Colonel Purcell got a call from Colonel Hill asking about his progress. He got the information needed and told Lieutenant Colonel Purcell his men and instructor would be arriving on Monday and they would be ready to start hands-on training the following week.

After the call from Colonel Hill, Lieutenant Colonel Purcell called Honda and Polaris to confirm shipping dates of the trainers. Both said that the quads would be shipped in time for the deadline. Lieutenant Colonel Purcell wouldn't relax until men and machines had been placed together.

CHAPTER 4

The following Monday was somewhat hectic. The civilian instructors showed up, all of them towing trailers with their personal quads on them. They weren't their race quads, just their practice quads. Others would take their race quads to the races. The instructors would fly to wherever their race was on Fridays and be back Sunday night. The concept was for the instructors to work Monday through Thursday. They were contracted to instruct for a minimum of eight weeks and possibly as much as twelve weeks, depending on the progress by the soldiers. They all met at Colonel Hill's office. Captain Davis took charge of them. He gave them a quick briefing. He told them the first day would involve billeting, medicals, uniforms and visits to the training site. They were told of the training schedules and also told that when they were teaching they had total control of the class. The captain told them that all the soldiers were special forces trained, they were volunteers and that they ranged in rank from specialist to captain. They would have over forty soldiers to train. The unit would receive its own designator, they would have their own supply and mess facility. Once the training started they would break up into teams. The instructors would specialize in certain areas and the soldiers would rate from instructor to instructor. Instructors would work in pairs. He suggested the paired instructors also billet with each other. He said they would be introduced to the troops at 1700 hours (5:00 p.m.) and initial training to start the next day. They would receive more information at the meeting with Colonel Hill later. The captain said "Now if you grab your personal gear we'll get you over to billeting." The men grabbed their bags and loaded into a couple of vans waiting for them. On the way over to billeting the captain had realized that he had not introduced the instructors to each other. Most already knew of some of the instructors either by racing with them or read about them in one of the magazines. Therefore, when they arrived he introduced the instructors to each other and they chose partners before they went to their rooms. Twenty minutes later they were back in the vans heading over to supply to get their uniforms. They were issued tan desert boots, desert camouflage, fatigue pants and belts, black t-shirts—with the words Special Forces printed in white—, and blue ball caps with red lettering that said instructor on them. They all dressed out and looked sharp.

They then walked a short distance to the mess hall to have lunch. They sure got many looks from the soldiers inside the mess hall. At first they were nervous but soon realized they were looks of admiration.

After a quick lunch of hamburgers, fries and sodas, they loaded into the waiting vans and headed to medical. They received extensive physicals from head to toe. They were examined by several different doctors and were even given psychological examinations. They were all in top shape physically and mentally. They were all well behaved and seemed to be enjoying themselves. They were a light-hearted group of guys cracking jokes the whole time. A couple of hours later they were back in the vans heading to the training site. Some of the guys had already seen the training site but for some it was their first look. The training site had several buildings including a mess hall, headquarters, barracks for the soldiers, a supply building and a very large maintenance and storage facility. The men were very impressed with the maintenance building. It contained state of the art facilities. Top of the line tools, computer terminals, hydraulic work stands, you name it they had it, all neat and well organized. They talked to the mechanics assigned there. Most seemed knowledgeable mechanics and some had been trained pretty well on quads. They told the instructors that a team of factory mechanics would be in to teach them what they needed to know. The instructors offered to assist the mechanics if needed. The mechanics thanked them and appreciated their offer. The instructors viewed the rest of the area and then headed over to the big meeting with Colonel Hill and the troops. While Captain Davis was attending to the needs of the instructors, Staff Sergeant Ketcher was in processing the troops, assigning barracks, handing out schedules, getting the troops fitted for their new uniforms, both fatigue and riding uniforms. By the time for Colonel Hill's meeting everybody had been processed. When the instructors arrived at the meeting they were greeted by Colonel Hill and welcomed. They were asked to sit at a row of tables on a large stage facing the auditorium. He told them he would join them shortly. Captain Davis and the instructors found seats on the stage. They were joined by a few more officers and enlisted men. The room started filling with the trainees and the rest of the support staff, about seventy men altogether. After everyone entered the room Staff Sergeant Ketcher walked in and called the room to attention. Everyone stood to attention as Colonel Hill made his way to the podium. Once there he told the men to take seats. He started by saying "My name is Colonel Don Hill. Welcome to the first ATV special operations training camp. I would like to start out by saying everyone in this room is a volunteer. That means you all want to be here. Our mission is to train and equip you for missions that are suited for ATV. You may have missions where you are the only unit involved or you may be part of a multi unit mission. We have brought in expert riders to train you and we are building special ATVs for you to use as tools to complete your missions, whatever they may be. You will be trained and evaluated by the staff. Some of you may not be suited to this new form of warfare. That doesn't make you less of a soldier. You are all heroes in my book. Simply by being here proves that. Initial training will last four weeks. After that some of you may be reassigned. Failure in this first class won't preclude you from reapplying in the future. As you know, we are at war with terrorists and it is my mission to produce a highly skilled ATV attack unit. It's plain and simple. We want men that can be counted on. The training here will be tough and at any time you want out, if you feel like it's not for you, just tell us. We don't want to waste your time and we don't want you wasting ours. During your first four weeks here you will receive extensive rider training, weapons training and physical training. If you are good enough to make it past the first four weeks, we move to unit training. During this segment of your training you will be given different situations or missions that you complete as a unit—no cowboys or John Waynes. Everything is to be coordinated and every man can feel he can count on the others. This is a brand new form in a way to conduct the business of warfare and it is our hope it proves to be an effective tool against our enemies. I know we have other units that use special tools and vehicles to accomplish missions, so most of you have an idea of what's to be expected from you. Well, enough said about that. You all have your training schedules. These are subject to change. If any changes are made we will do our best to inform you in advance. However, you must realize that this being a brand new unit there may be glitches. Nevertheless, be assured, this is no half ass unit. Everything we do or don't do will be for your benefit. Now I would like to introduce you to the staff. Like I said before, my name is Colonel Hill. I'm in direct charge of this unit. My boss is Brigadier General Robert Johnson. To my left, please stand when I call your name—Lieutenant Colonel Purcell along with Major Dobson. These men are in charge of ATV development. Once you start training on the ATVs they will be coming to you for input that may be needed to improve machine performance. You see, we are so new our machines need training too." The crowd laughs. "Next to Major Dobson is Captain Davis. He will handle day-to-day operation and will be in charge in my absence. He will be assisted by Staff Sergeant Ketcher who is standing in the back of the room. Next is our company First Sergeant Holliman. His major function is to coordinate all activities and the welfare of the men. Next is Staff Sergeant Golihare. He is in charge of supply. Then there is Master Sergeant Duane Hill. No he is not kin to me. He is in charge of weapons and weapons training. Next is Staff Sergeant Tisdale, motor pool. Then there is Master Sergeant Miller, head ATV mechanic. Then down on the end is Staff Sergeant Vaughn, head cook. Now on my right are the instructors. These are contract civilians and are expert ATV riders, who have volunteered to train you men. They all will hold temporary rank of warrant officers so you will address them as sir or mister. First Bobby Duck, then Johnny Hale, Harvey Light, Buddy Bishop, Chad Duncan, Chad Hubanks, Will Valance, and Mick Smalley. Thank you gentlemen" They all sat down. "You trainees will be divided into four squads to maximize training time. At times you will all be together but at other times you will be training separate. Well, that's all I have for you right now. Are there any questions?" A hand came up. "Yes", said Colonel Hill. The man stood to attention. He said "Sir, when will we get our first look at the ATVs?" "Good question" said Colonel Hill and turned to Lieutenant Colonel Purcell who stood and said "The training ATVs will be here in a couple of days and the actual combat ATVs will be here in about a month." "Thank you" said Colonel Hill. "Are there any more questions?" No hands went up. Colonel Hill said "First sergeant." At that First Sergeant Holliman stood to attention and called the room to attention and then dismissed the men. As the room was emptying out he turned to his instructors. He knew they weren't used to the military way of doing things and he wanted to know if they were having any problems. They all seemed okay. They were all eager to get started. Colonel Hill approved of their enthusiasm and said "It's the Army way, hurry and wait." They all laughed but knew what he meant. The meeting broke up and they all headed to the mess hall for dinner. The instructors had worked out among themselves who would team with who. Bobby Duck and Johnny Hale would team together and would specialize in teaching jumping the ATVs. Chad Hubanks and Harvey Light would work with the larger support ATVs. Chad Duncan and Buddy Bishop would concentrate on high-speed turns and Will Valance and Mick Smalley would put it all together in cross-country training.

After dinner they returned to their rooms. Bobby and Johnny decided to go off base and have a beer. Well, the next thing you know all eight instructors were loading into the vans and heading out the gate. One of the staff NCOs had told Buddy about a place not too far from camp that the young men would like. He told him the music was cool, the beer cold and women were hot. So they headed for a place called Pete's Party Palace. They pulled up to this place which was a large barn converted into a club. They could tell by the number of cars that it wasn't a very busy night. They walked in to find a very plush looking set up. It was divided into three sections. On the left was a large room closed off from the rest of the bar that contained several pool tables. Only a handful of people were playing pool. In the middle was a large dance floor flanked on one side by a long bar and a stage on the other side. To the right were several sets of tables and chairs. The music was good but not too loud. The men headed for a couple of empty tables near the dance floor. Soon after sitting down they were approached by a tall waitress with short frosted hair. She said "Hi boys. My name is Charlotte. What can I get you?" Chad Duncan spoke up. "Bring us a couple pitchers of Bud to start with and your phone number." Everybody laughed. Charlotte just smiled and winked, whirled and headed for the bar. The men talked amongst themselves. Bobby and Johnny noticed a couple of good-looking girls standing near the bar. They kept looking over at the men. Soon Charlotte returned with two pitchers of beer and eight frosted mugs. She looked at Chad and said "You want to run a tab or what?" He smiled and said "Or what." Charlotte blushed even though she had heard that line a million times. Then he said they would pay as they go. They exchanged looks and then Johnny spoke up. "Excuse me miss, would you mind getting those two girls at the bar a drink for us?" Charlotte turned to get the drinks. Chad, Bobby and Buddy remained seated. The others got up to play pool.

The girls got their drinks and came over to thank them. They asked them to join them and they did. They started with usual small talk – names (both were named Amanda), Bobby and Buddy introduced themselves. Chad was sitting there but he kept reviewing Charlotte. Soon Bobby, Buddy and the two Amandas were up dancing. Charlotte came by the table. Chad asked her to take a break and join him. She did. She said "You aren't soldiers, who are you?" Chad said "We are professional ATV riders contracted to the Army." She said "I knew it, my ex-husband Jerry thought he was good enough to ride motorcycles professionally, he wasn't." Chad said "Did you say ex-husband?" She said "Yeah, we've been divorced for two years and Jerry has moved on. I do still like watching the races." Chad said "Maybe you could come watch me race sometime." She smiled and said "I'd like that." The other men returned with girls. There was Lori, Brenda, Edna, Debbie and Sherry. They all worked in a clothing store in Big Springs and were on their way home from bingo when they decided to stop for a drink. Charlotte got up and said "beer all around." Oh yeah. Well they drank and danced for a couple of hours then headed back to camp, only to return several times over the next few weeks. Chad and Charlotte became close and she even went with him to one of his races.

The men knew they had a demonstration to put on at nine a.m. the next morning. They thought they could get up about eight, eat breakfast, check out their quads and be good to go. What they didn't know was that Fort Hood got up at five-thirty. It sounded like the world woke up at five-thirty. The men thought that Fort Hood was under attack. Men were running and yelling everywhere. Fort Hood gets an early start.

Physical training or P.T., as they call it, had everyone doing push-ups, sit-ups, running. The ATV riders decided to stay up. Later they would even join the soldiers for P.T. However, for today they just showered and headed for the mess hall.

By 8:00 a.m. they were at the training site. They checked out their quads, filled them with gas and put them on line for the demonstration at 9:00 a.m. They had already worked it out amongst themselves who would do what. At 9:30 everyone was assembled for the demo. Bobby and Johnny were first up. Chad Hubanks was the first speaker. He started out by telling the class, "Gentlemen, the demonstrations today are to show you pretty much what these quads can do. We will demonstrate several different things. These men have hundreds if not thousands of hours riding and racing. We've all had to learn everything the hard way. In no way do we expect you to master these machines in a few weeks. What we hope to do is teach you what to do and what not to do. We have not seen the quads you will be training on. No doubt they will not be as fast and nimble as our race machines. Our first two demonstrations will show you how these machines can be jumped." He then flagged Bobby and Johnny. Bobby came first with a series of high speed low level jumps. He hit the jumps and the landings with smooth precision. The wrong amount of power could result in loss of control and crashes. He made two or three runs then Johnny hit the gas. He made the higher jumps landing perfectly on the down hills. The soldiers watched with great intensity studying their every move. After Johnny was done he and Bobby did a series of tandem jumps, trusting each other to do what was expected. They were good.

Chad got in front of the crowd again. He said "Next we will have Will and Mick. They will demonstrate high speed cornering. "Pay close attention to how they use the quads and themselves." Will and Mick then began their show. Their quads were extremely fast as they both came flying down a straightaway, slowed just a little by using the front brakes forcing the rear in around to make it through the corners then back hard on the gas. They controlled the momentum of the quad by using their bodies to counteract the rollover force. They would move from side to side to keep all four wheels on the ground. After several minutes they pulled off the track. Bobby then got up in front of the men and said "Sometimes you don't want all four wheels on the ground. We will show you a few moves that will help control the quads when they are on two wheels." Harvey and Chad Duncan came down the straightaway with their quads up in the air just riding on the rear wheels. They made it look easy. Nevertheless, it requires a lot of balance and practice. They showed how to turn and control their speed. Next came Chad Hubanks and Buddy. They were both riding on two wheels also. With a twist Chad was on his front and rear left tires and had his right ones up in the air. Buddy was just the opposite with his left tires in the air. Soon the demonstrations were over. All eight men did a high-speed pass then they did some figure eights that were modified where half were going one way and half going the other way. They then parked in front of the soldiers and invited them down to look over their quads. After the soldiers checked out the quads they went into a large room where a big screen television had been set up. They spent the next two hours showing videos of themselves riding and racing. Each instructor took a turn at speaking to the soldiers, explaining in detail some tricks they had learned about riding.

They then broke for lunch. After lunch the soldiers were back in the classroom. They were beginning a basic maintenance course. The quad instructors weren't conducting this class but thought they might be helpful so they attended. They were about a half hour into the class when Captain Davis came in and asked the quad instructors to join Colonel Hill and Lieutenant Colonel Purcell in the maintenance building. When they arrived they found forty brand new quads. There were twenty Honda 500s and twenty Polaris 500s. In addition, there was a team of factory mechanics there to train the Army mechanics. Lieutenant Colonel Purcell came up to the instructors and asked if they would put the new quads through their paces and evaluate their performance. He explained to them that these were just the training quads and did not contain a lot of the equipment the attack quads had. He did, however, say that extra weight was added to the trainers to simulate the weight of the attack quads. The men said sure. Bobby, Johnny, Will and Mick each grabbed a Honda, while Chad, Harvey, Chad and Buddy each grabbed a Polaris. They started slow just getting the feel of the machines, which were quite different from their own bikes. Soon they were putting the new machines through hell. They spent the next four hours solid riding and abusing the new quads. When they finished Colonel Hill, Lieutenant Colonel Purcell and Major Dobson were anxious to hear from them. They all said the new quads were reliable, had good balance despite the added weight. They were concerned about the quads' lack of power in both the whisper mode, which by the way was very quiet, and the full power mode. The factory technicians took offense to the last statement. Bobby spoke up. "We know you build a quality machine, but we feel they can be improved." He said "I know a mechanic back in Tulsa, Oklahoma that is very good at improving performance. We can get him down here and, depending on how much modification you are willing to do, I feel he can greatly improve the performance level of both the Hondas and Polaris." Lieutenant Colonel Purcell asked how to contact this guy. Bobby said "His name is Lonnie Eubanks. He runs a performance shop called 'Sand Trax'." Some of the other instructors said they had heard of him and he had a real good reputation within the quad world. The instructors were thanked for their candor and dismissed the men for the day. He told the instructors that he would like to get the men on quads as soon as possible. A few minutes later Lieutenant Colonel Purcell was on the phone talking to Lonnie Eubanks. He told him who he was and how he got his name. At first Lonnie thought someone was playing a practical joke on him. He said it sounds like something Bobby Duck would pull. Lieutenant Colonel Purcell assured him he was legitimate and would like to come see him about doing some work. Lonnie, still not sure, told him to come on up. He would be glad to talk to him.

Lieutenant Colonel Purcell and Major Dobson were on a plane that night to Tulsa. They took along some pictures of the new quads and specs for Lonnie to look over.

The next morning they were at Sand Trax, a small shop but loaded with quads and high tech equipment. Lonnie then realized they were on the up and up. Lieutenant Colonel Purcell showed Lonnie the pictures and specs. They told him what the quad instructors had said. Lonnie said he was flattered by what Bobby had said about him. He hesitated though. He told the soldiers that he was covered up with work and didn't think there was any way he could break loose and work on the new quads. Lieutenant Colonel Purcell told him about the tools and equipment they had on hand. He also told him that he wouldn't actually have to do the work. They had trained mechanics and factory technicians on hand. He would only have to look at the machines and advise them what to do. He would only be gone a few days. They told him his country needed him and besides, it would boost his stature with the quad world. Lonnie reluctantly agreed to take a look at the quads. He said he wasn't sure what could be done but he had a few ideas that had worked on similar motors. He said he would tie up a few things and be at Fort Hood Thursday night or Friday morning. He told the lieutenant colonel to have his mechanics ready to work all weekend if necessary. Lieutenant Colonel Purcell agreed and thanked Lonnie. Then he and Major Dobson left.

Meanwhile back at Fort Hood the trainers were getting some riders training. The instructors loaded all the trainees on the quads and went on an extended ride across the vast area of Fort Hood, avoiding other areas of the post that were conducting other training.

32

They were out all day riding over all kinds of terrain. They had fuel trucks waiting for them at various locations. When they refueled they ate MREs. By the end of the day the soldiers were worn smooth out. The machines held up better than the men did. These were special forces men used to hard training but there were still a lot of blisters, mostly on hands but some in a few other places. They continued this until Thursday evening. That's when the quad instructors left to go do their racing. All but one of the instructors had races and that was Chad Duncan who decided to stay and spend the weekend with Charlotte, the waitress from the bar.

The trainees spent that Friday in weapons training with Master Sergeant Hill.

Lonnie showed up Friday as promised and he had a Polaris expert with him. His name is Art Brown. Lieutenant Colonel Purcell met with the two men and took them to the maintenance center. They hopped on a couple of quads and took them for a spin. When they finished they agreed with the instructor's evaluation of the lack of power. Lonnie did say he was impressed with the overall performance. He talked with Art and the head Army mechanic, Master Sergeant Miller. They decided they wouldn't tear into the motors but would try a few other things. First they would rejet the carburetors and add a better air intake system. This would take some doing because of the snorkel system on the air boxes. Then they would change out the sprockets. This would allow them to get the most out of the existing horsepower. They wanted to be able to swap motors in a hurry if needed. Lonnie also suggested that they extend the front A arms one inch on each side. Art agreed and replaced the stock shocks with adjustable custom shocks made by Axis. This would allow the riders to adjust the suspension easily for the different load factors and terrain. Reluctantly the factory technicians agreed with Lonnie and Art's modifications. Some of the things had to be ordered and overnighted. This would be rough since it was Friday afternoon. However, the suppliers assured them of overnight delivery on most of the parts if not all of the. Lonnie and the rest of the mechanics spent the rest of the evening making modifications. They also prepared the quads for the other mods. Even though Lonnie's agreement was advisory he couldn't help but get in there with wrenches in his hand. As he and the other mechanics were working he gave them many tips on repairs that make things easy. The next morning the other parts came in. They worked hard to complete the mods on all 40 quads but by Sunday afternoon they finished. Lonnie and Art headed for the airport. At the airport they ran into a few of the instructors coming back. Included was Bobby Duck. They shook hands, traded a few humorous insults and asked how the other was doing. Lonnie told Bobby of the mods they made. Bobby nodded in approval. Lonnie then told Bobby how proud he was that he was helping train the soldiers. He said "Teach 'em good, so they can take out them terrorist sons of bitches." Then Art chimed in "Give 'em hell Bobby, don't hold nothin' back." The two men smiled and shook Bobby's hand again, told him to keep in touch and left. It was just then that Bobby thought he may really be doing some good. His chest puffed up just a little bit more as a feeling of pride came over him. He hooked up with the other riders and headed back to the base. When they arrived they met Chad Duncan just returning from his weekend with Charlotte. He was really falling for her. The rest of the guys noticed this and started giving him some good-hearted ribbing. Chad just went along with it. He couldn't let them get to him.

The next morning they met with Captain Davis for a quick briefing. They all asked him if there was any way they could be included in some of the other training. The captain told them he would check with Colonel Hill but didn't see a problem with it. Especially because it would only enhance their ability to properly train the others.

That day they split into four groups, Alpha, Bravo, Charlie and Delta. They would begin specialized training. Each group would spend two days in certain aspects of the training. This is where they really start evaluating the trainees. Bobby and Johnny worked with the men on their jumping skills. That proved to be very hazardous. There were a lot of tumbles and spills as the men tried to master the art of jumping. They would make notes about the progress and the lack of the soldiers. Chad Hubanks and Harvey worked on rough terrain negotiation, creeks, hills, rocks, etc. Mostly low speed stuff but hard on the machines. Will and Mick worked on high speed maneuvering. They utilized both manmade and natural terrain in their training. Chad Duncan and Buddy worked on stealth manoeuvring. This proved to be the easiest of all because of the special forces training they already had. They would train on quads half a day. The second half would be used to train on weapons, tactics, assault, hand-to-hand, navigation and communication. At the end of the day everyone's butt was dragging. For most of the men the evenings were used to relax and get ready for the next day. Everyone that is except Chad Duncan, who managed to slip away a couple of hours every night to visit Charlotte down at Pete's Party Palace. Well then came Thursday night. Every one of the instructors but Chad left for their races. Chad left Friday morning with Charlotte. She was off on Friday, Saturday and Sunday.

They flew to New Orleans where Chad had been entered into a race along with Harvey and Buddy. Charlotte really liked watching the races. She fit right in. All the racers seemed to like her.

Well, the weekend went well. Many of the pro riders had heard about the special forces quad training. They all expressed their support for Chad, Harvey and Buddy. When they got back to Fort Hood on Sunday, they told their friends about the support. They all said the same thing. Word had gotten out. When Colonel Hill found out that so many people knew about the unit he was concerned. Then he realized he could use the unit for good public relations. Anyway, the next week was a carbon copy of the previous week. The soldiers were getting better. Some of them were getting very good. The instructors were pleased with the progress the soldiers were making. Likewise, the instructors caught on real quick in the other training. A quality team was forming. By the next weekend some of the soldiers showed interest in the races the instructors took off to every week. Will and Mick, having the most influence with the big money sponsors, talked to some of them. One sponsor, ITP, noted for tires and wheels sent airline tickets to the soldiers that wanted to watch a race. Several soldiers took them up on their offers. About a dozen soldiers went to this race. It was a GNCC (Grand National Cross Country race). The soldiers watched the races intently mostly to compare what they learned to the other racers. Overall, they had a good time and enjoyed meeting all the people involved with quad racing.

Back at Fort Hood the following Monday, everyone met for a briefing. They were told by Colonel Hill that this was make or break week. He said there would be competition missions given to each team. Although these would be team competitions and part of the evaluation would be based on team work abilities, individual performance would be the determining factor on if you make the final team or not. He told the men if they did not make the first team he appreciated all of their hard work and dedication. He also said they hoped to start another class in a few months, for them not to give up hope of being on the quad force. After this meeting, he told them they would report to the first sergeant for their operation orders. He said the quad instructors would be monitoring their quad skills and would participate in some of the non-quad competitions. He wished the men good luck and dismissed the men. All the team leaders report to First Sergeant Holliman for their operation orders. The leaders were given sealed orders to be opened in team presence and not to be discussed with other teams. Team Alpha received their orders to draw weapons and quads and to report to quad town, a mock town set up for simulated attacks. Their mission would take them up some very rough and steep terrain. They would take up positions overlooking the town. The support vehicles were positioned to aid the attackers. Five men would approach the town. Two would dismount and search two possible locations for injured soldiers. They then must return to the base and avoid enemy patrols. This would be an all day mission. Bravo team's mission would also involve drawing weapons and quads and attack an armor supported patrol then return. It was a twenty-five mile trip and would have to take great pains not to be detected. Charlie's mission was totally on foot. They would have to use machine pistols on a range then move five miles, repel down a two hundred foot cliff, cross a river, walk another three miles, then before they are done they hit an obstacle course. Delta had to wait until nightfall, draw weapons and quads, and then navigate to several different points along a fifty-mile course. The quad instructors took turns at predetermined observation points. They all took turns at the walking course, which was very demanding. Well, the operations all went well. The rest of the week was spent rotating the four groups into the four different operations. Friday morning the operations had all been completed. By noon the decisions had been made. A list was compiled and without ceremony the names of the first quad special forces group were posted on a bulletin board. On the attack quads were First Lieutenant Mike Randolf, Staff Sergeant Bill Royce, Staff Sergeant James Fomby, Sergeant Mike Shipman, Sergeant Doyle Stockstill, Sergeant Jackie Higgonbotham, Sergeant Keith Wright, Specialist Jeremy Mangrum, Specialist Josh Upton, Specialist Jeremy Taylor, Specialist Aaron Bookout and Private First Class Luke White. A little side story about how Private First Class White got into the unit. He has only been in the Army about nine months. He had heard about the new quad unit being started up. He was supply clerk in a special forces unit but wasn't special forces qualified. He volunteered for quad unit as supply clerk. On day after hours, Captain Davis was taking Johnny Hale out to work on his personal quad. They found Private First Class White riding one of the Honda training quads. He was riding the hell out of it, doing jumps and wheelies. He was a far more advanced rider than any of the other trainees. Captain Davis started to get on to him. Johnny stopped him and suggested if Private First Class White could perform all the other tasks that he be placed on the team. Well the guy worked hard and earned a spot on the team. Now for the guys who were assigned to the support quads. Second Lieutenant John Wooley, Sergeant First Class Brent Kroker, Staff Sergeant Butch Culp, Staff Sergeant Rick Prince, Sergeant James Firey, Sergeant Jeff McFarlane, Specialist First Class Eric Martin, Specialist Scott Baiers, Specialist Phil Hughes, Specialist Cheyenne Allen, Specialist Jamie Wolf and Specialist Matt Dameron. Well, these were the members of the first A.T.V. unit. They would continue to train. The new attack quads would be here sometime during the weekend.

That night none of the instructors had a race. They decided to celebrate a little with a few beers at Pete's Party palace. They showed up about 9:00 p.m. The place was packed. None of them had been to the bar on a weekend. They had a real good band on stage. There were many soldiers there. Even though everyone was in civilian clothes, you could tell by the haircuts. The men found a couple of tables and ordered some beers. Chad Duncan was just arriving because he went by and picked up Charlotte. When they arrived things turned nasty. They had just sat down when a group of highly intoxicated men approached, led by a big tall guy. They were tankers from Third Armor. They sized up the quad riders. Charlotte asked Chad to let her handle them. He reluctantly agreed. Well, the big guy started in on Charlotte by saying "So this is the guy you dumped me for." Charlotte said "Now wait a minute Jim. You and I had some laughs but it's over." The big guy said "The hell it is you bitch, you owe me." Harvey started to get up and one of the drunks poured a beer on him. Well all hell was fixing to break loose when out of nowhere about half dozen men jumped the drunken tankers. The fight was on. They were special forces guys that hadn't made the team. One of them turned to Chad and said "Take her and the rest of the guys and get out of here." He said "The cops will be here soon and you guys don't need to go to jail, the unit needs you." So Charlotte and all the quad riders left. As they were pulling out of the parking lot, several police cars and military police Hummers were pulling in. They knew that the special forces guys would be in big trouble. They dropped Charlotte off and headed back to the base to find Colonel Hill. By the time they found Colonel Hill and told him what had happened, Captain Davis and First Sergeant Holliman were already at the Military Police Station. When Colonel Hill and the quad riders showed up, Captain Davis already had the six soldiers standing at attention. He was doing a lot of yelling. Colonel Hill calmly walked up to Captain Davis, said something to him and Captain Davis turned and walked out with the First Sergeant. Colonel Hill then turned to the six special forces men and said "I appreciate what you men did tonight. You will get your new assignments by Monday morning. That's all." All six saluted Colonel Hill. He returned the salute and said "Now get out of here. I'm going home." Colonel Hill turned to face the quad riders, winked and smiled. Then he left the room. The quad guys thanked the six soldiers. The soldiers told the quad guys that it had been an honor and a privilege to serve with them.

Well, the next morning the quad guys got the word. The new attack quads had arrived. They beat a path to the maintenance building only to find everyone there.

CHAPTER 5

Well, the men couldn't wait until Monday to try out the new attack quads. They were fierce looking machines. They sported Kevlar instead of plastic. They even had Kevlar in the tires. They had Kevlar wheel covers to conceal composite wheels. The color scheme was dark green with black tiger stripes. There was even Kevlar protecting the engines exhaust and drive train. The modifications that Lonnie Eubanks and Art Brown had come up with had already been incorporated into the new quads. They were ready to go. Only the guns and rockets needed to be installed. There were 40 quads, 20 attack bikes and 20 support bikes. In addition, the new uniforms and helmets had arrived. Colonel Hill was there with the base photographer. He had all the riders, including the instructor's dress out in the new gear for a pose for a group picture with the men on the quads. The riders spent the rest of the day helping the mechanics check out the quads. They were told however they would have to wait until Monday to do any riding. The next morning, Sunday, it was raining and they all went to church. After the service they asked Chaplain Jimmy Noe if he would bless their unit. This wasn't an unusual request in the military. Chaplin Noe did as they requested. The instructors spent the rest of the day riding at a nearby river. That is, all but one. Chad Duncan had gone to see his girl Charlotte. Chad and Charlotte had become quite an item. Charlotte knew Chad would be heading home in a few weeks. She tried not to fall for Chad in fear of a broken heart. She couldn't help herself though, and prayed that Chad felt the same about her. Then Chad floored her when he asked if she would like to fly home with him the next weekend to meet his family. Of course she said yes, and saw this as a good sign. She asked Chad if he would teach her to ride A.T.V.s. Chad said sure, that he would have another one of his quads sent down for her to ride. Meanwhile the rest of the quad guys were having a ball down at the river until one of them took a big spill on a blind corner. It was Harvey. He flipped several times knocking him unconscious. That wasn't the worst of it though. He also had a compound fracture and broke a tooth. They took him straight to the hospital. He got his leg in a cast. He was in a lot of pain, not from his leg but from his broken tooth. Being Sunday there was not a dentist on duty. They had to call one in. Soon the dentist showed up. Her name was Captain Dana Ross. She went right to work on Harvey and soon had his pain relieved. Harvey would have to stay in the hospital a couple of days due to the severity of his leg injury and watch for the possibility of a concussion. He knew along with the other riders he was through. He not only would not be an instructor, he may not even be able to race again. The quad guys told Harvey they would see him later. He tried to joke off the incident but inside it was tearing him up. When the men got back to their rooms they told Chad what had happened. He was disappointed that he wasn't there with them. They all understood.

The next morning they showed up at the training center, still a little down about losing their friend. Soon, they began to bounce back because they were getting ready to enter the final phase of training. The soldiers expressed remorse over losing Harvey. Finally one of the soldiers said "There were eight, now there is seven." The rest of the soldiers cheered. That seemed to break the down spell. Soon the soldiers and the seven settled into some serious training. For the next three weeks it was train, train, train. The soldiers were becoming good quad riders and the quad riders were becoming good soldiers.

The first week they spent putting the new quads through their paces. They performed magnificently and they owed it all to the magnificent seven. They took the quads over the roughest terrain Fort Hood could offer. Later toward the end of the week they were in a grove of trees taking a break. Two tanks came up on them and stopped. Out jumped the big guy that had caused all the trouble in the bar. He walked straight up to Chad Duncan. He had no expression on his face. He stuck out his hand to Chad and said "I owe you a big apology. I let the booze do my talking the other night." He said "Charlotte is a sweet girl." Chad said "Thanks, I know Charlotte is sweet and I'm going to ask her to marry me." You could have heard a pin drop. Then the big tanker smiled and said "Good luck" to him. He turned to the other quad instructors and said "I think what you guys are doing is great, thank you." They acknowledged him, he turned, walked back to his tank and left. Then Buddy said "Chad are you serious? You're gonna get hitched?" Chad said "Yes, if she'll have me." They all congratulated him. Then they got on their quads and began riding again.

That night they all headed to their pro races. Chad Duncan took Charlotte with him. Harvey had gone home the day before. He was accompanied by both Colonel Hill and Lieutenant Colonel Purcell. They had expressed to him their deep appreciation for his help. They told him and his family if he needed anything just contact the Colonel at his office. Bobby, Johnny, Buddy and Chad Hubanks went to California for a motocross race. Will and Mick went to Ohio for a cross-country race. Even with all the training they had done they were still rated one and two on the national circuit.

Some of the soldiers were doing a little moonlighting at some of the area races. Three of them entered a race as far away as Anadarko, Oklahoma. It was a highly publicized charity race. The three, Mike Shipman, Brent Kroeker and Jeremy Mangrum met a half dozen Air Force guys. These guys were strictly amateurs but liked to race. They told the soldiers of a big multi-style race that was coming up at the end of the month in Wyoming. They said it was a four-day event, which included all kinds of races. There would be a grueling cross-country event, flat track racing, motocross, hill climb and stuff even for utility quads like mud bogging, log pulling and a cross-country event that involved many creek crossings. They said thousands of people would be there and maybe even some television coverage. The Air Force guys challenged the soldiers. The soldiers said that was scheduled for their last week of Phase II training, but that they would talk it over with the superior officers. The Air Force guys said that they hoped they could make it. They asked the Air Force guys where exactly the race was. They said it was at the base of the Big Horn Mountains near a town called Buffalo.

Meanwhile Chad and Charlotte were having a great visit with Chad's family. They were a close-knit bunch that worked construction. The little town that Chad was from was very pretty and the people there were friendly. Charlotte just loved it there. Everything was so green, not anything like the area around Kileen, Texas. They were busy visiting everyone. Chad did have time Saturday night to be alone with Charlotte. That's when he asked her to marry him. Charlotte started crying and said "Yes, of course I'll marry you." They decided they would get married in two weeks at the chapel at Fort Hood. After all, that's where most of Charlotte's friends and family were from, around the Fort Hood area. Chad's folks would fly down for the ceremony.

Chad and Charlotte told Chad's family the news. They were so happy for them. Chad's mother told Charlotte she wasn't worried about the short romance. Chad always had a good head on his shoulders. He was quick to make decisions. She could tell by what he had told her that he had made a good decision. They both cried. Sunday night everyone was back at Fort Hood. The guys couldn't wait to find out what Charlotte said. When they saw Chad they didn't even have to ask. Chad just looked at them and said "Two weeks." They all laughed and congratulated him. The next day they started week two of Phase II training. The three soldiers that had found out about the big race in Wyoming told the instructors. They figured they had more pull with the top brass than they did. They were right. The instructors said that they would have to wait for the right time to bring it up. The week started out good. They spent the first three days doing high-speed assaults on a mock village. They used live ammo in the machine guns and smoke in the rockets. Everything was going well. By Wednesday morning the teams were getting pretty salty in their coordination and communication. They were preparing another coordinated attack when Colonel Hill and Lieutenant Colonel Purcell showed up. They were going to evaluate progress. They were getting a briefing on the upcoming exercise when General Johnson showed up. He had two congressmen with him—Congressman Jack Gregory of Oklahoma and Congressman Monte Hanson of Wyoming. The instructors perked up when they heard Wyoming. The general had told the congressmen about the special unit and they wanted to see it for themselves. They were told they arrived just in time to watch an exercise. The general said "Fine, get to it son." Well, the exercise went off without a hitch. The general and congressmen were very impressed. The soldiers had become very good on the quads. The general asked how close they were to completing Phase II training. Only two and one-half weeks left. Bobby Duck spoke up. "General sir, how would you feel about showing this unit off to the public?" The general asked "Are they ready?" "Well" Bobby said, "I think they are better than most." "What would you suggest?" said the general. Bobby said "There is a monster race and rally in Wyoming during the final week of training. We could take the whole show up there. Show off our attack quads and the men could compete on the trainers." The general turned to the congressmen. "What do you think?" Congressman Hanson said "You know I'm an avid sportsman, I ride A.T.V.s. I think it would be a great idea and I know the recruiters would love to see this." Congressman Gregory said "I think it shows just how far we will go in our fight with terrorists and the American public would love it." The general said to Colonel Hill "Make it happen." The general then asked about the injured instructor. "How's Mr. Light doing?" Colonel Hill told him he should fully recover in a few months. General Johnson then turned to Chad Duncan. "I heard you are getting married, and right here on post." Chad grinned "Yes sir, I would be honored if you could attend." "Wouldn't miss it for the world" then shook his hand and said "Congratulations." Then he said "Well, we've got to go. The congressmen want to see what else we are doing." He spoke up to men gathered around "You men are doing a hell of a job. You should be proud of yourselves. I know I'm proud of you." Then General Johnson, the congressmen and their driver, Staff Sergeant King loaded up in a Hummer and left. Colonel Hill turned to Captain Davis and said "Well, I guess you better start rounding up some tractors and trailers. Oh by the way, find me a map. I want to know where Buffalo, Wyoming is." Colonel Hill spoke to the men "You men know this puts a kink in our training schedule. I hope you're ready to pick up the pace to complete training a week early." The men cheered. Colonel Hill turned to Lieutenant Colonel Purcell and said "We've got some work to do. Let's get at it." They got in Colonel Hill's Hummer and left. The men, tired from the intense training, seemed to find another gear and pressed on with the training. They pushed on with their daylight assault drills and after dinner came back to begin setting up for night training. By Friday morning their butts were dragging. The instructors had been scheduled to pull out Friday morning leaving Friday to the soldiers. They all cancelled their races that weekend and stayed so they could complete the required training. The men were really working well as a unit.

Charlotte was busy preparing for her wedding the following Friday night. She quit her job at Pete's Party Palace. She arranged for a caterer and she and Chad met with Chaplin Noe after service on Sunday. Everything was coming together.

By Wednesday of the following week the men had completed all the required training and spent the next two days practising with their quads and preparing for the wedding and the trip to Wyoming.

Meanwhile Captain Davis had found four good-looking tractor-trailer rigs to haul the quads and equipment needed for their trip. He also got a couple of buses to haul the riders and mechanics.

By Friday afternoon all of Phase II training was complete. The training facility was empty. Everyone was getting ready for the wedding. The ceremony was scheduled for 7:00 p.m. By 6:30 the chapel was packed. Everyone was there. Colonel Hill, Lieutenant Colonel Purcell, even the general and his family were there. Chad's family, Charlotte's family and friends and of course all the men, wives and girlfriends from the unit were there. It was a beautiful ceremony. Chad and Charlotte seemed so happy together. After the ceremony they all went next door for the reception. There was cake and punch. The owner of Pete's Party Palace sent over a couple of kegs of beer. Everyone danced and had a good time. Colonel Hill even danced a two-step with Charlotte. It seemed like the crowd was thinning out. They didn't notice that all the riders had left. Then as they were preparing to leave they found out why. Instead of a car waiting outside they found a quad. Not just one quad though. They had a thirty quad escort. They were all dressed in their battle gear. Chad and Charlotte loaded on their quad. They were led all over Fort Hood, with Military Police cars in front and rear, lights flashing, quad rumbling. They weren't on whisper mode. People came out to see what all the noise was and cheered as the couple and their escort came by. Finally they ended up at the main gate where a limousine was waiting. Chad told his friends that he would see them in Wyoming in a few days. He told them he had some business to take care of first. They all laughed and cheered as Chad and Charlotte Duncan got into the limousine and drove away. The men rode their quads back to the maintenance building. Someone had placed one of the unused kegs of beer there. They all grabbed a couple of beers. They knew their time together at Fort Hood would soon be over. They told jokes and made a few toasts to each other. After about an hour, they started leaving. They were all tired from the intense training the last few days. The trainers were the last to leave. Things had quieted down and the men were quietly sipping on the beer. It seemed everyone was reflecting on what had been done the last couple of months. Johnny spoke up "I don't know about the rest of you guys but this has been one of the best experiences of my life." They all agreed. He continued "I count you guys as friends for life and if you guys ever need me, I'm there for you." With that Chad said "Oh, let's not get all sentimental. Let's get to bed; we've got a lot of work to do tomorrow." They all laughed and headed back to their rooms. On the short walk back one of them started whistling the Army song. Soon they were all doing the same. They kept it up all the way.

Saturday morning came fast. The quad riders ate breakfast and made their way down to the maintenance building. There were people everywhere. Parked out front were three shiny rigs, three black trucks and three trailers. They were also shiny, black with the words U.S. Army in yellow on the sides. The first two trailers were to be loaded only with quads. The trailers had been rigged to carry the quads double decker. One trailer would carry the fully equipped attack quads. They would be used as a static display. The other trailer contained the training quads and the pro quads the trainers had brought with them. The trainers had replaced the plastics on their quads to more resemble the Army's quads. The remaining trailer was used to carry the rest of the equipment needed. Tools, tents, fuel tables, chairs, cots, you name it. There wasn't going to be an empty square foot of space left on the trailer. It took the men all day to load and pack the trailers. By dark they had everything ready to go.

The trucks would pull out the next morning along with a van full of men to set it all up. The rest of the men would follow on Monday. Sunday was a day of rest except for the men packing up their personal gear to get ready for the trip. They had all gone to church to hear Chaplin Noe's sermon. It was great. He preached about love of your fellow man and what God had planned for them. After church Colonel Hill invited them to an old fashion Texas Bar–B-Que. The food was great and they listened to country music. Afterwards they left and finished packing. The next morning they loaded onto the buses and headed to Wyoming.

CHAPTER 6

The bus trip was uneventful. Most of the men slept, still recovering from the training they had done, others played cards or read. They stopped in Childress, Texas, for lunch. Somebody said this was Colonel Hill's hometown. Their next stop was Fort Carson, Colorado, where they spent the night. Next morning they were on the road again stopping in Windsor, Colorado. Soon they were in Wyoming. They stopped one more time in Casper, Wyoming for dinner. It was right before dark on Tuesday when they arrived at the race site at a ranch just outside of Buffalo, Wyoming. The events weren't scheduled to start until Thursday. There were already thousands of people there. There were small pop up tents to the large corporate tents, motor homes of every shape and size. Some stayed in the cargo trailers they used to haul their ATV's. It had been a nice day in the seventies but with the sun going down and so was the temperature. Not cold but cool, it dropped into the low 50s and colder still in the mountains just to the west of them. After unloading and stowing their gear in one of GP medium tents that had been set up for them. The soldiers and trainers split up. They were just wandering around checking out all the people. There were large displays set up by ATV manufacturers, also those that made and sold accessories. At the grandstands where the flat track and motocross races were to be held, a band had set up and people had drifted over to watch them perform. Some people were even dancing. Everywhere you looked people were relaxing around campfires. Some had their quads up on stands checking them out, tightening bolts, checking tire pressure, oil levels, etc. Bobby and Johnny ran on to a couple of guys they had ridden with back in Oklahoma. They told them that Lonnie Eubanks was there somewhere. They continued to wander around for a while. By 10:00 things had pretty much settled down for the night.

The next morning the men woke up early. By the time the sun came up all the soldiers were in a nearby field doing exercises. There were several curious onlookers watching them do P.T. After about a half hour, the men lined up for a two-mile run. That's when the onlookers gave up. By 0630 they had all showered and were sitting down to breakfast. You could smell breakfast cooking all over the campsite. Bobby, Johnny, Private First Class White and Sergeant Shipman had sat at a table near the edge of the Army's dining area. Two small girls about five years old stood watching them. Bobby offered them some of his breakfast. The girls came right over. They were hungry so Bobby got them both a full plate. The men talked with the girls for a while. The girls were from Kansas; their dad was a flat track racer. Soon the girl's mother showed up. She said she had been cooking breakfast when the girls walked off. Bobby told her the girls were fine and they had just had a good Army breakfast. The woman apologized and left with the girls. Bobby turned to Johnny and said, "I want two kids of my own some day." Johnny laughed and said, "You ought to get married first." Bobby said, "Yeah. I guess that would help." All the men laughed. Then they finished their breakfast.

The only event scheduled for that day was what they called a poker run. It really wasn't a race; it was more of a ride, a forty-mile ride that would take most of the day. You could ride it fast or slow, it didn't matter. Right after breakfast the newly weds showed up, Chad and Charlotte. They checked in to see what was happening. They and a few of the soldiers decided to go on the poker run. You go from checkpoint to check point and at each check-point you would receive a card. At the end whoever had the best poker hand won prizes, which were mostly quad related items from helmets to ball caps, tee shirts to gloves and so on. It was just for fun.

Sign-up for the various competitions were starting. Captain Davis and Staff Sergeant Ketcher were taking care of all the sign-ups for the Army that left the soldiers free to practice and check out their quads.

That afternoon Bobby got a big surprise. His mother, Sandy, and father, Eddy, his two sisters, Brandee and Julie, along with Julies's husband, Mike, his grandmother, Betty, and her boyfriend, Harley, showed up to watch Bobby race. His grandmother had a cabin near there in the mountains. They decided to spend a few days there. Bobby was very excited to have his family there and spent as much time with them that he could. He showed them the Army's quads and introduced them to everyone. Colonel Hill and Bobby's dad, Eddy, hit it off real well. They had met once before when the Colonel had recruited Bobby. By early evening his family left for the cabin but said they would be back the next day to watch him race. That evening after dinner the Air Force guys that had told them about the races showed up. They were a cocky bunch. They issued challenges to the soldiers and even bet with them. The soldiers agreed but weren't about to tell them about the pro riders that were with them. It would be like taking candy from a baby.

Not long after the Air Force guys left, guess who showed up? It was Lonnie Eubanks. He had just arrived. He couldn't wait to look at the attack quads and maybe take a little test ride. Several men went with him. After first seeing one, his first word was, "Wow." Johnny said, "That's the fewest words I've ever heard you say." They all laughed. Lonnie then opened up with questions. He asked so many questions the men couldn't keep up with him. When it was all said and done Lonnie was please. He talked with the men way up into the night. Finally realizing how late it was, he excused himself and everyone went to bed.

The next day things would really get started. First thing would be a two-hour cross-country race. Will and Mick were entered in this race long with Lieutenant Randolf, Sergeant Mangrum, Staff Sergeant Fomby, Sergeant Wright, Specialist Bookout and Sergeant Stockstill. This proved to be an extremely tough race. There were hundreds of entries. Vallance and Smalley had entered the pro class, the rest of the men had entered the advanced novice class in the modified division. There were many different classes. Each class would take off in staggered times. However, they would all be out on the track at once. It was a ten-mile loop. The start was a half mile straight away then it was into the woods with steep hill climbs and steep valleys, through creek beds into open fields. There were some tight twists and turns—spots just wide enough for quads to fit through. There were rocks, stumps, sinkholes and natural jumps. They even had to watch out for the deer and pronghorns. As expected, Mike and Will took the lead in the pro class. The rest of the men were doing well, they had good starts. They weren't winning but were close, especially First Lieutenant Randolf. He was running in third, Sergeant Mangrum had moved into sixth, Sergeant

Wright eighth, Sergeant Stockstill ninth, Sergent Bookout thirteenth and Staff Sergeant Fomby fourteenth. There were thirty-five riders in this class. Several had broken down but the military quads were holding up very well.

At the end of the race everyone moved up one spot after the guy in second place bent a tie rod knocking him out of the race. Only one Air Force guy even finished the race and he finished tenth. In the pro class Varlance finished first, followed closely by Smalley, barely separated by a couple of seconds.

Next came the hill climbs. Only two soldiers entered this event, Second Lieutenant Wooley and Sergent First Class Brent Kroker. The hill was very tall and very steep. Many would try, only a few would make it to the top. If you were lucky enough to make it to the top you would be timed. Second Lieutenant Wooley was the first soldier to try. When he made his attempt he choose what he thought was a good line. It wasn't, he was having a hard time and then missed a gear. That ended his attempt. Sergent First Class Kroker made it to the top and finished a respectable sixth. Lonnie Eubanks took top honors in the Hill Climb contest. His quad was specially designed for the event. He was impressed with Special First Class Kroker's attempt.

The next event would be the Log Pull. This was a relatively new event. It was a team event in which pairs hooked onto logs. They would have to drag the longs a predetermined distance in the shortest amount of time. · Several soldiers participated in this event. Sergent Jamie Wolfen and Sergent Matt Dameron, Specialist Cheyenne Allen with Specialist Scott Bairers, Sergeant James Firey with Staff Sergeant Prince and Sergeant McFarlane with Specialist Martin. Six two-man teams all together. Coupled with the powerful quads, the strength and stamina training from the Army made this an ideal event for the soldiers.

They took the top six spots with Sergeant McFarlane and Specialist Martin taking top honors. By that afternoon the preliminary flat track races would start. There were so many entries they had to have a series of heat races that lasted the rest of the day and into the night. Sergeant Higonbotham, Specialist Upton, Chad Duncan, Buddy Bishop and Chad Hubanks managed to finish high enough to get to the quarterfinals the next day. The top brass were happy with the day's results and looked forward to the next day's events. The men that didn't race that day were at all the events of the men that did race, cheering them on. Bobby and his family went with Charlotte to watch all the races. They all had a good time.

The next morning, Friday, would bring on another great day of racing. There would be a special opening ceremony before the races were the Star Spangled Banner would be sung. It normally is every day before a race but this would be special. Vice-President Dick Cheney and Congressman Monte Hanson would be there. We knew it was more than a rumor the Vice President would be there by presence of the Secret Service. The soldiers had been asked to provide a symbolic escort with the attack quads from the helicopter-landing zone to the stage in front of the grandstands. It was a quarter mile trip. Soon the thumping sounds of helicopters could be heard. Several helicopters landed, the Vice President and his entourage loaded into Hummers and headed toward the racetrack stage. The crowd at the races had grown from about ten thousand to over twenty thousand. The race promoter was concerned about there being enough sanitary facilities to handle such a large crowd. The stands were full, the racetrack was full and people were everywhere. Congressman Hanson approached the microphone. "Good morning, I'm Congressman Monte Hanson. On behalf of the great people of Wyoming, I would like to welcome all our visitors. What do you think of our beautiful state?" A loud cheer went up from the crowd. "I hope you are having a good time and I hope you can take the time to see more of it. We think it's one of the best kept secrets in our country." Another cheer came up. "I'm honored to be here today to represent our great state and introduce to you one of our favorite sons. He is a native of this great state and epitomizes the people of Wyoming. So without further comment, a man that really needs no introduction, I'd like to present to you, the Vice President of the United States, Mr. Dick Cheney."

A deafening roar erupted as twenty thousand people cheered their vice president-even the democrats. Most people judge politicians on merit, not by what party they belong to. In fact, most people are turned off by partisanship. They just wished the politicians would realize that.

Mr. Cheney came to the microphone. "Good morning." The crowd cheered again and finally settled down. "I'm proud to be here. I hope everyone is having a good time. This is what America is all about—freedom. Here you are all free, bought and paid for by those who came before us. We are under attack by those who would take our freedom away. I wonder if you would join me in not only saying but believing in the Pledge of Allegiance to our great country." Everyone stood and turned to the flag and when Mr. Cheney started they all joined in saying the Pledge of Allegiance. Afterward the crowd again erupted into a cheer. "Thank you. I also think we should thank the thousands that put their lives on the line to protect our freedom. Like these men here from the Army competing in these races. The quads that they ride here are for fun. But these special quads are designed to look out for our interests. They are just a part of the tools we use to fight our enemies, gentlemen." He looks down at the soldiers, comes to attention, "I salute you." He then throws up his arm to salute the men. The soldiers snap to attention and return the salute. The crowd of twenty thousand goes wild. The clapping, cheers and whistles seem to last for several minutes. Bobby Duck's folks, standing near by, are clapping and tears of pride are flowing down their faces. Mr. Cheney's speech had hit a home run with the crowd. The media had lots of good stuff to put into the nation's papers. Soon Mr. Cheney concluded the speech. "Well, I'd like to conclude by saying I wish you all well. Enjoy America, it's bought and paid for. Thank you." He then steps back from the microphone. But before the crowd totally erupts again, he steps back to the microphone and says, "God Bless America." He steps away again. Another round of cheers comes from the crowd. Then country music star Tobie Keith steps to the microphone and asks the crowd to join him in singing the Star Spangled Banner. They do. At the completion of the National Anthem, the cheers erupt again along with all the quads at the race firing off. It was a moment to remember. The vice president was escorted back to the helicopters but before he boarded he motioned for Colonel Hill to come see him. He told the Colonel, "I wish I could stay and watch the races but something hot is going on and I've got to get back to Washington." He said, "I think what you and your men are doing is great, keep it up." Colonel Hill snapped to attention and saluted the vice president and said, "Thank you sir." The vice president then boarded the helicopter and left.

Because of all the ceremonies and speeches the races would not start until after lunch at 1:00 p.m. The rest of the afternoon would be the flat track races. The soldiers that had made it to the quarterfinals began to prepare for their races. Chad Duncan and Specialist Upton were in the first races. They did very well finishing first and second. That assured them a spot in one of the semifinals. A couple of races later Sergeant Higgenbothom and Buddy Bishop raced. Only Buddy finished high enough to move on. Chad Hubanks raced in the next race. It was a good one until Chad was bumped causing him to spin out. They still had a chance in the TT races. They are like flat track races but with a couple of bumps in the track. Chad Hubanks ended up finished in second place on the TT's.

Late that afternoon came the semi-finals of the flat track. Only Chad Duncan and Specialist Upton made it to the finals. Buddy Bishop had trouble with his tires. This knocked him out. They broke for dinner. Afterwards they had the finals of the flat track and would begin the motocross. It was a tight race with Chad and Josh changing places several times during the race. In the end, Chad claimed the victory. Charlotte was so excited. After the race Chad said to Josh, "You have really gotten good." Specialist Upton said, "I had a great teacher."

Now it was time to start the motocross. There were literally hundreds of entries in several different classes, from the little riders on beginner quads to the open pro division. Johnny Hale and Bobby Duck were in that division. The soldiers had entered in the open novice class. This class was right below the pros. These guys had been training hard for the last two months but none of them had raced motocross before. The soldiers were Private First Class White, Sergeant Shipman, Specialist Hughes and Staff Sergeant Royce. The pro class would have four heat races, each rider would race twice. The same was for the open novice class. The biggest class, the beginner class, would have six heat races but the racers would only get one shot at making it to one of the two semifinals. They would strive to complete all the heat races that evening. The semifinals would be the next afternoon and the finals Saturday night. Johnny and Bobby were in different heat races at the start. Both won their first heats. They both spoke about how tough the track was. It had very rough whoops, tight turns and an almost impossible jump. Most of the jumps were OK but one would only work for the most experienced riders. Only two of the soldiers did very good on their first heats. Sergeant Shipman finished fourth in his first heat, Private First Class White got a third in his heat, Staff Sergeant Royce flipped on the whoop section. He got last on his first heat. Specialist Hughes was just plain outrun, he did get seventh out of twelve racers. He would have to do a lot better in his second heat. Finally by 9:00 p.m. the first heat had been run. Staff Sergeant Royce and Specialist Hughes ran together in their second heat. Staff Sergeant Royce got fourth and Specialist Hughes fifth but neither was good enough to make the semifinals the next day. Johnny and Bobby did manage to advance to the semifinals. They also raced their second heat together. Both machines were running good. However, there was stiff competition. Johnny got third, Bobby fifth. With Bobby's first place win in the first heat he did make it to the semifinals. All the soldiers were pulling for them. By the time the races had finished that night it was 1:00 a.m. The temperature had dropped into the upper forties. The cook had put on a big pot of coffee. It was late and they didn't need the caffeine but that hot cup of coffee sure tasted good. The men sat up for another hour reflecting on the day's events. It had been a great day and I guess they just weren't quite ready to let it end. They slowly made their way to their cots. They knew morning would be there too quick.

The next morning, Saturday, it was a crisp morning but soon the sun warmed everything up. Bobby, Johnny, Sergeant Shipman and Private First Class White borrowed a Hummer and drove into the town of Buffalo to meet Bobby's family for breakfast. Colonel Hill and Captain Davis soon joined them.

They had a good time. Colonel Hill talked with Bobby's mother, Sandy. He told her Bobby and the other instructors were what made his project work. She should be very proud of her son. She was. After breakfast they all headed back to the racetrack for the day's events.

There were two other events that day besides the motocross that would begin that afternoon. There was a mud bog contest and a creek contest. These events were mostly for utility quads but many sport quads were entered into it also. The mud bog contest was first and it was hilarious to watch. They had a one hundred yard pit filled with a marsh like substance. The rules were this: the quads would enter the mud and try to get to the other end in the shortest amount of time. The bottom was soft and it had drop offs in it. Several of the soldiers entered this event and a couple of the pro's. Mud was slung everywhere. Not many people made it all the way through, mostly the four-wheel drive utilities. Only three sport bikes made it. Only one soldier made it and that was Sergeant First Class Kroker. At least we think it was him. He had so much mud caked on him we really couldn't tell who it was. Everyone had a good time though except the guys who had to wash the quads when they were done. Some people washed their quads by entering in the creek race. It was a half-mile course that went up and down steep creek banks, down the creek through some very deep holes, up and over rocks and a speedy section of shallow water. The name of the creek was Crazy Woman Creek, which was perfectly named because Chad's wife entered the race. Chad had been teaching Charlotte to ride and she wanted to try it. She didn't get far though. She hit a deep hole in the creek and flooded out. Chad had to bail off into the creek to save his bride. Buddy, Bobby and Johnny were standing nearby. They laughed so hard they had tears running from their eyes. Sergeant Stockstill did very well, winning the event, which was timed, followed closely by one of the Air Force guys. Chad got Charlotte dried off and joined Bobby, Buddy and Johnny for lunch. They revisited Charlotte's mishap over and over. They really had a good time at her expense. She took it very well and said she would do it again. Chad and Charlotte were happy together.

After lunch Bobby and Johnny went and double-checked their quads along with Private First Class White and Sergeant Shipman. They too had managed to make it to the semifinals. Staff Sergeant Ketcher came by and wished them good luck. He had worked hard behind the scenes to try to make things go smoothly. He had done a great job. The soldiers recognized this and thanked him. He said, "You guys can thank me by winning this race. I've got money on you guys." They all laughed. Private First Class White, feeling a little cocky said, "It's in the bag." The others knew better. They knew the competition was tough. It was any one's race at this point. Private First Class White tried his best to finish high in his semifinal. He tried a little too hard though. He tried to clear the big jump and nosed in. He and his quad were separated from each other. Nothing was hurt but his pride as they say. Sergeant Shipman however took third in the semifinal assuring him of a spot in the final race. Soon the pro semifinals got started. Johnny easily took first. Bobby looked on. He was thinking to himself, boy, Johnny is good. Bobby raced next. He had the tougher of the two semi races. He was lagging behind in fifth when the two guys in front of him were tangled up in a corner allowing Bobby to get by them. He finished third getting him into the final. He had the last semifinal race. After a short break the finals would begin.

Later as the quads began assembling for the finals it was nearing dark. It seemed the whole camp was there. Bobby and Johnny both seemed nervous. This was the largest crowd Bobby had ever performed in front of. Johnny had been on the pro circuit for quite awhile. They started running all the classes and there were some great races. The crowd was really getting into it. Sergeant Shipman's race came next. He was surprised he had made it this far. The race started and he got a terrible start. His quad died on take off. He tried desperately to make up time. He had managed to pass several people. He was running fifth when all of a sudden three guys in front of him were tangled up. He slowed down to avoid the collision and got a little sideways. The guy behind him was too close to avoid hitting him. They bumped, not hard enough to flip but just enough that it knocked his chain off his rear sprocket. Stick a fork in him, he was done. As he pushed his quad off the track several people standing near him applauded his efforts. He knew he had done his best and there would be other races.

Now came the main event, the pro class final. There were ten quads on the line. The flag went up, the gate dropped and they were off. Bobby and Johnny both got great starts. It was a ten-lap race. Into the first corner, Johnny was running second and Bobby in forth. They were as they say hauling the mail. Their positions stayed the same until the eighth lap. That's when Bobby made a move for third. He grabbed on in the whoop section and passed the guy in third. He closed the gap on Johnny who couldn't get around the guy in first. By the last lap it looked like they were going to end up that way when the unexpected happened. Going into the last turn with Johnny following the leader, Bobby just to his rear on the outside, the guy in front suddenly slowed down. Johnny plowed into the back of him. Bobby managed to swing wide and pass them both. Over the last jump and Bobby was the winner. The crowd went wild at such a dramatic finish. Bobby couldn't believe he had won. Johnny ended up in second after making a great recovery from the mishap on the corner. Bobby later found out that the guy was down shifting for more power and accidentally went into neutral. All the soldiers were waiting for him in the pit area to congratulate him. Johnny pulled up and also congratulated him. He told Bobby he deserved the win. Bobby was asked to go back on the track for a victory lap. He told his parents it was the best race of his life. He then made the victory lap. The crowd loved it. This race would later be recalled by Bobby as a major launch to his race career. They all celebrated way up into the night.

Not just Bobby's win but how the whole team did. The next morning after breakfast everyone started packing up. There was an awards ceremony at 9:00 a.m. All the racers and officers attended the ceremony. Bobby was with his family. He was telling his dad that he would soon be home. The awards ceremony was not even half way through when First Sergeant Holliman came and got the colonel. He left in a hurry. The men didn't think much of it at the time. After the ceremony the men started returning to pack for the ride home. Captain Davis called all the instructors together. He told them that Colonel Hill wanted to see them. He was in the only tent that hadn't been taken down. After all the men had entered the tent, he started talking. "Men," he said. "I know we are at the end of your contracts and you are all looking forward to going home, but I have a favor to ask. We have a possible situation unfolding in Montana along the U.S. Canadian border. We've been ordered to assist. I feel I can't order you to go, but we really need your help." Before he could continue, the men collectively said, "Say no more Colonel. We're there." The colonel smiled and said, "I knew I could count on you. We leave in an hour." Bobby told his parents it may be a few more days—something had come up. He told them he would call when he could. He kissed his mother and left to go pack. Chad made arrangements for Charlotte to return to Texas without him. He told her he would be a few days, for her to prepare to move back to his hometown when he returned.

The soldiers quickly finished packing, loaded on the buses and headed north.

CHAPTER 7

The buses and trucks were headed north. Nobody knew exactly what the mission was all about. The instructors were anxious and tried to conceal it. It wasn't working. The veteran soldiers didn't seem as nervous about the mission as they did about the races they just left. Sergeant First Class Kroker sensed his instructor's nervousness. He sat down to talk to some of them. He tried to reassure them that they would probably just go into the mountains, get some fresh air and go home. They were starting to feel a little better. These guys weren't scared, in fact they didn't scare easily, that's why they ride so well. As they were travelling, Colonel Hill tried to get as much information on the mission that he could. He spent a long time on the radiophone getting specifics. He wanted his men informed on what they may be up against. After about four hours on the road they needed to stop for fuel and food for the men. They stopped at a truck stop. The colonel had the big trucks refuel first. The drivers grabbed a sandwich to go and took off. The rest of the men went into the truck stop for a sit down meal. That is everyone but the colonel, all the officers and the First Sergeant. The colonel was briefing them on the mission and later back on the road the men would receive the same information. The colonel didn't stay to eat. He, Lieutenant Colonel Purcell and Major Dobson, along with Staff Sergeant Ketcher as their driver, pulled out and headed north. That left Captain Davis in command. He and the two lieutenants were the only officers left. Most of the men had the special chicken fried steak and truck stop cobbler. They ate heartedly because they figured they would be eating MRE's the rest of the way. The MRE's would fill you up, but they weren't chicken fried steak with mashed potatoes and gravy. Forty-five minutes later they were back on the buses heading north. Captain Davis got onto the bus with the ATV riders. He said, "OK men, this is the situation. We are going to be a part of a multi unit force. When I say multi unit, I mean not just the Army. However, there are a number of special forces units already in the area. There's Air Force and Air National Guard flying cover. There is also FBI, CIA, Border Patrol, Highway Patrol, County Sheriffs and Canadian Law Enforcement working this mission. As it stands now our job will be observers." "Observing what?" one man said. "Well, if you won't interrupt any more I'll tell you. It seems our own CIA along with and in cooperation with the Canadians has been monitoring several small groups of Islam's not so fine young men, possible terrorists. They felt like they might lead them to something so they didn't move in immediately. Well, sure enough, all of these small groups joined together to make one larger group of about twenty-four men. That's when the intelligence people lost them at a small town just north of the border. Our satellites and high flyers have been unable to locate them. It is believed that they are on foot and heading our way through the mountains. Our helicopters have been searching for them but haven't had any luck. That's where we come in. We are going to split into four-man teams and cover as much ground as we can. They figure our mobility and our use of infrared we might be able to spot these guys and call in the cavalry. As of now our only function is that of a fire ranger more or less. We are due to arrive at the command post in about four hours. You will be issued food, water, maps, coordinators, communication gear, weapons enough to sustain you for two days. We will re-supply as needed probably by air. Oh yes, I almost forgot. Your quads will be fully armed just in case. More than likely they will wait until early morning to send you out but that's subject to change along with everything else. Remember right now all these men are wanted for is illegal immigration. The CIA believes that they are heavily armed and may have bombs or bomb making material with them. Some of these guys are confirmed al-Qaeda so they do mean business. If confronted they won't hesitate to die for Alla and take you with them. Well, I think that about covers it. "Any questions?" Sergeant First Class Kroker spoke up. "Sir, have group assignments been made?" Captain Davis said, "No, they haven't sergeant and I would like you to make out the rosters. Please divide our volunteer instructors up between the most experienced soldiers. I know you men have trained hard and we can count on you but you haven't had any combat experience. We try to cover all the bases in training but true combat experience is all but impossible to beat." The quad trainers understood. "Now if there are no more questions I'll let Sergeant

First Class Kroker make out the duty roster." The captain turned and headed for his seat in front of the bus. Most of the men sat in silence, soaking in what they had just heard. Some openly talked about the mission. Sergeant First Class Kroker set to work making out the duty assignments. A half hour later and it was complete. There would be seven groups of four and one group with three. The three-man group would act as sweepers going where they were needed. They would be alphabetized for ease of communication.

A (Alpha): First Lieutenant Randolf, Sergeant McFarlane, Specialist Martin and Will Vallance.

B (Bravo): Second Lieutenant Wooley, Sergeant Firey, Specialist Bookout, and Mick Smalley.

C (Charlie): Staff Sergeant Fomby, Sergeant Higgonbotham, Specialist Mangrum and Johnny Hale.

D (Delta): Staff Sergeant Culp, Specialist Hughes, Specialist Allen and Bobby Duck.

E (Echo): Staff Sergeant Prince, Sergeant Wright, Specialist Wolfe and Chad Duncan.

F (Fox trot): Staff Sergeant Royce, Sergeant Stockstill, Specialist Dameron and Chad Hubanks.

G (Golf): Sergeant First Class Kroker, Specialist Baires, Private First Class White, and Buddy Bishop.

H (Hotel): Sergeant Shipman, Specialist Taylor, and Specialist Upton (the sweepers).

An hour later the buses turned off the highway. The mountains they were headed for were rough looking. Soon they came upon a large field. Tents had been set up everywhere. It was a beehive of activity. As they were unloading from the bus a Blackhawk helicopter was taking off loaded with heavily armed men.

As they were getting off the bus Staff Sergeant Ketcher handed them photocopies of a rough drawing of the camp. They were instructed to go to a tent nearby and take a seat. First Sergeant Holliman walked in. He had a large map pinned up behind him. After everyone was seated he gave his briefing. He began, "Welcome to Camp Mike. We are just one of several camps located along a two hundred mile stretch of the border." He pointed to the map behind him. "This is our Area of Operation. As you can tell it has very few roads and the terrain is very rough. It's too rough for any conventional vehicles. That's why you are here. You will be patrolling this area. We already have several teams in the area. They have been helicoptered in and have set up observation posts. After this meeting you will be issued your gear. Everyone will familiarize yourself with the maps you'll be provided. Other agencies are operating here. We will do our best to keep you informed of their locations. If you spot the bad guys radio it in. We have three Blackhawks assigned to us. Call it in and we will send in a strike force to take them. After you have eaten and drawn your equipment and weapons you and your quads will be trucked to your disembarkment points at 0230. Each point will have coverage areas. I will tell you our helicopters and planes have been ineffective. They hear our motors and hide, that's where you guys have the edge with your quads in whisper mode. Be prepared for changes in orders as the situation requires.

After a quick meal the men set about the business of preparing for the mission. They dressed out in full camo gear. They drew the necessary equipment needed from a supply tent and checked everything out. Then they checked it again.

The men, after checking all their personal equipment, went over and checked the quads—weapons to motor oil, tire pressure to electronics. By midnight they were completely ready. Captain Davis came by. He said the Brass had decided to wait until daylight to deploy the team. They didn't want them to be victims of friendly fire by the troops already in the field. So everybody kicked back and waited. Some were even able to get a little sleep. The rest of the night was quiet. By 5 a.m. the men were loaded onto the trucks and were fixing to head out to their drop off points. The truck pulled out for the short fifteen-minute ride to the first drop point. A few miles up the old logging road they were following, the trucks came to a sudden halt. The radios were blaring with activity. First Lieutenant Randolf was on the radio with Colonel Hill. Everybody wondered what was going on. When First Lieutenant Randolf got off the radio he ordered the trucks to be unloaded. Everyone gathered around him. He said, "The mission has been changed. The terrorists have been spotted. One of our operations spotted them. Unfortunately the terrorists spotted them too. They are under attack by a split off group so the others can continue. We sent up a Blackhawk with an assault force. They shot it down with a shoulder fired SAM (surface to air missile). They seemed to have several of these. The second Blackhawk had mechanical problems and the third had returned to its base for refuelling. Other helicopters were in the area but it would be an hour before they could get there. By that time the terrorists would have wiped out the operation and the survivors of the crashed Blackhawk. The whole thing was unfolding just ten miles from our location. We are those guys only hope of survival and we needed to cut off the escape of the rest of the terrorists. We will split into two groups. Second Lieutenant Wooley will lead the rescue mission and take out the terrorists attacking them. He will take Charlie, Bravo and Golf with him. The rest of you with me. Let's go," he said, "we will have to figure this thing out as we go. Everyone monitor communications." The men scrambled to their quads, fired them up and headed up a narrow trail toward the action. The terrain was rough but the men were making good time. Sergeant First Class Kroker and Buddy Bishop had taken point. Within fifteen minutes they could hear gunfire. First Lieutenant Randolf contacted the operation and told them that they were coming in. They radioed back the main body had moved down a trail just to our west. havining about a forty-five minute head start. First lieutenant ordered his group to head for the trail. Second Lieutenant Wooley had one-half of his men dismount and the rest to take up positions on a high point overlooking the battle area. The men on foot closed in behind the terrorists. When they were in position they opened fire. They dropped six terrorists on their first volley of fire, the other four remaining terrorists ran right into the men on top of the hill. They finished them off. Ten terrorists down, fourteen to go. Second Lieutenant Wooley contacted the base about the rescue mission's success. They checked on the men from the downed Blackhawk. Miraculously they were still alive but some had life threatening injuries. They needed to be evacuated as soon as possible. Chad and Bobby reached the guys at the operations first. They were surprised to find the guys that had helped them in the bar fight. They were sure glad to see their old instructors. Bobby asked if anyone was hurt. They said, "Yes but nothing too serious." Second Lieutenant Wooley showed up to check on the guys at the operations. He told them help would be here soon. Second Lieutenant Wooley's group stabilized the injured including two terrorists that survived with only superficial wounds. They guarded them but they weren't going anywhere. Second Lieutenant Wooley rounded up his men and remounted their quads to help First Lieutenant Randolf and his men.

Meanwhile First Lieutenant Randolf was hot on the trail of the remaining terrorists. They had gone to whisper mode on their quads to try to keep from warning the terrorists. Even in whisper mode they were gaining ground.

The trail they were following had deep crevices and very high walls. No wonder the choppers couldn't spot them even with the infrared. All they had to do was duck under one of the may outcroppings of rock and they would be invisible. They had planned their route carefully. In the direction they were going was in the same general direction that the soldiers had followed. A brief look at the map confirmed this. First Lieutenant Randolf radioed Second Lieutenant Wooley. He told them to take his men back down the trail they had come up. He said to follow the old logging road up and they may be able to cut them off but they would have to hurry. First Lieutenant Randolf continued to follow the terrorist's trail. He knew they couldn't be too much farther ahead of them. Staff Sergeant Culp was running point, he radioed that he was seeing movement up ahead. First Lieutenant Randolf told him to back off, that they would have to find a better place than this to attack. He stopped and looked on his map again. There was a clearing a quarter mile ahead where the old logging road crossed the trail. They would attack there. He contacted Second Lieutenant Wooley to find out his location. He was too far away to be part of the attack. First Lieutenant Randolf's men would have to do. Staff Sergeant Culp reported in. "Lieutenant, you're not going to believe this. There is a building across this opening. It's hidden by trees and all the terrorists went in there." First Lieutenant Randolf surveyed the situation. He spread his men out to cover the building. He called into Colonel Hill. The colonel told him to sit tight, tow Blackhawks loaded with assault troops were on there way. Their ETA was ten minutes. Second Lieutenant Wooley called in they had reached the old logging road and were working their way to him.

The terrorists had other ideas. They had spotted First Lieutenant Randolf's men and opened fire on them with automatic rifle fire. First Lieutenant Randolf ordered his men to return fire. The twin-mounted machine guns on the quads were making Swiss cheese of the building that was made of tin. Four terrorists tried to break for the woods. Chad Hubanks and Will Valance gave chase. They stopped three with their machine guns and just as the fourth was about to enter the woods they locked onto him and both fired missiles. When the smoke cleared the terrorist was dead. The battle really heated up, bullets were flying everywhere. Then out of the building came two off road vehicles. It seemed like there was bad guy shooting from every window. Private First Class White had the angle the rear and fired a missile at them, flipping the vehicles on impact. The other one got away but not too far. The other team was waiting for them. There was an explosion, then a series of louder explosions. First Lieutenant Randolf called to see what happened. The reply was they had taken the vehicle out with a missile and hit their cache of SAM's, all four terrorists had died. They did manage to capture three terrorists from the first vehicle that Private First Class White had taken out. A couple of minutes later the Blackhawks came in. They were told they weren't needed. They were told by the pilot of one of the Blackhawks that the injured men from the operations and the downed Blackhawk were being airlifted out. Colonel Hill called in he had been monitoring all the conversations on the radio. He told the lieutenant that they would be relieved by a team of CIA and FBI Agents. He asked about casualties. Not one man on the quad force had been injured. Some of them said they needed to change drawers but nobody got hurt. The quad team gave first aid to the captured men and rounded up all their weapons. Soon two more helicopters showed up with the FBI and CIA along with Colonel Hill. The quad team was relived. Colonel Hill walked over to his men shaking his head and smiling. He said to them as a group, "I knew you guys were good, I just wasn't sure how good. Now I know. You men really earned your pay today." He asked if they needed anything. Buddy spoke up. "Yes sir, a hot meal and a shower." They all laughed. The colonel said, "You got it." You men can take the Blackhawks back down to the command post. I'll send someone for your quads." Specialist Upton spoke up. "Sir, if it's all the same to you we would like to take the quads down to the command post." The colonel said, "Of course. Lead 'em out, lieutenant." First Lieutenant Randolf turned to his men and said, "Let's roll, " a term coined on 9-11 by the passengers of ill-fated flight that cost them their lives saving others. The quad team headed down the logging road and back to the command post.

As they rolled back into camp they were greeted with cheers and whistles. It was a heroes' welcome but the men didn't feel anymore like heroes than the rest of the men doing the clapping and cheering. They felt like they were just part of a team. It took everyone to make it happen. There were reporters there and they told them the same thing. The civilian instructors that had taken part were singled out by the reporters. Mick Smalley spoke for the whole group. He said, "We are proud of our Army, it has been both an honor and a privilege to serve with these guys. All America should be proud." The soldiers that were nearby and heard his remarks clapped and cheered them.

After cleaning up and eating the men checked their equipment and began packing to go home. All that remained was debriefing by Colonel Hill. He was in another meeting that seemed to last for hours. Most of the camp had been packed up by the time the colonel came out of the meeting. He called his men into another tent. Instead of a debriefing he was going to give them a briefing on another mission. He started by saying, "Congratulations on impromptu but successful mission here today. You saved many lives by your actions. You have proven yourselves worthy of being called special forces of the United States Army. I know you are all tired and are ready to go home. Unfortunately Uncle Sam needs your help again. It seems that our country is due even another attack. One of the guys you captured was more than willing to talk to us. He said he didn't want to be part of the attacks on the U.S. but was forced to. He told us of a plot to bring in a dirty atomic bomb. There is an Islamic fundamentalist leader that is in the Philippines. He is surrounded by hundreds of his followers, make no mistake· about it. These guys are out to ruin your day. This guy, Abdullah, is the only one that knows where, how and when this bomb is to be brought into the U.S. We must capture him. It won't be easy. He is in the hills on one of the Philippine Islands. There is only one road in and it's heavily defended and even if we got through the defenses there are so many avenues of escape it would be impossible to track him down. Air assault is out of the question. The area is surrounded by radar guarded SAMs. Bombing is out because of the civilian population in the area and like I said, we want to get this guy alive. That's where you guys come in. You can get those quads of yours up those mule trails, hopefully without being detected and grab this guy for us. I need all of you on this, even you civilian types. We really need your expertise on the quads. You have proven yourselves here today. I can't order you to go and if any or all of you want to go home, I'll understand. If you want to go home please leave now before I go on." Nobody left, not even the newlywed Chad Duncan. "Well alright then, thank you. From here you will be bused to Helena. There a C-5 cargo plane will take you and your equipment to Manila. You will receive more information on the plane. I'll be going with you. That's all I have right now." First Sergeant Holliman called the men to attention. The colonel left. Sergeant First Class Kroker said "Let's roll." Roll they did.

CHAPTER 8

The bus ride to Helena was uneventful. Most of the men slept. Some used cell phones to call their families. They told them not to expect them as planned. They said they would call when they could. The families of the professional soldiers understood. They had been through this many times before. Charlotte talked to Chad. She tried to not be overly concerned. The rest of the citizen soldiers called their families. Some had their families contact their race sponsors to cancel races they were supposed to be at. Nobody could say where they were going or what they were doing. They did say they had a successful mission in Montana, which the whole world would find out anyway from the newspapers that covered it.

Once at the airfield in Helena, it took about an hour to unload the trucks and load and secure the quads and equipment onto the C-5 cargo plane. This was the biggest plane the Air Force had to offer. It had been flown in from Tinker Air Force Base in Oklahoma. The men boarded the aircraft. They were met by the flight crew. They couldn't believe it, they were the Air Force guys they had raced and bet with in Wyoming just two days earlier. One of the Air Force guys said "I guess we owe you guys some money from our bets." All the soldiers started laughing. Sergeant First Class Kroker said "You guys were set up. We have seven professional riders with us. We'll call it all square if you get us to the Philippines and back in one piece." The same Air Force guy said "You got it. Just sit back and enjoy the ride."

The guys boarded the plane. They were CIA agents. They were both big men and introduced themselves as agents Gary and Kevin Smith. Colonel Hill thought, yea right, two guys named Smith. The agents were there to brief the colonel and his men. The plane took off and would make one stop in Hawaii for fuel and then on to Manilla. They provided detailed maps of the island they would be going to. They gave them detailed information on enemy size and their defenses. They told them that this would be a joint operation with the Air Force, Navy and Marines. The actual assault and abduction would be the job of Colonel Hill's men. There were back up plans in case the Army failed. The other forces were mainly used for support of the guys on quads. The actual assault plans would be worked out by the colonel and his other officers. After the CIA completed their briefing the soldiers went to work on their assault plan. Three hours later they came up with a plan. They checked and rechecked the plan and then presented it to the men. The plan included the main assault plan and several contingency plans in case something went wrong. Colonel Hill would be in charge of communication and coordination with the other units involved. The plan was for the special forces unit would be taken by sea to a remote area on the backside of the island. The area was rugged and had little or no inhabitants. They would have to travel twenty miles to the village. After about ten miles they would split up into three groups. Second Lieutenant Wooly would take Sergeant Firey, Specialist Dameron, Will Vallance, Mick Smalley and Specialist Bookout with him. Their mission would be to take out the radar station along with the remote controlled sam site. This would enable the helicopters to come in and pick up the captured terrorists leader. First Lieutenant Randolf would lead his attack squad close to the village. The attack squad would include himself, Staff Sergeant Royce, Staff Sergeant Fomby, Sergeant Wright, Specialist Mangrum, Specialist Upton, Specialist Taylor, Private First Class White, Bobby Duck, Johnny Hale, Chad Duncan, Chad Hubanks and Buddy Bishop. Also joining the attack squad would be Sergeant McFarlane who would transport the prisoner. The remaining support quads would take up positions on high ground to cover the attack quads escape from the village. The quad force would take the captured terrorist to a landing zone. If Second Lieutenant Wooly had been successful, a helicopter would land, taking the prisoner and any wounded soldiers. The rest of the quad force would link up there and make their way five miles to a more secure pick up point. There they would be safe behind three companies of Philippine soldiers who would then attack the village in force. The team studied the plan, the maps and the pictures of the village until they all had it down pat. The veteran soldiers acted more nervous about this mission than they did the last. The civilian soldiers noticed this, which made them even more anxious. They all spent the rest of the flight checking and rechecking their equipment and the maps.

After several hours on the plane it finally started their descent into the airfield at Manilla. After they landed two trucks with cargo containers backed up to the plane. They loaded the quads and equipment into them and they took off. After the trucks left four fifteen-passenger vans picked up the soldiers. They took them straight to a Navy ship that was docked. It was still dark and there wasn't much activity going on in the streets between the airstrip and the small Naval shipyard. Once the men and equipment were on board they headed out to sea. They would spend the entire day at sea. An aircraft carrier located nearby would provide the necessary air support. Colonel Hill would soon fly to the aircraft carrier along with all the support staff, which included Lieutenant Colonel Purcell, Captain Davis, First Sergeant Holliman and Staff Sergeant Ketcher. They would coordinate the mission from the carrier. When the mission was over the quad force would be airlifted to the carrier. Most of the men enjoyed the ride the Navy was giving them. Some didn't like it one bit. The Navy fed them and they all were ordered to get some sleep. For the civilian soldiers sleep was hard to come but they all managed to get some rest. While they were resting the Navy loaded their quads onto amphibious assault vehicles. Right before dark the men had reached their destination. The soldiers geared up and loaded onto the assault craft. They would have a forty-five minute ride to the beach. The assault crafts were operated by Marines. There was a small contingency of Marines with them to cover their landing if needed. Bobby Duck got to looking at the driver of the assault craft. He turned to face Bobby. Bobby said "Christopher, is that you?" Christopher said "Bobby? What the hell are you doing here?" Bobby said "Oh, just going for a little ride with these quads." Christopher laughed. Then Bobby said to the rest of the soldiers "Hey guys. I want you to meet someone." They turned their attention toward Bobby. This is a good friend of mine from back in my hometown. This is Christopher Strickland." They all smiled at him. "He and I used to play little league ball together. His mom works with my mom at my mom's consignment store." Buddy Bishop said "Hey Christopher, do you really claim to be Bobby's friend?" The rest of the soldiers laughed. Bobby asked "Christopher, how have you been?" He said "Oh, pretty good. I miss everyone at home." Then he said "You still playing on these quads?"

Bobby said "Yeah, they are even paying me to ride now." Christopher said "I bought me a dirt bike, but haven't been able to ride it much lately." Bobby said "Well, when we get back home we'll go riding." Christopher said "I'd like that. Well, we're almost there, you'd better get ready." Bobby said "Yeah, I guess I'd better." Soon they were on the beach. The men mounted their quads and started unloading. Bobby turned to his friend. "remember we've got a riding date" he said. Christopher waved at Bobby and said "Good luck and be careful." After the soldiers unloaded the Marines pulled back off the beach and back into the ocean.

Meanwhile Colonel Hill, back on the aircraft carrier, had met with the ship's captain, Captain Rick Parker. He had met all the colonel's needs. He told the colonel that all aircraft and men were ready when he was. Captain Davis monitoring communications got the word the package was delivered, meaning his men were on the beach. It was now up to the twenty-seven quad riders. First Lieutenant Randolf checked his map and ordered the men to move out. They were all in whisper mode. They moved slow, five meters apart along a four-foot trail. The moon and stars were bright with no clouds. They could see pretty well, so they didn't use their night vision. Specialist Upton was right behind the point man that was monitoring his infrared system. They would know if anyone was in their path.

It was slow but steady going, constantly uphill. They crossed streams and hugged sheer cliffs but were making progress. After about two hours they reached the point where they would split up. They all checked their communication systems. Everything checked out all right. As they split up they all wished each other good luck. First Lieutenant Randolf reported to the colonel that everything was OK and that the team had just made their split. Second Lieutenant Wooly would have the hardest time getting to his destination. That's why he took the most experienced cross-country riders with him. He knew that if anyone could get them there in time it would be Will and Mick. He was right. These guys had the uncanny ability to find the right lines for their journey. The radar site was about three miles from the village. First Lieutenant Randolf took his attack force straight to the north side of the village. The road to the village came up from the south side. Sergeant First Class Kroker headed for the high ground on the west side. First Lieutenant Randolf's group was the first to reach their objective. His men dismounted, they were going into the village on foot. They included himself, Staff Sergeant Royce, Sergeant Stockstill, Specialist Upton and Specialist Taylor. They moved to the edge of the village and waited for the other units to be in place. It seemed to take forever. Sergeant First Class Kroker reported in. His men were in place to provide maximum support. A few minutes later Second Lieutenant Wooly called in. They were ready. First Lieutenant Randolf told him to wait until they had their package before he took out the radar/sam site. First Lieutenant Randolf and his men began moving into the village. They silently took out about a half dozen sentries. Everyone else was asleep. As they were doing that the rest of his men moved their quads and the comrades' quads closer to the edge of the village, getting off and pushing them the last one hundred yards. They were still fifty yards of the village edge. Sergeant First Class Kroker called his commander. He said from his vantage point that there was no more outside movement other than theirs. The lieutenant and his men made it to the building that housed the terrorist leader. They found the building. There was a light on inside. Sergeant Stockstill got up next to the building and looked inside. What he saw was a single man sitting at a small table going over some papers in a briefcase. This was the guy they were after. Sergeant Stockstill reported this to First Lieutenant Randolf on his helmet microphone. Everyone heard him and knew things were about to get dicey. First Lieutenant Randolf slipped inside the building with Sergeant Stockstill while the rest of the team covered them. First Lieutenant Randolf, using a tranquilizer gun, shot the man. Specialist Upton came in. He and Sergeant Stockstill grabbed the man and began carrying him out. First Lieutenant Randolf looked over the papers in the briefcase. He thought they might be important so he grabbed them and the briefcase. As he was leaving the building along with his two men and the terrorist, a man carrying an AK47 came walking out of a small building across the street. He spotted the soldiers. Staff Sergeant Culp took him out with a shot from a silenced automatic pistol. Unfortunately he had his finger on the trigger and fired two rounds on his way to the ground. Lights began coming on all over the village. Men came out and began firing at the soldiers. Quads came roaring into the village giving cover fire to the soldiers. The support quads up on the hill opened up, keeping at bay the terrorist soldiers. Sergeant McFarlane came in with his quad. They loaded the captive onto his quad. First Lieutenant Randolf told Bobby, Johnny and Buddy to cover the Sergeant on his ride to the rendezvous point. More and more bullets began to fly. Bobby recalls at least two bullets hitting his quad with no damage. The rest of the attack quads buzzed around firing their machine guns and rockets at the enemy while the soldiers on foot raced back to their quads. An RPG was fired, causing Sergeant Shipman's quad to flip. He was OK except for a broken leg. Several quads rushed to his rescue. Private First Class White was the first to reach him. He dismounted his quad to help his friend. As he was helping him on his quad he caught a bullet in the back, mortally wounding him. As he was falling Sergeant Shipman took out his attacker with a missile. Chad Hubanks grabbed Private First Class White's collar and dragged him out of the line of fire. He then placed him on his quad. By this time First Lieutenant Randolf and the other men made it back to their quads. They all headed for their escape route. Chad Duncan placed a hand grenade on the downed quad so the enemy couldn't use it against them. Sergeant First Class Kroker's men kept up heavy fire while the rest of the men made their exit. Meanwhile, as soon as the firing started, Colonel Hill ordered the aircraft into the air. Second Lieutenant Wooly had already placed charges on the radar site. As soon as First Lieutenant Randolf cleared the village he set the charges off, destroying the radar site and all the men inside. They then loaded up and headed to the helicopter pick up point. They would get there before anyone else. Sergeant First Class Kroker pulled his men back, regrouped and made for the pick up point.

Second Lieutenant Wooly arrived at the pick up point in just a few minutes. The helicopter was just a few minutes away. They set up a perimeter defense. A few minutes later they heard quads coming. It was Sergeant McFarlane with the terrorist leader. Buddy Bishop was leading him in. Bobby and Johnny were lagging back to cover them. Sergeant McFarlane and Buddy reached the pick up point about the same time as the helicopter. They were loading the prisoner onto the helicopter when a patrol of seven men opened up on them. They hit the door gunner on the helicopter. Bobby and Johnny fired their missiles at the patrol as well as Second Lieutenant Wooly and his men. Within seconds all seven terrorists lay dead. A couple of minutes later Sergeant Shipman showed up along with Chad Hubanks who was carrying the body of Private First Class White. Sergeant Shipman was helped onto the chopper and a couple of men helped Chad place Private First Class White onto the chopper. The helicopter was just fixing to take off when

First Lieutenant Randolf showed up with the rest of his attack squad. He handed one of the helicopter crew members the briefcase and told him to get it to Colonel Hill. A call came in on the radio. More terrorists had been spotted in the area. The helicopter took off. A charge was placed on the abandoned quad. First Lieutenant Randolf and his men would have to travel five miles to a safe pick up point. Attack helicopters would cover their escape as best they could. The Philippine soldiers were on their way. Will Valance and Mick Smalley, along with Staff Sergeant Culp would lead the way. Soon they were joined by the support quads of Sergeant First Class Kroker's group. The rest of the attack quads would supply cover. Staff Sergeant Fomby and Sergeant Wright would bring up the rear. The trail down the mountain was interlaced with other trails. The jungle growth made it all but impossible for air cover to be effective. On their way down they ran into several small groups of terrorist soldiers. In most cases they just rode right through them before the enemy could launch an attack on them. There was on spot that a small enemy patrol was in their path and they had to fight through them. For the most part the guys in front were doing the most firing. They would fire their twin machine guns, taking out everything in their path. They must have killed or wounded fifteen to twenty enemy soldiers on their descent. At one point two enemy soldiers had high ground on them. They peppered the quad column, striking several quads but their men had somehow avoided being hit. Bobby Duck did an amazing thing. He wheelied his quad and with a sweeping motion took out the two bad guys with his machine guns. They had closed to within a mile of safety when they received a call from a helicopter. At a crossroads ahead of them a large number of enemy troops were located there. There was no alternative route at this point. They didn't know whether to just fight their way through or wait on reinforcements from the Philippines. They didn't wait long for the answer. A couple of F14's made the decision for them. They would hit the enemy on either side of the crossroads, allowing the quads time to get through. They were barrelling down on the crossroads and starting taking fire. Then the F14's came in and cleared a path. The quads were less than one hundred yards from the crossroads when the F14's dropped their ordinance. The soldiers could feel the heat off the blasts. It kept the enemies' heads down long enough for all twenty-five quads to fly through the area. The quads were flying down the path, weaving in around obstacles in the trail. Once through the crossroads the quads reached safety in less than five minutes. They were going so fast that it caught the Philippine soldiers completely off guard even though they knew they were coming. Another mile and they reached the helicopter-landing zone. Two big Chinook helicopters were hovering when they arrived. The soldiers quickly loaded their quads into the cargo containers hooked underneath the helicopters. Once loaded the Chinooks lifted off, taking the quads directly to Manila where they would be loaded into the C-5 cargo plane.

Two blackhawk helicopters came in and picked the soldiers up and took them to the aircraft carrier. After reaching the aircraft carrier, they were taken to the mess hall where they ate. This also gave them time to unwind from the mission. Afterwards they went into a briefing room where Colonel Hill was waiting. The colonel said "You guys did one helluva job. I believe you are responsible for saving maybe thousands of lives. We haven't got much out of terrorist general, but the papers you sent back told us plenty. We got a list of names of terrorist operatives operating in the United States. What was even better than that, a cargo ship with a Panamanian registry was transporting three dirty bombs to California. The ship is to transfer the bombs to a yacht twenty miles off the coast near San Francisco. We have a Navy ship intercepting that ship as we speak. A team of Navy Seals will stay aboard the cargo ship in case the people on the yacht don't hear about what you guys have done. The Coast Guard will also be there in case they try to get away. IN a few minutes we all will be flown to Manila for the ride back home. Sergeant Shipman will join us. They have set his leg. As for the loss of Private First Class White, I know you are all saddened by his death. As am I. His body is being flown back to Washington, D.C. where he will be buried at Arlington with full honors. Men, your country owes you a great debt of gratitude. You should be proud of yourselves. I know I'm proud of what you accomplished. Your families have already been notified of your return.

You soldiers will be given thirty days leave and you civilian types will finally be allowed to go home with our sincere thanks.

I would like to get reports from all of you to help us in the future on what went right and what went wrong. From what I can tell this was pure textbook. I salute you." The colonel snapped to attention and saluted his men. They all stood and returned his salute. Soon they boarded the helicopters for the flight to Manila and boarded the C-5 for the ride home. They were exhausted.

CHAPTER 9

On the flight to Hawaii the men were quiet. Some tried to sleep but mostly they reflected on what had happened and mourned their fallen comrade, Private First Class White. He wanted so much to be part of the unit. They were all feeling grungy. They were still wearing the clothes that they had worn on the attack. After a few hours they landed in Hawaii. While the plane refueled, the men went and took a shower and put on clean clothes. Black t-shirts and tan pants, new boots and baseball caps that said special forces. The men also had hamburgers. They looked and felt a lot better. After the plane took off again the colonel brought out a couple of ice chests. They were full of beer. The colonel said "Here, have one on me." The men all grabbed a cold one. Specialist Mangrum said "Now, this is worth fighting for." They all laughed. After a few beers the men started opening up to each other. Sergeant Shipman held up a beer and said "Here's to you Luke." The rest of the men held up their beers and said "To Luke."

Soon they were all pretty loose. They still had eight hours to Fort Hood. They started toasting each other. The officers, the attack quad riders and then the support quad riders. Sergeant Wright even toasted the general for his idea about forming the unit. Sergeant Stockstill said "Boys, we are coming to the end of our journey together. Most of us will continue to grow our quad force but we are losing key members of our force and they surely will be missed. I've never served with such dedicated individuals as the Magnificent Seven." All the soldiers stood and raised their beers to their instructors and comrades.

They all laughed and told stories on each other. After awhile they started settling down. They were still four hours away from home. They all fell asleep and slept well.

When they were about thirty minutes from touchdown, they were awakened. They slowly started getting around some, threw water in their faces to regain sharpness.

When the plane touched down it taxied to a stop. Before the door opened Colonel Hill came to report to them. He said "I thought you guys might want to know. We captured the three nuclear bombs. They were to be set off in three cities on the Fourth of July. You guys are heroes."

That made the men feel proud. Then the door opened on the airplane. When the men began walking down the ramp a big brass band started playing but was soon drowned out by cheers of the hundreds of people gathered to greet them. They marched proudly in front of the friends and families there. They marched to a stage set up for them. General Johnson shook each one's hands and he walked up the steps to the stage. Behind the hundreds were two full battalions lined up for review. The general went to the microphone. "We are here today to honor these men. They have shown what the American soldier can do. They serve as an inspiration to us all. But I'm not the one to stand here before you. Ladies and Gentlemen, I give you the President of the United States. From behind the stage and up the stairs came President Bush. As he walked up to the microphone, he stopped to shake hands with the men. The crowd clapped and cheered. The president finally got to the microphone. "I hope you men don't mind me stopping by. I was on my way to my ranch and I found out what an incredible job you have done for the rest of us. I understand you just completed training. In fact, seven of you are not even soldiers. As of today you seven will be on the honored rolls of the military. It's the least we can do. I hear you went up to Montana and stopped terrorists from crossing our borders. Then you stopped even more terrorists from bombing our cities, saving thousands of lives. I think Colonel Hill did a superior job in recruiting you. It just goes to show the world what our people are capable of doing. Also, I would like to thank the private sector for stepping up to the challenge of developing a quality tool for these men to use. Thanks to Honda and Polaris, these men had quality vehicles for these young men to use. Terrorist threats against this country will not stop us. Thanks to these men and thousands more just like them, we will stop any enemy that tries to ruin our way of life. I know if you ask these men if they are special they will deny it. They will tell you that hundreds of men were involved in their successful missions. I'm here to tell you that's all true but you are still heroes. You inspire us all in spirit and in action. We are here today to honor you, not embarrass you. You are all heroes on quads." The crowd went wild. Bobby Duck later recalled he thought winning that race in Wyoming was great. But the president honoring him and the rest of the men would never be topped. The president continued "I would like to honor this unit with a presidential citation. First Lieutenant Randolf, would you please step forward." First Lieutenant Randolf approached the president. "This citation says on the behalf of a grateful nation I, George Bush, President of the United States, acknowledge the superior efforts of the First Special Forces Quad Unit. Thank you." The crowd again cheered. The president handed him the citation and shook his hand again. The president then asked "Is there anything you would like to say?" First Lieutenant Randolf stepped to the microphone. "I had a lot to say to you but one thing keeps popping into my head." He hesitated for a moment, then said "Let's roll." The crowd went wild. The president smiled and said "That pretty much says it all. Thank you." The president left the stage while the crowd was still clapping and cheering.

General Johnson returned to the microphone. "Thank you, Mr. President." He turned to the soldiers being honored. "The president was right. You men are heroes on quads. To show you the appreciation of a grateful nation, I would like to present to all the soldiers the Silver Star." The crowd cheered again. "I am also authorized by the president to bestow one our nation's most prestigious awards to the Magnificent Seven. The Medal of Freedom. You men personify American. Congratulations." He presented the medals to each man. He returned again to the microphone. "Now I know you men want to get to your families. I know they want to get to you. Thank you men." At that the band struck up the Star Spangled Banner. The soldiers saluted as everyone sang. Afterwards the men left the stage to be with their families. The families were all over the men congratulating them and telling them how proud they were. There were a lot of hugs and kisses. Chad Duncan found his new wife Charlotte. They embraced so hard that you thought that they were Siamese twins.

Bobby walked by, tapped Chad on the shoulder and said "Get a room." Chad laughed and said "I am." Bobby found his family in the crowd. They were so proud of him. All the men stood around and visited for a while. They introduced family and friends to each other. Sergeant First Class Kroeker came up to Bobby. He said "I know you guys are ready to get out of here and go home." Bobby said "You got that right Sarge." Sergeant First Class Kroeker said "Well, you've got to pack, right?" Bobby nodded. He said "I plan to eat dinner with my folks and head for Oklahoma." Sergeant First Class Kroeker said "Well, I'd like to buy all of you guys a drink after you pack and before you go to dinner." Bobby said "Sure." Sergeant First Class Kroeker said about 6 p.m. at Pete's Party Palace." Bobby said "I'll be there." Sergeant First Class Kroeker asked the same of all of the Seven. They all said they would be there. Bobby and the rest of the men headed back to the B.O.Q. to pack. All the men found large envelopes taped to their doors with their names on them. Bobby and his roommate Johnny took the envelopes inside to open them. Inside they found a letter of appreciation from Honda and Polaris. It read, 'You have done us and our country a great service. You have saved us from terrorist attacks on our city. We would like to offer you our sincere thanks by offering a token of our appreciation. When you return home you will find two new 500cc quads, race ready and full of gas. Also you will need a new trailer to haul them in and a new pick up truck to pull the trailer. If there is anything else we can do for you please contact us. Bobby and Johnny couldn't believe this. They began hollering and laughing. The other men up and down the hall did the same thing. They were almost too excited to pack. But they did pack. Before they went to Pete's they all decided to visit the training site one more time. When they got there on one was around. They were going to take one last look at the attack quads but everything was locked up. They decided to head on over to Pete's. They arrived promptly at 6:00 p.m. or 1800 hours military time. As they walked in they were surprised. Everyone was there. All their families and all the soldiers from their unit. From the colonel to the supply clerk. There was a catered meal waiting for them along with lots of beer. The men came in and were shaking everyone's hands. Charlotte had set the whole thing up. They were ushered to the dance floor where Colonel Hill was waiting for them.

The colonel said a few words. "You men are the heart and soul of this unit. If ever you get tired of racing, come on back, we'll make room for you." There wasn't a dry eye in the house. Not even tough Sergeant First Class Kroeker. Bobby said "I know I speak for all of us. We will never forget. This will be the stuff we tell our children and grandchildren about. If they don't cry, we will beat them." The crowd laughed. "I know personally you guys are the best. I'm so proud to have served my country with men like you. We can go home knowing that we will be safe in our beds because of you and many more like you. I'm so glad Colonel Hill asked me to help out." The crowd applauded. Bobby and the rest of the men nodded their heads as if to say that's the way they feel also. First Lieutenant Randolf stepped forward. In order to honor you we have adopted a song that will be our theme song from now on. The jukebox came alive with the theme song from the old movie 'The Magnificent Seven'. It sent chills up and down everyone's spine.

After the song Buddy Bishop, eyeing the food, started walking towards the buffet and said "Let's roll."

PART II

PREFACE

In Part I you were introduced to a new tool that our military uses to fight the enemies of our country. Along with these tools we were introduced to the men that made them work. You were taken from an idea through training and onto a couple of successful missions that probably saved thousands of lives. In these uncertain times we live in it's good to know there are people out there putting it on the line for us every day. In this book you will revisit players from the first book and meet some new ones. I will try to show you the versatility of our machines and men in some different ways. You know war is hell. People getting maimed and people dying. Let us not forget those who died for us. I encourage all Americans to be the best that they can be. Don't be afraid to show your love for your family, for your country and for your lives. Live it to the fullest. I hope you enjoy reading my book. If you do, tell a friend. They might like it too. This is just my way of showing others what I feel about us.

Eddy Duck

CHAPTER 1

It was late August. Tulsa, Oklahoma was still in the grips of a heat wave. A few more weeks the heat would give way to some cooler temperatures.

Bobby Duck is back in school and working, spending every spare moment working on or riding his quad. He had become quite a celebrity with the locals in his town named Sand Springs, located just west of Tulsa. He had several offers from big name companies offering to sponsor him in his racing. The company he worked for even offered to pay for his schooling. He worked for American Airlines. They were hit hard because of the events on 9-11 and Bobby and the others had gotten some pay back for them. They were proud of him and he was proud to be a part of them. Bobby didn't make much money, but he hoped to be able to make a good living after he graduated A&P (Airframe and Powerplant) School. He loved being around the big planes almost as much as he liked riding quads. Bobby's family supported him both financially and emotionally. All in all though things were going his way.

It was Friday night. Late after school Bobby stopped by to visit with Lonnie Eubanks. He knew others would also be there, all with the same things on their minds. Tell jokes, work on quads, pick up a few tips and talk about girls. When Bobby got there he was really surprised. His friend Johnny Hale was there and so was Lieutenant Colonel Purcell. He was the design engineer from the Army. There were several other guys there as well. They were all gathered around a couple of brand new quads. Lieutenant Colonel Purcell came over and shook Bobby's hand. "It's good to see you again Bobby" he said. "I asked Lonnie the other day if he would mind looking at our newest quads." Bobby turned to Lonnie and said, "You knew he was coming and didn't tell me." Lonnie laughed and said, "I didn't think you would be interested." Bobby said, "Yeah right." Johnny said, "Hey Bobby, let's take these things up to my place tomorrow and try 'em out." Bobby said, "Sure, what time?" Johnny said, "About six. I'll get my grandma to fix us breakfast." Bobby said, "Sounds good. Will it be okay if I bring my dad?" "Sure" Johnny said. "Oh yeah Lonnie, you and Lieutenant Colonel Purcell come too." Lonnie said, "Okay, but tell your grandma I'm a hearty eater." Bobby said, "I won't have to tell her, I think she will be able to figure that out on her own." He then patted Lonnie on the belly. They all laughed. Bobby asked the lieutenant colonel "What's going on back in the unit and with the rest of the guys?" Lieutenant Colonel Purcell said, "Well, all hell is breaking loose. We have grown to two full platoons of quads and have incorporated two other mechanized platoons using dune buggies and motorcycles. Half of the men are preparing to ship out and the rest in a few weeks. Colonel Hill is still in charge and doing a bang-up job I might add. The guys you trained are doing the training now. They are doing a good job but they could really use the help of The Magnificent Seven." (The name The Magnificent Seven was given to the original instructors which included Bobby Duck, Johnny Hale, Will Valance, Mick Smalley, Chad Hubanks, Chad Duncan and Buddy Bishop. There was an eighth member, Harvey Light, who suffered a career ending injury.) Bobby said, "Just say the word and I'll be there." Lieutenant Colonel Purcell said, "Watch what you say, we may just take you up on that." Johnny said, "Don't forget about me. I'm there too. Somebody has to watch out for Bobby." They all laughed. Johnny said, "Well, it's getting late and if we are going to ride in the morning I'd better get some shut eye." Bobby shook his head in agreement. They said their good nights. Bobby and Johnny went home. Lieutenant Colonel Purcell went to a motel after he got directions to Johnny's from Lonnie. Lonnie ran the rest of the guys off. He stayed up all night checking out the new quads. They weren't all that different in basic design than the originals. He hooked one of the machines up to dyno. He checked it in both stealth and full bore. He was amazed at the results. Horsepower had been dramatically increased. After further checking he discovered changes in the carburator. The overall size had been increased. The snorkel system had been modified with a quick release. With the snorkel disconnected a ram air system was used allowing more air to the intake. The valves had also been changed along with a higher compression piston. The frame and suspension had also been changed. The front end had been raised to make access to the weapons systems easier.

The true test would come when Bobby and Johnny rode the quads. Lonnie had been up all night but he wasn't tired. He was, however, very hungry, so he loaded up the quads and headed to Johnny's. He was the first to arrive. Johnny's father and grandfather were sitting at the kitchen table drinking coffee. Johnny's grandmother was busy fixing breakfast. After being offered a cup of coffee Lonnie said, "Boy, them eggs and bacon sure smell good." Mrs. Hale said, "Well, set yourself down there, it will be ready in a few minutes." Johnny came in, kissed his grandmother and poured himself a cup of coffee. Soon Lieutenant Colonel Purcell showed up along with Staff Sergeant Ketcher who had stayed at the motel the night before. They all shook hands. Johnny said, "Well, we're all here except Bobby." He no sooner said that when the knock came at the door. It was Bobby. He came walking in and had a big grin on his face that really showed off his dimples. He said, "Good morning Mrs. Hale, good morning men." Johnny's grandfather asked where his dad was. Bobby said, "He's parking his truck, he'll be in here in a minute." Johnny said, "Sit down, we're fixing to eat." Soon Bobby's dad joined them. The men ate breakfast, even Lonnie got his fill. Soon they were all outside. Johnny and Bobby suited up and hopped on the quads. They rode for two solid hours, stopping only for water and fuel.

Afterwards they all went into the Hale's garage. Mrs. Hale brought iced tea to all of them. Bobby's first words were "Wow what a ride." Johnny said, "Ditto." They all laughed. Lieutenant Colonel Purcell said, "Well, that pretty much answers my question." He then asked for a breakdown of wow. Bobby said, "Well I was really impressed with the extra horsepower. The throttle response was great." Johnny said, "Yeah, I also liked the way the bike handled. At first I was a bit concerned about the raised front end, but it handled incredibly well. It will make it easier to operate the weapons system." Lonnie and Bobby's dad took the quads for a spin. Both were good riders, Lonnie was really good. They had fun. Lieutenant Colonel Purcell was impressed with their riding skills. Bobby's dad was a little apprehensive on the jumps but he was a skilled rider nonetheless. Bobby and Johnny spent the time watching and talking with Lieutenant Colonel Purcell. They found out that half the quad force was heading to Turkey. They were part of a pre-invasion force in Iraq. They were hooking up with Kurd forces to find out information before the invasion to throw Saddam out of power and eliminate the nuclear and chemical threat to the rest of the world. Bobby and Johnny both offered their help again. Lieutenant Colonel Purcell asked the two men about the others. Bobby said, "Well, I've kept in touch with them and with the help of Johnny's computer it would take no time to find out about how the others felt."

Soon Bobby and Johnny were on the computer. They typed in one message and instantly zipped it to the other five members of The Magnificent Seven. The message simply said 'The Magnificent Seven ride again' followed by a question mark. They almost immediately received two responses. They came from Buddy Bishop and Chad Hubanks. Chad's response was "What's up? I'm ready." Buddy's response was "When and where." Lieutenant Colonel Purcell was impressed. The other three had not yet responded. Bobby said, "They must be out of town, they will check in later." It turned out Will and Mick were working with the INS (Immigration and Naturalization Service) border patrols and were out on a training run. Their responses came later that evening and were similar to that of Chad and Buddy.

Chad Duncan was out of town on a construction job. His wife Charlotte relayed the message on the computer to Chad. He didn't hesitate. He got on the phone and called Johnny directly. Johnny explained what was going on. Nothing was for sure yet. When they found out more they would. get in touch with him. Johnny told him about the improved four-wheeler. Chad was excited to hear from his friend and told him to keep him informed. Later that evening Bobby and Johnny joined Lieutenant Colonel Purcell and Staff Sergeant Ketcher for dinner. Lieutenant Colonel Purcell had been in contact with Colonel Hill. He told them that Colonel Hill had agreed with him the men were needed. With half his force going into harm's way he could really use their help getting some of the others up to par on the new quads. If Bobby, Johnny and the others were willing, orders would be issued for them the following week. Both agreed. They could be there in about three days. They weren't sure about the others. Lieutenant Colonel Purcell said he would contact them personally. After dinner they all headed back to Sand Trax to visit with Lonnie. It was around ten o'clock p.m. Lonnie had just arrived. He had gone home earlier after leaving Johnny's to take a nap. Bobby told him about his upcoming trip to Fort Hood. Lonnie said, "Well, this calls for a drink." He opened a refrigerator and pulled out Cokes and Dr. Peppers for everyone. They sat around for the rest of the evening and early into the next morning talking and telling jokes. The next day Lieutenant Colonel Purcell and Staff Sergeant Ketcher loaded up and headed for Fort Hood.

Bobby and Johnny began making arrangements to make their trip back to Fort Hood. They contacted the other guys to let them know what was going down. Chad Hubanks had just broken up with a girlfriend again. He said he needed a change of scenery. Buddy Bishop said he wouldn't be able to be at Fort Hood until Thursday. Will Valance and Mick Smalley said to look for them when they see them. Now Chad Duncan was another story, he was married now. He had more than himself to think about. He was all set to back away. Charlotte had other ideas. She told Chad he would not back off because of her. She told him to go and there would be no more talk about it. Chad and Charlotte loved each other very much. He knew she was right. He had to go. The others would be there for him. It was only for a short time and Charlotte would go with him so she could visit family and friends.

Bobby made arrangements at school and work. There would be no problems. His mother Sandy cried the day he left, but not until he left. His dad said he was proud and wished he could go with him. This would only be for a few weeks so Bobby and Johnny decided to fly. They left on a Tuesday afternoon. It would be late when they arrived at Kileen, Texas. Staff Sergeant Ketcher picked them up at the airport and took them to their rooms at Fort Hood. It was late at night but Fort Hood was a beehive of activity. It seemed like everyone there was awake and busy. Bobby knew it was just a matter of time these men would be in harm's way.

When they got to the BOQ (Basic Officers Quarters) they were met by Will and Mick. They had arrived earlier that evening. They were hungry so they decided to try to find a mess hall that was open. They found one. The only thing they were serving was cold sandwiches. That was fine for them. Staff Sergeant Ketcher had told them he would be by after breakfast the next morning to pick them up. There seemed to be a sense of urgency in the air. Tension was high. Chaplin Noe came by and welcomed the men back. He said, "Things around here are hopping, ain't they." The men just laughed. Boy was that an understatement.

They visited with Chaplin Noe for awhile then had to leave. The four men walked back to their rooms. They were all tired but couldn't sleep. But they must have, because before you know it they were awakened by Fort Hood physical training.

CHAPTER 2

It was a beautiful morning. The temperature about seventy degrees but it promised to be a hot one with the humidity increasing due to a weak front moving in.

Bobby got out of bed and put a pot of coffee on. Before he had gotten involved with the military he never drank coffee. Now he started each day with a cup or two. Soon the coffee started perking, that got Johnny up. After each had a cup they talked about being excited about being there. Soon came a knock on the door. It was Will and Mick. They stumbled in and asked for a cup.

Bobby asked Mick about his INS (Immigration and Naturalization Services) adventure. Mick said, "It was fun, Bobby. We helped teach some border patrol guys how to ride. After seeing our quads operate on the Canada thing, they decided that they would be a good thing for them to use. The quads they use are a scaled down version of the Army's support quads. What they really like though is the infrared scanners." Bobby asked, "What about your racing? Where's that at?" Mick said, "We've been on summer break. We have a race scheduled about the same time we finish up here. It looks like the timing is perfect. Will and I are still battling it out for first." Bobby said, "Cool." Mick asked Bobby, "What about you ol' buddy?" Bobby said, "I've been so busy with work and school I haven't had much chance to do much racing. I've been able to make a few motocross races. But, if Johnny's there I've been getting blown away." Bobby looked over at Johnny. Johnny laughed and said, "Well, I'm still trying to make up for your win up in Wyoming." Bobby said, "That seems like such a long time ago." They all agreed, when in fact it had only been a couple of months. Will asked, "Well, what do you all think the game plan for us will be?" Bobby said, " I don't know. I guess we'll find out after breakfast." Johnny said, "Speaking of breakfast, let's go eat." They all headed over to the mess hall.

They were about halfway finished eating when in came Staff Sergeant Ketcher followed by Chad Duncan and Chad Hubanks. They came straight over to the table. They shook hands with everyone. Bobby said, "Hey, when did you guys get in?" Chad Hubanks said he drove in last night and decided to stay in a motel. "When I went in to check in, Chad and Charlotte were checking in. The motel operator was Charlotte's cousin, Dean Bennett. We got a real good rate." They all laughed. Staff Sergeant Ketcher said, "Well, when you guys finish here, I need to take you to administration for processing and then to Lieutenant Colonel Purcell's office." The men ate their breakfast, talked over what's been happening. Chad Hubanks had gotten a job and was doing some racing on weekends. Chad Duncan said that he had been busy getting settled in with Charlotte and was working a lot of hours. He told the men that this would be a break for him. " half hour later they were in the van heading to the administration building. Their first stop would be the JAG office to fill out the contracts and other related papers that were necessary for them to get paid. When they walked in they were surprised to find Buddy Bishop waiting on them. He said, " You didn't think I'd let you start without me, did you?" Bobby said, "The Magnificent Seven ride again." Johnny said, "Let's roll." After they filled out the papers they stopped by medical to update their files and get a set of shots. Nobody seemed to know what they were for. All the nurse said was they were ready to go. While they were in medical, Bobby complained about a tooth that was bothering him. They sent him across the hall to the dentist office. He was terrified of the dentist, always had been. Anyway, he just had time for a quick exam. He and the others were due in Lieutenant Colonel Purcell's office. It was the same dentist that had worked on Harvey Light, Dr. Dana Ross. She asked Bobby about his friend. Bobby told her he was doing okay. Dana gave Bobby a quick exam and took x-rays. She told him he needed some work done and scheduled him for Friday afternoon. Bobby reluctantly said okay.

Bobby then rejoined his friends. They all headed over to Lieutenant Colonel Purcell's office. When they arrived they were sent right in. Lieutenant Colonel Purcell was on the phone. He was talking with General Johnson. The men overheard part of the conversation. " I don't know sir, I can ask. Well, okay, sir. Yes sir." He then hung up. He said, "Boy, I sure am glad you all made it. Things have really been hectic around here." He stood up and walked around his desk to shake hands with the seven men. He asked, "Did you get checked in okay?" They all nodded or said yes. "Good," he said. "I've prepared a training schedule for you. Check it out and see what you think. I was just on the phone with General Johnson." He began handing out the schedules. "General Johnson is on his way over. He wants to talk with you . It seems our schedule has been moved up. As you know, Colonel Hill has already taken half the company to Turkey. The rest of the company was scheduled to join them in three weeks. That's been moved up a week." Bobby interrupted, "Sir, does that mean you only need us for two weeks?" Lieutenant Colonel Purcell said, "Well, that's what the general wants to talk to you about. He is going to ask you to go to Turkey with us." The men all looked at each other. Lieutenant Colonel Purcell said, "I should let the general talk to you guys about this. I just wanted you guys to know what's going on." Lieutenant Colonel Purcell could tell by the look on their faces they had a million questions. But nobody said anything. He continued, "I know you guys hadn't figured on this and you have a lot of questions and concerns. Maybe the general can clear it all up." No one said anything. You could feel the tension in the room. Each man was pondering the situation. All of a sudden the phone rang. Lieutenant Colonel Purcell answered it. It was Staff Sergeant King, the general's aide. He said that the general had something urgent that had come up and asked the men to join him later for lunch at the Officer's Club. Lieutenant Colonel Purcell said okay and hung up. "Well, guys," he said, "it looks like you've got a couple of hours to kill." Johnny said, "Good, I'd like to check in at the training site to see what's going on." Lieutenant Colonel Purcell said, "That's fine. Why don't you all go and I'll meet you at the Officer's Club at 12:30. I've got a couple of things to do before then." The men left his office and loaded into the van.

On the way over, they talked amongst themselves. Bobby said, "I really hadn't figured on a longer stretch. But, if they need me, I guess school can wait." Will said, "You know that would pretty much end the race season this year." Mick said, "Yeah, but it would give someone else a chance to win for a change." They all laughed. The van pulled up to the training site. No one was around. They walked into the Company Office. There sat Sergeant First Class Kroeker. When he saw the men he grinned, jumped up to shake hands and said, "The Magnificent Seven returns. It's good to see you guys. We've missed you around here. We sure can use your help." Bobby said, "That's why we're here. It looks like all hell is breaking loose," Sergeant First Class Kroeker said. "You don't know the half of it. At least half the Special Forces units have received orders and are on their way to the Middle East." Johnny asked, "Where's everyone else?" "They're over at medical getting some shots," Sergeant First Class Kroeker said. "We got the word we're shipping out in two weeks from Friday." Chad said, "That doesn't give us much time, does it?" Sergeant First Class Kroeker said, "No it doesn't. We'll take what we can get." He asked, "Have you guys seen the new quads?" Johnny said, "Bobby and I have but the rest of the guys haven't." Sergeant First Class Kroeker said, "Well, let's go look at them." He grabbed a portable phone then he and the others walked over to the maintenance building.

When they walked in and got their first look at the new attack quads, the first thing they noticed was the raised front ends. Will asked Bobby, "How did they handle?" Bobby said, "Surprisingly well and they have really increased the horsepower to the wheels. Lonnie Eubanks checked them out on the dyno meter. They've got forty horse in stealth mode and seventy in the full attack mode." Chad and Will both said together, "Wow." The others laughed. Buddy said, "I can't wait to try them out." Mick asked, "Did they do anything to the support quads?" Sergeant First Class Kroeker said they are due in tomorrow. "We heard they didn't do anything to the frame but increased the horsepower on them as well. Not as much as the Honda's but still quite a bit. They will outrun any stock quad being built." Bobby said, "Yeah, I guess so." The men marvelled at the machines for quite a while. Sergeant First Class Kroeker said he would arrange for test rides after lunch. Bobby said, "Oh, yeah, lunch. We are supposed to meet with the general at 12:30. What time is?" Buddy responded 11:45. "Time for my lunch," said Sergeant First Class Kroeker. "I'll see you guys this afternoon."

They all left the maintenance building. Bobby and the rest decided to walk to the Officer's Club. It was only a mile away and they needed the exercise. The temperature was really climbing. It was sunny and eighty eight degrees. The humidity was really up there, also. They walked past a company of two hundred men carrying full battle packs and weapons. There was so much sweat pouring off these guys you could float a boat. Still, they marched proud. They sang cadence that the sergeants were leading them in.

If you've never been around soldiers singing cadence, you're really miss-ing something. The quad riders were impressed with the resolve of the American military. Even if it meant just marching in the hot Texas sun.

Soon the men were at the Officer's Club. They were all dressed in their instructor's uniforms which contained no insignia. They were stopped at the door. " sergeant asked if he could help them. Bobby said jokingly, "Why yes, my good man. We are here to have lunch with General Johnson and Lieutenant Colonel Purcell." The sergeant going along said, "But of course gentlemen. Your party awaits you." He opens the door for the seven men. Once inside they quickly locate the general's table. They approach the gen-eral and he stands to greet them. "Welcome, guys. Come sit down. I've taken the liberty to order for you. The food will be out in a few minutes." They all find chairs and sit down. He continues, "I want to thank you men for answering the call for your services again. I know that puts great hard-ship on your lives at home. This is a very stressful time for all of us. We are preparing to send thousands of young men like yourselves in harm's way. That's why we need you. We need to train our men on the ATV's. They may be the difference if they live or die. The terrain they we'll be operating in is very treacherous. We don't want to lose men because they can't ride prop-erly." Lunch arrives and interrupts the general. Patty melts, fries and iced tea all around. The men started eating immediately. As they were eating the general continued. "Well, the bottom line is in two and a half weeks the balance of the special quad unit will leave to join the others. They will be based in Turkey but will operate in Iraq. Before I continue I must know if you would be willing to accompany them and continue the training in Tur-key. Your length of service will depend on the progress of your students. You did a fantastic job with the first group and I'm sure you can accom-plish the same thing with the newer men. The first group has done okay teaching but you guys have so much more to offer. I can't or won't just arbitrarily order you to go. It's strictly voluntary." Bobby spoke up, "Sir, when Lieutenant Colonel Purcell told us about this I was not sure. I was thinking only of myself and my own self interests. I was on the verge of turning you down. Then something happened on the way over here. We passed a proud company of soldiers marching down the road. I thought, these guys are just like me. They are willing to put it all on the line for me. I was very humbled. That got me to thinking. If there was anything I could do to help them, I was going to do it. If that means going to Turkey you can count me in. I can't speak for the others, just myself." Johnny said, "You just did." They looked around the table, each man held a thumbs up. Bobby's speech had touched them all. Bobby added, "Besides, the Army is going to fix my toothache." They all laughed. The general then said, "You guys truly are heroes in my book. For your age you have a good understanding of what America is all about. Thank you. Now, down to business. As you know, Colonel Hill has taken half the company to Turkey. They will set up two camps, one a base camp in Turkey. The other a forward camp. His mission is two-fold. One, help coordinate and arm the Kurds. Two, obtain as much intelligence on troop movements, defenses, strengths and weaknesses of the Iraqi Army. Sounds simple enough, doesn't it. Believe me it's not. The environment is totally hostile. From our forward base camp we will send out several patrols to man observation posts. Most of our movements will be done under the cover of darkness. Our quads, motorcycles and special dune buggies will be the backbone of our operations. We will only operate aircraft in the region if we are attacked. Men and equipment will be parachuted in to secure zones set up by us and the Kurds. We can expect support from the Turkish Army but only on a limited bases. You men will be assigned to the rear base. There you will conduct your training as the men rotate in and out. Your time there will largely depend on how well you train the men. Well, that's pretty much it. Do you have any questions for me?" No one said anything. Then he said, "Oh yes, Lieutenant Colonel Purcell will be your Commanding Officer until you leave. Major Dobson will accompany you to Turkey. He will officially be the Company Executive Officer but his real function will be the maintenance of the equipment. Your old comrade, First Lieutenant Wooley, will be senior officer in operations. He was promoted after the Philippine Operation. First Lieutenant Randolf is now Captain Randolf. Well guys, I need to go. I hope to get to visit with you before you leave. Good luck and God speed." He stood up to leave. All the men stood also. He said, "Sit back down and finish your lunch." He turned and left with Staff Sergeant King in tow.

The men finished their lunch. Will said, "Well, I've got some phone calls to make this evening. There's going to be some very unhappy people." Mick said, "Yeah, but what can they do? Send us out of the country?" They laughed. Bobby said, "At this rate I'll be retired before I finish school."

Again they laughed. Chad Duncan said, " I don't know how I'm going to tell Charlotte. She's been so supportive this far." Buddy said, "You know I feel good about this. If we had said no, I think it would have haunted us from now on." Chad Hubanks said, "Bobby, what you said to the general was exactly what the rest of us were thinking." Johnny said, "Yeah, and that's scary that we are all thinking like Bobby." They laughed. Bobby said, "Let's roll, I need to ride." They got up and headed back to the training site.

When they got back the place was empty again except for Sergeant First Class Kroeker and First Lieutenant Wooley. They congratulated Wooley on his promotion. They told the two of them about the meeting with the general and that they would be accompanying them to Turkey. First Lieutenant Wooley said, " I knew you guys couldn't say no. The rest of the men are at weapons training. What do you say to a little riding and check out these new quads."

The men walked over to the maintenance shed. They geared up, gassed up and loaded up for an afternoon of riding.

The rode until almost dark. The new quads performed great. They had plenty of power and handled great. By the time they finished they were dogged tired. They turned in the quads and headed back to their rooms. They were hot and sweaty. " shower and some food was what they needed. After dinner they all went back to their rooms to make some phone calls.

Bobby called his parents. His mother was upset but his dad understood. He told Bobby that his mom would be okay. He said, moms are supposed to be like this." He told Bobby that they would pray for him and his safe return. Bobby told his dad thanks. He told him he wasn't coming home this weekend because he was getting his tooth fixed. He would try to come home before he left for Turkey. His dad asked him if there was anything he needed. Bobby told him he had wished he had his truck and quad. His dad said, "Yeah, I bet you do." They soon ended the conversation. Booby's mother got back on the phone and told her son she loved him and was very proud of him. When Bobby hung up the phone he thought to himself. My parents have been the best. He loved them very much. Soon he drifted off to sleep. The others made similar phone calls.

The night went by quickly. At 0430 the next morning Fort Hood woke up. They needed to get up early to beat the heat and do physical training. The seven joined in. It was still pretty warm for that time of day, seventy six degrees and the sun wasn't even up. After a half hour of push up, sit up and other exercises they went on a five mile run. Most units only run two but this was Special Forces. By 0600 the men had cooled down, took showers and were headed for breakfast. By 0700 they were at the training site. There were seven familiar faces and seventeen new ones. They all had been training for about a month on the trainer quads. Today would be the first time for any of them to be on the new more powerful machines.

The schedule called for the first half of the day to be spent on quad evaluation. All the men seemed excited about the new quads and to get some advanced training from the pros. Introductions were made then they all headed to the maintenance building to get their machines. " half hour later they were ready to go.

They all had the light colored desert camo on. The quads had already been fuelled, the oil and coolant levels checked. While they were getting ready Bobby asked Chad Duncan, "How did Charlotte take the news?" Chad said, "Better than expected. She supports me one hundred percent." He then asked Bobby, "Since you are staying here this weekend, why don't you join us at the lake. There will be lots of people. Good food and beer." Bobby said, "Sounds good, I'll let you know. It depends on how it goes at the dentist tomorrow afternoon." Chad said, "Cool." Soon they were ready to go. They all took off. " long course had been laid out for the men to follow. Sergeant First Class Kroeker and First. Lieutenant Wooley led the way. The seven pros mixed in with the rest of the men to check them out. At first some of them seemed a little intimidated by the more powerful machines. Soon they were getting the hang of it. Some of the riders were pretty good and some were struggling just to keep up. They all were riding hard. After two hours they stopped for a break. First Lieutenant Wooley asked the pros, "Well, what do you think?" Will said, "Some of them are catching on pretty good, they just need more time to get comfortable." Johnny said, "They all need more work on the jumps." Bobby said, "Let's split into small groups on the way back. Maybe we can show them a few things." First Lieutenant Wooley said, "Good Idea. Each of you take one of us veterans with you and two or three of the new guys. I know every time I ride with you guys I learn a better way to ride. Hopefully they will too." They split into seven groups. All the soldiers were eager to learn. They knew their lives may depend on how well they could ride. Bobby took

Sergeant First Class Kroeker and three others with him. They did well in manoeuvring and overall acceleration but were timid in jumps. He purposely chose terrain with a lot of jumps. He would lead the way flying over jumps effortlessly, as well as did Sergeant First Class Kroeker. The other three watched and tried to emulate the pro. After tackling several small jumps they started getting more confidence. Bobby started hitting some bigger jumps. After a few crashes by the others he backed off. After about an hour they stopped near a medium sized jump. Bobby said, "You guys are doing just fine, especially no longer than you've been riding. Jumps are the hardest thing to learn. After awhile you will be able to determine the speeds that are needed for each jump. Braking in the air can control your angle. It just takes practice." Sergeant First Class Kroeker said, "These men aren't afraid to jump. In fact, we are going to jump ten thousand feet tomorrow. Want to join us?" The others were waiting for him to respond, "Sure," Bobby said. "I'd love to give it a try." One of the soldiers said, "Cool." Bobby made several jumps on that mid size jump. Hitting it at several different angles and speeds. He was able to land perfectly each time. Finally he pulled up and said, "Your turn." The soldiers must have been paying close attention because they all successfully negotiated the jump. Bobby thought, cool. They finally made their way back to the training site and joined the others. He reported his progress as did the others.

They all headed to lunch. Bobby told them about being asked to sky dive. The others said the same thing. They had been set up.

After lunch they all headed to the towers. There they were taught about how to land and how to control the parachutes. The soldiers were impressed about how easy the pros caught on.

That night at dinner Chad confessed his fear of jumping. Buddy said, "Hell, we're all scared. I'll probably wet myself." Bobby said, "You do that anyway." They all laughed so hard they almost threw them out of the mess hall. Charlotte came by and picked up Chad. They all agreed to meet at Pete's Party Palace for a beer. The men went back to their rooms and cleaned up.

It was about 7:30 when the men got to Pete's. As they were walking in, Bobby leading the way, a good looking blonde was walking out. She bumped into Bobby as she was turning to wave to Charlotte. Bobby walked over to the table where Charlotte and Chad were sitting. He said, "Who is that?"

96

Charlotte said, "Who is what?" Bobby said, "That blonde," and pointed at the door. Charlotte said, "What blonde? I don't see anyone." Bobby turned to the door, the girl was gone. Bobby said, "This is going nowhere." Charlotte and Chad smiled at each other. Charlotte said, "You must have hit your head today. You better sit down and have a beer." Bobby said, " I believe I will, thank you." He and the others sat down and Charlotte poured them all a beer. Charlotte said, "Chad told me he taught you guys a few things today." She winked at Buddy. He said, "He sure did, he was awesome today." Chad's face turned beet red. They all laughed. " group of men from their unit came in. They spotted their instructors. They came over to the table and offered to buy them a beer. The pros turned them down and instead bought the soldiers a beer. One of the soldiers, a Sergeant John Allen, asked, "Are you guys ready for tomorrow?" Bobby said, "Sure we are." "Well," the sergeant said, "don't drink too much. Beer doesn't taste as good coming up as it went down." Charlotte said, "He's right, one more beer and that's it." Not knowing any better, they agreed. Charlotte asked Bobby, "I hear you might join us Saturday at the lake." He said, "I'm going to try." She said, "Well, if you make it I'll introduce you to that imaginary blonde." Bobby said, "I'm there." He grinned. She asked, "What about the rest of you." They all had plans of going home after they jumped tomorrow.

Soon they all finished their second beer. Buddy said, "I guess we'd better go." They all got up and said their goodnights and headed for the door. Chad said, "I'll hook up with you guys at physical training in the morning." They waved at him and walked out.

Later that night Chad had a long talk with Charlotte about what was going to happen. She told him just to stick with the others and nothing would happen to him. She felt the seven of them could accomplish anything together. She said she had seen a lot of men come through the doors at Pete's but there was something magical when those men were together. They were like the Three Musketeers only there were seven of them, all of the same mind, ready to take on the world. Others around them felt the same way about them. Several soldiers commented on how well they worked with each other.

The next morning there they were doing physical training with the rest of Fort Hood. When they finished, they got cleaned up, ate a light breakfast and headed to the airfield. They joked to hide their fear. At the airfield they went to a hangar to draw their parachutes and to get a final briefing. Meanwhile back at the training site, a guest was arriving. It was Bobby's dad. He had brought down Bobby's truck and quad. He had contacted Lieutenant Colonel Purcell and he gave him directions to his office. He arrived just in time to watch his son's first parachute jump. Lieutenant Colonel Purcell took him out to the drop zone. "" pair of C-130 cargo planes flew overhead. In the first one was the ATV's. They would be dropped first in special crates. The second plane has the soldiers and your son," said Purcell. Bobby's dad told him, "I'll bet he's about to mess his pants." Lieutenant Colonel Purcell said, "I think I messed my pants on my first jump." Back up in the plane the men were preparing to jump. The ready light came on, the men stood and hooked their static lines to the cable in the plane. Most jumpers don't use these anymore. Mostly because of the different altitudes they jump from. New parachutes are pulled open by the individuals at set altitudes. This allows the men to free fall to this point increasing the accuracy of the drop. There was an experienced jumper next to each quad pro.

The green light came on. The jumpmaster told the men to go. They began to pile out the back of the plane. When Bobby got to the door he hesitated. The man behind him just grabbed him and pushed him out the door. Almost immediately his chute opened and he began drifting slowly to earth. He looked around, he was surrounded by others drifting too. His fear was being replaced by the thrill. He was having fun.

Soon the ground started getting closer and the fear started to drift back in. " few seconds later Bobby had both feet on the ground. There was a little jolt but he was alright. He began gathering in the chute. He felt great. He felt so alive at that moment he was ready to do it again. Soon he was joined by the others. They felt the same way he did.

Back where Bobby's dad and Lieutenant Colonel Purcell were watching the men drift to earth, Lieutenant Colonel Purcell heard Bobby's dad saying a prayer, not for just his son but for all the men. This touched him deeply. He thought no wonder these guys are the way they are, with people like Bobby's dad pulling for them. They stood and watched all the men land. Lieutenant Colonel Purcell said, "Well, it looks like they are all down. We'd better go, they'll be back at the company area soon."

The men secured the parachutes, unpacked their quads and headed back to the maintenance shed. They were all excited about the jump. Lieutenant

Colonel Purcell walked in with Bobby's dad. One of the soldiers called the room to attention. They all snapped to attention. Lieutenant Colonel Purcell said, "As you were." They relaxed. Bobby spotted his father and said, "Dad." He came over to him and asked, "What are you doing here?" His dad said, "I brought your truck and quad to you." Bobby said, "You did. Why?" "You said you wanted them so I took a day's vacation and brought them to you." Bobby said, "You missed it Dad, we just parachuted in. It was great." Bobby's dad said, "No, I didn't. I saw the whole thing. It sure looked like fun." Bobby said, "Dad, it was a real rush. Excuse me for a few minutes while we finish up here." Lieutenant Colonel Purcell replied, "Go ahead, we'll finish up here. Besides, don't you have a dentist appointment?" Bobby said, "Oh yes, thank you, sir." Bobby and his dad left together.

Bobby asked where his mom was. "She's in Dallas, shopping for her store," Bobby's dad said. "She told me to tell you she loves you. I'm going to fly up there and meet her. She's got her car. She followed me to Dallas. When is your dentist appointment?" Bobby said, "In a couple of hours. I'll be fine, Dad, you don't need to stay. I'll take you to the airport. We can stop and have lunch." Bobby's dad said, "Okay then. Lunch sounds pretty good."

The two men left in Bobby's truck. They drove to the airport and ate lunch. Bobby told his dad he would be home next weekend.

Bobby was soon headed back to the base and the dentist office. Dana Ross, the dentist, was ready for him. She asked him his deployment status. He told her he was going to Turkey in a couple of weeks. She told him that she would temporarily fix the tooth and when he returned he would have to have it fixed permanently. Bobby told her okay.

An hour later he was done. His whole face was numb. He returned to his room to recuperate. He found a couple of notes. One from Johnny saying he will see him Sunday night. The other from Chad Duncan giving him directions to the lake. Bobby suddenly felt all alone. He decided to take a shower and hit the sack.

CHAPTER 3

The next morning, Saturday. Bobby got up. His mouth felt good. He got ready and headed to the lake. It was about forty miles south of Fort Hood. He made several twists and turns. He followed the directions to the letter. After being on the road for about an hour, he came upon a tree lined lake. He found his friends Chad and Charlotte. There were close to fifty people at their picnic. Chad was playing volleyball. Charlotte was busy spreading food on a nearby table. Charlotte called Bobby over to the table. She handed him a cold beer. She asked, "How's your tooth?" Bobby said, "Good, real good." He asked, "Who are all these people?" Charlotte said, "Family, friends, and friends of friends. But we are all family here and so are you. Relax and have a good time." Bobby said, "This reminds me of Memorial weekend with my family." Chad came running over and said, "Come on Bobby, we need you in the game." Bobby turned to Charlotte and said, "Duty calls." He went with Chad to play volleyball. The picnic site was beautiful. It was located where a creek ran into the lake. Several kids were in the water swimming. Chad and Bobby were having a ball playing volleyball. After about a half hour Charlotte said, "You guys take a break and come get some of my famous fried chicken." Chad laughed. Bobby said, "What's so funny?" Chad said, "We stopped and bought her famous chicken at KFC on the way here." Bobby laughed, "Well, let's eat." On their way to the table a couple of personal watercraft pulled up on the beach. Bobby glanced over at the machines. There she was. The girl from the bar. Bobby thought that girl is beautiful. I've got to meet her. Chad grabbed Bobby's arm. "Come on, dude, let's chow" he said. Bobby said, "Right, I'm starved." They started eating. The blonde girl came over to the table. "Charlotte" she exclaimed. She and Charlotte hugged. Charlotte said to her, "I've got someone here you've got to meet." She turned to Bobby who had just taken a bite of chicken. "Bobby, this is my cousin Jill. Jill, this is our friend Bobby." He was caught off guard. He tried to swallow the chicken whole and choked. Jill said, "I'm choked up to meet you too." Chad almost busted a gut. Charlotte hit Chad on the arm. Bobby finally got the chicken down, regained his composure and said, "I'm sorry. I'm pleased to meet you." She said, "Oh, that's okay. For a moment there I thought I was going to lose my future husband." Bobby said, "Husband?" Arelax" she said, "I was only trying to get a rise out of you." Bobby said, "You did that alright, in more ways than one." Charlotte said, "Jill, are you hungry? Do you want some chicken?" "Yes, thank you" she said. She sat down next to Bobby and fixed herself a plate. She said, "So, Bobby, you're a quad rider?" He thought, how did she know that. Charlotte must have told her about him. He said, "Yeah, that's right, I am." She said, "Cool. Maybe you can take me for a ride sometime." He thought, yeah I'll take you for a ride. He said, "I'd love to. Maybe after lunch. I've got my quad with me." She said, "Great, I'll show you the best places to go." Bobby was really fascinated with Jill. Bobby said, "Great." Charlotte said teasingly to her husband, "Don't you think we should go along Chad." He said, "Sure I do. But I didn't bring my quad. Besides, I've got some ideas of my own. Can I borrow one of your wet bikes Jill?" She said, "Sure, you can take them both if you want to." Chad said, "We only need one." Bobby finished eating. He said, "I'm going to go unload my quad, I'll be back in a minute." Chad said "I'll go with you." The two of them left to go to Bobby's truck. Charlotte then asked "Well, what do you think?" Jill said, "I'll let you know later. But so far so good." Bobby and Chad got the quad unloaded. Chad asked Bobby the same question. His response was exactly the same. Bobby checked the gas and oil and found a couple of helmets. Jill and Charlotte finished eating. Then they packed a small ice chest with beer and snacks. Bobby and Chad came walking back to the table. Bobby handed Jill a helmet and asked, "Are you ready?" Jill took the helmet and said, "You betcha, let's roll." Bobby and Chad looked at each other and smiled. The two of them got on the four-wheeler. It felt strange to Bobby. It had been a long time since he rode double with anyone. They rode up a trail for a few minutes. Bobby was going fairly slow. Jill said to him "I thought you were a pro. We're riding like my grandpa." That's all Bobby needed. He poured the coals to his machine. Jill screamed "That's more like it." She held on tight to Bobby. When he hit a corner she leaned right with him. After about twenty minutes Jill told Bobby to pull over. They were on a bluff overlooking the lake. She opened the ice chest and handed Bobby a beer. She said, "So what do you do when you aren't busy being a hero?" He told her "I'm going to school to learn to be an aircraft mechanic." She said, "That's cool." Bobby asked her "What about you? What do you do to make ends meet?" She said, "Right now I waitress in a pizza joint. But I'm going to school this fall. I'm going to try and get a marketing degree." He asked, "Where are you going to school?" She said, "Well, I've been going to junior college. This fall I'm going to Tulsa University in Tulsa, Oklahoma." Bobby said, "You're kidding, that's where I'm from." She said, "Cool, maybe you can visit me." He said, "You can count on it." Jill said, "I'll bet a good looking guy like you has a steady girl back home." He said, "Nope. Between work, school and racing I don't have the time. I date every once in awhile, that's about it." He asked, "What about your love life?" She said, "I've had a few boyfriends, but nobody serious." He then tried to shock her. "Well, that's all about to change with me." Instead it backfired. She said, "I know, we're getting married. I want my kids to have a father." Bobby blushed. He was speechless. He looked at her like he'd never looked at a woman before. He thought, could this be the one. He had to snap out of if. After all, he had just met her. She said to Bobby "I'm hot, let's take a swim." She pulled off shorts and top to reveal a swim suit. She walked over to the bluff that overlooked the lake. She turned to Bobby and said, "Come on." She took a couple of steps and jumped off the forty foot bluff into the lake. Bobby peeled off to his boxers. He stood on the bluff looking down at Jill. He asked, "Are you crazy?" He jumped to join her. The lake water felt good. He grabbed her and she felt good in his arms. She pushed him under the water, he let go and popped up a few feet away. She was laughing. They swam together for a few more minutes. She said, "Let's go for a ride. It will be dark soon and there's something I want you to see. They climbed back up the bluff, got dressed and started riding. They rode around to the east side of the lake. The arrived just in time to see the most beautiful sunset Bobby had ever seen. He'd seen sunsets before but not like this one. Maybe it was because Jill was with him.

They sat and watched together until the sun was all the way down. They didn't say a word. Finally she asked, "Well, what do you think?" He said, "Beautiful, and the sunset wasn't bad either." She blushed and reached up to him. She kissed him like he had never been kissed before. Then she said, "We had better go." They rode back to the picnic site. They had travelled a long way. They were about two miles from there when they ran out of gas. Luckily they were near a dirt road that led back to the picnic area. As they walked they talked. They talked about everything, family, friends, wants and desires. They talked about Bobby's experience with the Army and about his upcoming trip to Turkey. In no time they were back at the picnic area. They had a big fire going. Everyone was just sitting around telling stories. Chad spotted Bobby and Jill. He nudged Charlotte and pointed. She got up and came over to them. She asked, "Where have you two been? Where's your ATV? I've been worried sick." Jill said, "We're okay, we just ran out of gas a couple of miles from here." Chad walked up and said, "I'll go with you to take the gas back." Jill said, "No you won't, you stay here with your wife. Bobby and I will go get the four-wheeler. They got in Bobby's truck and drove down the dirt road to where they had left the quad. Bobby re-filled the tank and prepared to load it on the truck. Jill asked, "Do you mind if I ride it back to the camp?" Bobby said, "No, not at all. Do you know how to ride?" She said, "I think so." She got on the quad, fired it up and took off, pulling a wheelie for about twenty feet. Bobby shook his head and thought, well I'll be. He jumped in his truck and tried to catch her. She beat him back to the picnic area. Everyone was packing up. It was getting late. Jill had started saying goodbye to some of her friends and relatives. Chad had loaded the two waterbikes on the trailer behind Jill's truck. Bobby asked her if they belonged to her. She said, "No, they belong to my brother. He's down in Austin on a job." Chad offered to drive the truck home for her. They had ridden to the lake with Charlotte's sister and her family. He said, "I would appreciate some time alone with Charlotte." Jill said, "Sure, but what about me?" Bobby said, "You can ride with me." She said, "Okay, as long as we don't run out of gas again." Bobby laughed. Chad said, "Bobby, I'll see you tomorrow." Jill got into the truck with Bobby. Bobby asked her if she was hungry. "Starved" she said. "I know an all night restaurant not far from here." They talked all the way to the restaurant. They ate and talked some more. At one point Bobby asked her where she learned to ride quads. She told him she and her brother used to race cross country. Bobby was impressed. After they ate he finished driving her home. They sat parked in her driveway for several hours, just talking. Then she stopped talking and kissed him again. After the kiss he said, "I've never met anyone like you before. I feel like I've known you all my life." She said, "I feel the same way. It's kind of weird, ain't it?" He said, "Yeah, but in a good way." She said, "I hoped you would say that. Would you like to go to church with me tomorrow?" He said, "Sure, I'll pick you up about ten, okay?" She said, "That would be great. Well, I've got to get to bed. You've worn me out." She kissed him again and said, "Goodnight." Bobby waited until she was inside before he drove off. He had a hard time sleeping that night.

He was back at Jill's at 10:00 sharp. She greeted him with a kiss. "Come on in" she said. "I want you to meet my parents." Bobby suddenly got nervous. She sensed this and said to him Arelax, my parents are cool." He met her mother and father. They were real nice people. They talked for a few minutes, then went to church. After church they invited Bobby back to their house

for dinner. While Jill's mother was fixing dinner, Jill took Bobby out to the workshop. "There's something I want you to see" she said. She pulled a tarp off. Underneath was a mint condition 1986 250R four-wheeler. Bobby asked, "Is this yours?" She said, "It sure is. This is what I used to race on." Bobby thought, now I know she's the one for me. Soon dinner was ready. Afterwards Bobby and Jill sent for a walk. Bobby told Jill "I know we've just met but I really would like to spend more time with you. You know I'm leaving the country in a couple of weeks. I don't know for sure when I'll return." He said, "I know this may sound funny, but I think I love you." She said, "It doesn't sound funny at all." She kissed him and then started crying. She said, "I feel the same way." He said, "I'm going to be real busy the next two weeks, but I've got next weekend off. I told my parents I would come home. Would you come with me?" "I'd love to" she said. They talked into the afternoon. Then Bobby headed back to the base. When he got back he called his mother and told her about Jill. She was excited. They talked for several minutes then hung up. Bobby walked over to the training site. He could hear quads. He saw several of the soldiers busy practising jumping. He decided to suit up and join them. " few minutes later Chad joined them. The soldiers were getting better. They rode until dark. Chad and Bobby cleaned up and headed to the mess hall for dinner. Soon they were met by the returning men. They spoke of their weekends. Chad never said a word about Bobby and Jill. He figured it was Bobby's place.

Later that night Bobby went and found Chaplain Noe. He told him about

Jill and how he felt about her. Chaplain Noe told him sometimes that's the way it is. He told him he was happy for him. That made Bobby feel a lot better.

CHAPTER 4

The next morning, Monday, looked like another hot day. In fact the heat was on for the whole week. Once again it's up at 0430 to do physical training. After they finished and cleaned up they walked over to the mess hall. Johnny told Bobby about winning a motocross race. He said, "It was a close race, I had to ride hard." He then asked Bobby about his tooth. Bobby said it felt great. Johnny asked, "Hey dude, what did you do all weekend?" Bobby said, "I went to a picnic with Chad and Charlotte." He hesitated a minute and said to his friend "I met a girl, we had a lot of fun with each other. I think she might be the one." Johnny stopped and looked at him. Bobby expected him to start ragging on him. Instead he said, "Cool dude, she must be something for you to say that. Don't forget, we've got a job to do here." Bobby said, "It's cool dude, I'm all business." Johnny said, "Al-right then, don't get all freaky on me. I'm counting on you. What's her name?" Bobby said, "It's Jill. She's cool and she knows what's up with all of us." Johnny said, "Let's chow, I'm starving." Bobby thought that went better than expected. Bobby told the rest of the guys about Jill at breakfast. They were all happy for him. Chad Duncan said, "I was about to bust a gut to tell everyone." Bobby said, "Yeah, I know." Chad Hubanks said, "My girlfriend and I got back together this weekend." They all looked at him. Buddy said, "Cool, she must be something to put up with you." They all laughed. Will said, "We'd better go or we're going to be late for the morning training briefing." They all headed for the training site.

When they arrived at the classroom, most of the men were already seated. They found chairs and sat down. Lieutenant Colonel Purcell, First Lieutenant Wooley and Sergeant First Class Kroeker walked in. The room stood to attention. The three men walked to the front of the room. Lieutenant Colonel Purcell said, "Take your seats." They all sat down. He continued "I've got a briefing from Colonel Hill on his status. Things are going well. They have established a rear area base. Staff Sergeant Vaughn has got the mess hall up and running so we won't have to eat MRE's all the time. Staff Sergeant Gollihare is well stocked, we'll have everything we need. Thirty new quads have been delivered, Master Sergeant Miller and his crew are checking them out. Soon they will be swapping machines. Captain Randolf and Captain Davis are working on a forward camp and coordinating with the Kurds. They already have several observation posts in operation. Colonel Hill has over a hundred men working under him there. They are spread pretty thin and he's about ready for the rest of us. Any questions on Colonel Hill's report?" Buddy raised his hand, stood up and asked, "How many men are going with us sir?" Lieutenant Colonel Purcell said, "As of right now we are scheduled to take one hundred fifteen additional troops with us. Be aware, we are not the only unit over there. We already have one thousand special operations people in the region, that's not including support people from other branches." He asked, "Any more questions? If not, we'll do the training schedule for this week. First Lieutenant Wooley, you want to cover this? I need to be in the General's office in half an hour." "Yes sir" said First Lieutenant Wooley. "We had good results from Thursday's small group training. For the first half of the next three days we will continue this. We have also scheduled three more jumps. Another daytime jump and two night jumps. The first will be tomorrow afternoon. The first night jump will be Thursday and then again next Tuesday. This afternoon we will work on weapons training on the quads. Wednesday afternoon on small unit tactics. Thursday we will work in the morning on conditioning and survival tactics. Friday morning we will work on coordinated assault tactics. Our instructors will be allowed to leave early Friday. The rest of us will go on a forced march. That's all I have. Remember, we are subject to change anytime." Sergeant First Class Kroeker called the unit to attention. They all stood to attention. Then he said, "Let's go get on our quads." The men filed out and headed for the maintenance building. On the way over Bobby said to Johnny "Let's double up our crew. They all need to work on their jumping." Johnny said, "Cool. Two heads are better than one." The men suited up and checked out their machines. They hooked up with the eight soldiers assigned to them including two veterans, Sergeant Stockstill and Sergeant Higgonbotham. They spent the next two hours doing jumps.

It was hard work but fun, too. The soldiers really worked hard. Three of the men were really improving, Sergeant Grigsby, Sergeant Lowry and Specialist Money. Bobby said to Johnny "Don't you think Specialist Money reminds you of someone?" Johnny said, "Now that you mention it, he does. Specialist Luke White, the guy we lost in the Philippines." Bobby said, "Yeah, he has the same build, same riding style. They could have been brothers." Bobby and Johnny showed the soldiers a few tricks on the jumps. They used their helmet communication systems to talk the men through the jumps. After a couple hours they took a break. They got some water and refueled their quads. The next two hours were spent off track. Bobby and Johnny found some funky jumps, off camber stuff with sharp turns after landing. At first soldiers struggled. By end of the two hour session they were doing better. Their confidence level had jumped up tremendously. " couple of the guys couldn't quite get it. They were riding okay but there was just something about them. Bobby decided to recommend they stick to the support quads. After the training session the soldiers were eager to hear the pros' evaluation of them. Bobby and Johnny talked to each one of them individually. The young Specialist Money, his first name Luke, told them he was from Sapulpa, Oklahoma. Bobby said, "I knew there was something I liked about you." The men went to lunch. The pros compared notes. First Lieutenant Wooley joined them. He asked for a progress report. Overall, all the men were improving. They felt confident that they would be ready to go by the following week. That was good news.

That afternoon the men checked out their quads again. This time weapons had been mounted. They went to a range specially set up for them. They would go, one at a time, at a medium rate of speed. They would select targets and shoot their 9mm machine guns. Most of the men did really well. The pros did excellent. Their eye-hand coordination was phenomenal. After they completed that portion of the training, each was issued one training rocket. They would use their onboard targeting system to locate, lock on and fire. All of this while negotiating a series of twists and turns. Some of the men needed more practice. They were having trouble riding and shooting. They would concentrate too much on target acquisition and not enough on negotiating the trail. They needed to pick the speed up. All of this took most of the afternoon. When they finished they returned to the air conditioned maintenance building to clean their weapons.

Bobby called Jill's house. Her mother answered the phone. She said Jill was working late that night at the pizza joint. Bobby got the address from her. He invited all of his friends for beer and pizza that night. Those guys weren't about to turn down free beer. They all said they would join him. Even Chad, of course after he called Charlotte and included her in the deal. That evening after they cleaned up they all went to the pizza joint. Jill sure was surprised when they all came in. She took them to a table. Bobby said, "Jill, these are my brothers." He named them off. Then he said, "Guys, this is Jill, the future mother of my children." They all laughed. Jill said, "These are your brothers? Boy did I get the ugly one of the lot." Buddy said, "You got that right." Jill took their order. Soon she came back with a couple of pitchers of beer and eight glasses. Charlotte turned to Chad "Does this remind you of anything?" He said, "It sure does, you girls are good at carrying beer." It was a slow night so Jill sat down for a few minutes. Johnny said, "What made you pick this guy when you could have had any of us?" She said, "I felt sorry for the poor thing. Just look at that face. I used to get in trouble all the time for bringing home stray dogs. I guess I just couldn't break the habit." Another group came in and Jill had to wait on them. Johnny looked over at Bobby and said, "Son, you did alright." The rest of them agreed. You couldn't have knocked the grin off Bobby with a sledgehammer. They all drank their beer. Soon Jill came back with the pizzas. The men tore into them. Jill leans over to Bobby and says "Come with me, there's something I need to show you." Bobby got up to follow her. The rest of the men barely noticed as he left. They went to the parking lot. She didn't say anything. She wrapped her arms around him and planted a big kiss on him. He said, "Wow!" She said, "I just wanted to see if it was real." Bobby didn't understand, but there would be lots of things about women he wouldn't understand. She said her last day of work was Thursday. He told her that they would be ready to go at noon on Friday. "Great" she said, "I'll be ready." He asked, "How would you like to watch me race?" She said, "I'd love to." He said, "We're going to be pretty busy, I don't know if I will be able to see you again before Friday." She said, "Bobby, you have an important job to do. Don't worry, we'll have plenty of time together. If I thought I kept you from doing the best you can I'd drop you now. Okay?" He said, "Yeah, you're the best." This time he kissed her. She said, "Wow! We'd better get back in. I've got work to do." They went back inside. Bobby went back to the table and finished his meal. Will said, "It's getting late.

We'd better get back to Fort Hood." They all got up and Bobby grabbed the ticket to pay. Jill said, "It's been taken care of." She winked at him. They returned to Fort Hood.

The next day was a copy of the previous day, except the teams swapped around. The soldiers' riding skills improved each day. That afternoon Bobby and the others got to parachute again. This time they would free fall and use an altimeter on their wrist to determine when to pull the chute open. Mick said after their second jump "That's such a rush." Sergeant First Class Kroeker said, "Wait until you do it at night." By Thursday night the training had gone well. It was time for a night jump. " weak front had moved in causing the wind to pick up a little. It was still within jumping limits. However, a few of the jumpers drifted from the landing zone. One man was hurt. He broke his arm. Fortunately it wasn't anyone from the quad team. Somehow Charlotte found out that someone got hurt. She called Jill and she called Bobby. He told her everyone was okay. They talked for a few minutes and said, "I'd better call Charlotte and let her know. Don't tell Chad that she was worried." Bobby said, "Okay. I'll see you tomorrow" and hung up.

It was finally Friday. Light physical training and breakfast. The men were excited about the morning's exercise. It was a simulated attack. They had done this before. This time however, more than just the quads were involved. There would be ground troops that would use fast moving dune buggies and motorcycles in the assault. It was a simulated rescue mission. Lieutenant Colonel Purcell planned the whole thing. The soldiers were very proficient. Everything went without a hitch. No simulated casualties. Lieutenant Colonel Purcell was very pleased. General Johnson stopped by to observe. He told Lieutenant Colonel Purcell to give the men a well done. The quads performed flawlessly. First Lieutenant Wooley said, "I think we are about ready." He told Bobby to join the others. "You guys have helped a lot. I don't think we could have done as well without you guys." Johnny said, "We had good students. We just showed them a few things." The lieutenant said, "Well, I guess you guys are ready for a couple of days off. Get outta here. I'll check your quads in for you. They went back to their rooms, cleaned up and grabbed their bags. Everyone was going home. Even Chad and Charlotte. Charlotte and Jill met the men at the airport. Staff Sergeant

Ketcher dropped the men at the terminal. They all got into the same plane. They would split up in Dallas. Their spirits were high, even though they knew in a week they would be boarding a plane bound for Turkey. The men felt they had a good team together. Another short flight, Bobby, Jill and Johnny were landing at Tulsa. Johnny's grandpa picked him up. He had plans to race at Tulsa Saturday night. Bobby said, "We will try and catch your act tomorrow night." Johnny said, "I'll see you when I see you." Bobby's dad picked Jill and him up. Jill thought he was a real nice man. Bobby asked him "Where's mom?" He said, "She's fixing dinner." Jill said, "I'm starved. Bobby never feeds me." Bobby's dad chuckled "Well, his mom will take care of that." Soon they were in Sand Springs at Bobby's parents' home. Bobby and his dad carried in their bags. Bobby's mom Sandy met them at the door. She gave her son a big hug and then hugged Jill. She made her feel right at home. She had dinner ready and on the table. Jill and Bobby freshened up and sat down at the table. Bobby said, "Jill, I guess you're special. We don't eat at the table very often." Jill said, "It's the same way at my house." Bobby said, "Mom, Jill is going to Tulsa University this fall." Sandy said, "Great, my older daughter went to Tulsa University. She's a Certified Public Accountant." Jill said, "I'm going into marketing. But first I need to find a job to help pay for expenses." Sandy said, "I might be able to help you out there if you're interested." Jill said, "Sure, what do you have in mind?" Sandy said, "I have a couple of stores. " clothing store and a furniture store. I could use some help in my clothing store." Jill said, "That sounds wonderful." Sandy said, "Well, we will give it a try." They continued to talk while they ate. After dinner Bobby took Jill out to look at his ATV's. Jill said, "You've got five quads." He said, "No, just four." "There's four here and one back at Fort Hood" she said. He pointed at one and said, "This one's my dad's." "He races?" she asked. "Sure" he said, "but he only races cross country." He added "He'll race Sunday." She said, "You're racing cross country?" He said, "Yeah, I asked you if you wanted to go." She said, "I didn't know it was cross country." He asked, "Is there a problem?" She said, "Only if you don't let me race with you." He said, "Okay." She grabbed him around the neck and kissed him. He said, "Well, if you're going to race you probably should ride the quad to get used to it. We'll go riding in the morning." It was getting late. They went back in the house. The next morning they woke early, packed a lunch and loaded up the two quads. They headed to a nearby lake. They rode trails all day. She handled the quad really well. They had a lot of fun. Bobby felt closer to her than anyone he had ever been with. They returned home, loaded the quads in the big trailer along with Bobby's dad's quad. They cleaned up, went out to eat and then headed to the track to watch Johnny race. They were having a ball. Early the next morning they headed to Chandler, Oklahoma to the cross country race. Bobby, Jill, his mother and father all went. Jill told them she loved cross country racing. Bobby entered the Pro Class. Jill and Bobby's dad entered the Amateur Class. Bobby had trouble on the start but pulled out the win in the ninety minute race. His dad finished fifth and Jill finished seventh. They all had fun. They had to head straight home after the race. They had a plane to catch. Jill had a great time and looked forward to returning to Tulsa. Soon they were back in Texas. Staff Sergeant Ketcher picked them up at the airport. He took them back to the base. Bobby then took Jill home. He thanked her for going with him. He told her he had never had so much fun. She said, "Bobby, that's only the beginning." They kissed and said goodnight. Bobby drove back to the base. He was on top of the world.

When he got back he expected everyone to be in bed. They weren't, there was a note saying to come to the training room. He walked on over. Everyone was there. Bobby found Johnny and asked what was going on. Johnny told him he was just as much in the dark as he was. Lieutenant Colonel Purcell, Major Dobson and First Lieutenant Wooley were talking informally up front. All over the room men were talking amongst themselves. Something was definitely up. Finally Lieutenant Colonel Purcell said, "Take your seats. We have received a report from Colonel Hill that he is reporting increased activity in his area. It seems large troop movements all along the Turkish border. We are spread pretty thin up there and he has requested we move up our timetable. General Johnson has talked with him personally. As you know we were scheduled to leave Friday. I was hoping for coordinated night assault exercise but that has been cancelled. Most of the troops will leave now on Tuesday. The quad team and the rest of the support staff will leave on Wednesday. The only reason we don't leave on Tuesday is because I want to have another night-time chute drop with men and equipment. First Lieutenant Wooley has the modified schedule and he will put the information out later. All the news reports of the United States invading Iraq has made Saddam nervous, so he is moving his army around.

We are not expecting any conflict. Colonel Hill said he would feel better with reinforcements. You should pack any gear that you won't be using the next couple of days. " C-5 will take us out of here at 1200 hours Wednesday. Major Dobson will go with the ground troops. First Lieutenant Wooley will be in charge of the rest of you Wednesday. Do you have any questions?" No one answered. He continued "Good, I know you men are ready or I wouldn't be sending you. You have trained hard for this, you all will do fine." Sergeant First Class Kroeker called the room to attention again and then he said, "Dismissed." The seven pros looked at each other. Will said, "Well, here we go." They got copies of the new training schedule from First Lieutenant Wooley and headed back to their rooms. Chad Hubanks said, "Well, I need to call home and let them know I'm leaving Wednesday instead of Friday." Buddy said, "Well, the sooner we get over there the sooner we get back." Mick said, "Yeah, them Iraqis better watch out, The Magnificent Seven are on their way." Johnny said, "They should be shaking in their boots about right now." Will said, "I know I am." They all laughed. Bobby said, "It's cool guys. We just watch each other's back and we'll all come back home." Chad Duncan said, "You got that right brother." Soon they were all on the phone. They were telling their families of the change in plans. Bobby made arrangements to see Jill Tuesday night. They would all be going to Pete's for a beer. That is, if they had time. Their schedule looked pretty tight. Tuesday night was open for packing and personal time.

Monday morning the men were up and doing physical training. The weather had cooled slightly and the clouds were starting to thicken up a little. Rain was expected by Wednesday. They had a good work-out and did a five mile run. The seven men were in good shape. Will said after the run "I feel like I could run another five miles." Mick said, "Are you crazy?" Will said, "Well yeah, we all are, we're here aren't we?" Mick said, "Good point." The men showered and went to breakfast. Johnny said, "I hope we don't have to eat of lot of MRE's over there." Bobby said, "I know what you mean, that chicken a la king is gross." Chad Hubanks said, "I don't know, I kind of like the MRE's." Chad Duncan said, "You would." The morning schedule called for a couple of hours of riding. They loaded up and split into two groups. They practised simulated battles with each other, honing their riding and communication skills. After they finished and checked in their quads they headed to the classroom.

They spent the rest of the morning going over that night's mission. It was all pretty routine, except it was at night. It would be their second night jump. They were all glad to get extra practice in. After lunch it was back in the classroom. This time it was for the mission in Turkey. They were given maps that showed the locations of all the camps and operations. From looking at the detailed maps they could see a lot of elevation changes that meant lots of hills and valleys. They were shown actual photographs of the camps and surrounding terrain. They showed lots of rocks and sand. No trees were to be found in any of the pictures. They were issued code books to use in their communications. They were pretty simple. Mostly locations and numbers. The maps they had were also coded. They were told not to lose these and if they got in trouble to destroy them. They would be changed weekly and sooner if needed. That way if the enemy did get one it really wouldn't do them much good. They were released fairly early in the afternoon so they could rest for the night mission. Bobby couldn't sleep so he decided to call his parents. He called his mother's store because that's where she would be. She was upset about him going into harm's way again. He tried to assure her everything would be okay. His dad just happened to drop by the store while they were talking. His wife handed him the phone. He assured Bobby that his mom would be okay. He told his son that he wished he could take his place. Bobby knew that his dad meant it, he wasn't just saying it. He told him to stick with his friends and to think before he acted. He told his son he loved him. Bobby's mom got back on the phone. She sounded better. She asked about Jill. Bobby told her that Jill would be headed that way this weekend. She wanted to know if she could stay with them for a few days until she found a place. Sandy told him to tell her she could stay as long as she wanted. She then told her son that she loved him and she would pray for his safe return. They hung up. Bobby felt better and relaxed long enough to get a nap in.

The next thing he knew Johnny was waking him up. He said, "Better get up, we've got a half hour before we are supposed to be there." He put a pot of coffee on. Bobby got up and poured a cup. " knock at the door. It was the other five men. They walked in. Buddy said, "Is that coffee I smell?" Before they could answer he grabbed a cup. The others did the same. Bobby told his friends "Guys, I don't think I could do this if it weren't for you."

Chad Duncan said, "We know, we all feel the same way." Soon they were ready. They walked out together and headed for the training site. They loaded up on deuce and a half for the trip over to the airfield. They got their parachutes, listened to the safety briefing and loaded onto the plane. Soon the plane reached the desired altitude, the door opened and out they went. Each time they jumped it got easier. It was pitch black. The clouds had blocked out the moon and stars. They pulled the rip cords and drifted safely to the ground. There was no talking. The men gathered up their chutes and put them in a pile to be retrieved later. They located the crated quads. They all loaded and started the machines. They were in whisper mode but with that many quads they were pretty loud. They maintained a ten meter distance between them which made it look like a mile long train. No lights were seen. The men operated with night vision and infrared. Slowly they made it to the first check point. Their objective was less than a mile away now. Split into three teams, the men headed off in different directions. Voice contact remained but was kept to a minimum. Soon everyone was in position. Alpha grouped, dismounted and entered the target area. They were doing a simulated rescue. They entered a building, took out the dummy guards and grabbed the dummy prisoners. Alpha group was making their way out of the building. Major Dobson threw in a little surprise. All of a sudden flares started going off. There were simulated explosives. It sounded like all hell was breaking loose. Bravo team, Bobby and the other pros came in, guns blaring (blanks) to provide cover for the Alpha team. Charlie team remained on station covering the high ground and ready to cover their exit. Alpha team made it to their quads. All of them rejoined at the rally point. They then headed back to company area. The mission was complete. They ended the evening with an after action briefing. Everything went like clockwork. Lieutenant Colonel Purcell was impressed. He released the men. He told them they could skip physical training. They laughed, it was already two o'clock a.m. The rest of Fort Hood would be up in two and a half hours. They were told they didn't have to report until 0900. They all left and went to bed. By 0800 they were all up again. Bobby and Johnny had Chad sleep in their room. It had been too late for him to go home to Charlotte. They dressed and headed to the mess hall. Buddy said, "Our schedule says NBC training all day. What is that?" Chad Hubanks said, "I did some asking. NBC stands for Nuclear Biological and Chemical. It's been said that Saddam has lots of it. Will said, "Somebody needs to shoot that S.O.B."

Bobby said, "If I see him, he's dead." Johnny said, "I heard there is a bounty on him. If you get him we'll split it." Bobby said, "Equal shares for all of us." Mick said, "We'll be rich." Chad Duncan said, "I'd do it for nothing." Bobby said, ""men brother, "men to that."

After breakfast the men headed over to the company area. They walked into the maintenance building. Most of the equipment had been crated up and they were busy crating the ATV's. Major Dobson had already left with most of the men. Only the quad team and a few support personnel remained. It was almost 0900. Time to head to class. The NBC training was very in-depth. First they showed films of the effects of chemical and biological contamination. The films were very graphic. They skipped the nuclear film. The men were taught how and when to give injections to counteract some chemical exposures and how to test for them. They were issued chemical masks. In country they would carry these with them at all times. They were also issued chemical suits that were charcoal lined. They were taught what they would and would not protect them from. To most of the soldiers this was reinforcement training. To the quad pros it was new and very scary. One question kept nagging at them all. How would all of this protective gear work with their quad uniforms. The answer soon appeared with Lieu-tenant Colonel Purcell. He brought in several boxes, or at least he had them brought in. He told the men to keep their seats. He said, "What I have here is something I have had my team working on." He opened one of the boxes. "It's a lightweight chemical suit that allows moisture to escape but keeps chemicals out. It had been tested and it worked." He added "I also have a liner for your helmets that will allow them to seal off. Your gloves and boots are already designed against chemical contamination. Anytime you go on a mission you will wear these as part of your uniforms." He asked, "Any questions?" Chad Hubanks stood and asked, "Sir, what does Saddam have in his arsenal?" Lieutenant Colonel Purcell said, "Well, he says he has none. But our intelligence knows better. We know he is close to having nuclear capabilities. We can't let that happen. That's what all of this is about. We have to stop this crazy man from destroying the world. Some say we are overstepping ourselves. I'm not a politician, just a soldier like you do-ing what I'm told. I do believe, however, that this is a righteous fight. I want yours and my families to have a safe life." He finished by saying "Try these suits on for size and we'll go over to the post tear-gas chamber and try

116

them out. I'm sending these suits to the men already in country." He began handing out the suits. First Lieutenant Wooley helped him. The men went and got their quad uniforms and put the whole garb on. They were surprisingly comfortable. It was near lunch time, it was decided to eat first and then they would go try the suits out. They kept the suits on minus helmets and gloves. People looked at them kind of funny at the mess hall. One soldier said the Star Wars cast is here. The men did feel a little out of place. After lunch they headed to the tear-gas chamber. The suits worked great. To prove it, they were told to remove their helmets. It didn't take long for them to bail out coughing and hacking. Their skin burned and fluids came out their noses. This was only non-lethal tear-gas. They gained a lot of respect for chemical weapons. They returned to the classroom to complete the training. They were finally released to go pack and take care of personal business. The plan was to meet later at Pete's for a cold drink. The men were packed and cleaned up in a hurry. Before they went to Pete's they went and got a Texas sized steak dinner. Jill and Charlotte met them there. Both girls greeted their man with a kiss. Jill and Bobby's kiss lasted awhile, prompting cat calls from the others. Bobby turned beet red. Charlotte changed the subject. "So you all are ready to go take on the world." Buddy laughed "That's us, we're full of piss and vinegar." Chad Hubanks said, "Saddam better look out, The Magnificent Seven are on their way." Bobby recovered from his embarrassment and said, "We're ready for Saddam. I just hope he isn't ready for us." Reality check. Jill said, "No way. Nobody could get ready for you guys." Bobby smiled at her. She smiled back, desperately trying to cover up her fear. They all enjoyed their steak dinners. They joked and told stories on each other. Finally Charlotte said, "Well boys, let's go get a beer." Buddy said, "Sounds good to me." They paid the check and headed over to Pete's Party Palace. When they walked in most of the guys in their unit were there. The atmosphere was positive. They found a couple of tables together. Jill and Charlotte went for some beer at the bar. Jill asked Charlotte "When did you know Chad was the right one for you?" Charlotte smiled "Almost immediately. We didn't know it but looking back it was the first night he walked in here. It was kind of like chemistry. We've talked and he felt the same way." She asked, "You and Bobby?" Jill said, "I think he's wonderful, more than a passing fancy. I'm not sure, but I think he feels the same way by some of the things he has said." Charlotte said, "You know, you're just fighting it." Jill answered "Maybe so." They took the beer back to the table. The men all grabbed one. Before Bobby could take a drink Jill grabbed him and said, "Let's dance." Johnny egged him on "Bust a move brother." Bobby said, "Alright baby, let's see if you can keep up with me." They just started to boogey when the music changed to a slow song. Bobby grabbed Jill, held her tight and did some slow dancing. She was melting. She looked up at Bobby and kissed him. She looked deep into his blue eyes. While she was looking he was looking back at her. She said, "Let's get some air." They walked outside. They just wandered around the parking lot. She said, "Bobby, I'm going out on a limb here. I think I've fallen in love with you and I think you love me too." Jill was rarely this serious. Bobby stopped her, kissed her and said, "I've been crazy about you since you bumped into me here at the bar." She said, "We didn't even talk." He said, "We didn't have to. It's kind of weird, ain't it?" She said, "You sure are something." He said, "Well the timing sucks." She said, "Bobby, if you are what I think you are, we will have plenty of time together. I want you to get your head right. Don't worry about me or about us. I'll be here when you return. The others need you and you need them. Make me proud, make yourself proud. When this is over you will relive it over and over. I know, I've seen it before in my dad and in my uncles. If you are worried about me then you might make mistakes. I couldn't live with that and you couldn't either. I'm going to Tulsa this weekend to get ready for school. I'll be there for you when you return. Now kiss me before I..." He kissed her so passionately she almost fainted in ecstasy. He said, "I love you." She cried and said, "I love you too. Now, let's go get a beer." She pulled herself together and they both went back inside the bar. She was glad the bar was dark. By now the men were up dancing and having a good time. Bobby and Jill sat down and drank a beer. They watched the others dance. After the music finished they brought the girls over to the table. The girls were the same ones that they had met their first time in Pete's. Buddy introduced them to Bobby and Jill. "This is Edna, Lori, Sherry, Debbie and Brenda." Bobby said, "Oh yeah, the gamblers from the store in Big Springs. How are you all doing?" He pointed to Jill "This is my future wife Jill." They all said, "Hello." It turned out Jill knew a couple of the girls. They all had a wonderful time that night. By 11:00 the girls said they had to go. They thanked the men for the drinks and dancing. The men had one more beer with some of the guys from their unit. Most of them had already left for the base, but there was still a few of them there. Specialist Luke Money offered

118

a toast to their success in the Middle East. They all raised their glasses to him. Johnny said, "Well, I guess we'd better go too. The men were not drunk but were very festive still. All nine walked out of the bar whistling the tune for the theme song of The Magnificent Seven. Charlotte and Jill even joined in. Chad and Charlotte got into one vehicle. Chad said, "I'll see you guys in the morning." Charlotte said, "Yeah, we're going home to make a little Chad." The men laughed. Chad turned red and so did Jill. Jill had driven her car. She and Bobby got in that. Bobby said, "I'll see you guys in a little while." The rest of them loaded into the van. Jill told Bobby as they were driving back "One day I'll give you a little Bobby if you want to." Bobby said, "I love kids. I know my mom wants a grandbaby real bad." Jill had him pull over on a dark road just outside of the base. They kissed and hugged passionately. Jill said, "I want you so bad but we need to wait. Okay Bobby?" He said, "I feel the same way, I understand." She said, "We had better go before I lose control." He sighed, straightened up and said, "Yeah, I know what you mean." He drove onto the base. She was allowed to take him to his quarters. After he got out she said, "You take care Bobby Duck. I can't have the father of my kids getting hurt." He said, "Don't worry, I'm part of The Magnificent Seven." He added "I love you Jill." Before she could answer he walked off. She said to herself "I love you too."

Morning came too soon. Bobby had slept like a baby. He woke up before Johnny and started a pot of coffee. Johnny got up, poured himself and Bobby a cup and said, "Well, today is the day. Have you got your head on straight?" Bobby said, "I'm cool as an ice cube. I've got you covered brother." Johnny smiled, he knew Bobby was okay. They got dressed, finished packing and headed out the door with their bags. Chad and some of the others were already there. Bobby asked, "Who's not here?" Will said, "Buddy and Chad. They are on their way." Soon they were joined by their friends. They left their bags and headed to the mess hall. They had plenty of time. Soon they were joined by Staff Sergeant Ketcher. "I've got your bags in the van" he said. Johnny asked, "Are you going with us?" He said, "Well, yeah. Do you think I'd let you guys have all the fun?" Mick said, "Cool." They ate their breakfast and drove over to the training site to see if there were any stragglers. The place was empty. They drove over to the airfield. " big C-5 Galaxy was being loaded. Johnny said, "There's our ride. Where is everybody?" They walked into the large hangar. The men were seated in front of a stage. To one side was an army band. On the stage was General Johnson, Lieutenant Colonel Purcell, First Lieutenant Wooley, Sergeant First Class Kroeker and Congressman Jack Gregory. The men looked for a chair to sit down in. Before they could, however, Sergeant First Class Kroeker stood up and called the men to attention. The general approached the microphone. "At ease" he said. "Good morning. Today you men leave for a hazardous mission. You will be the eyes and ears for the upcoming assault on Saddam. The intelligence you provide us with is essential to our success. Our hopes and prayers go with you. But before you go I understand something needs to be taken care of. Will the following Warrant Officers please report to the stage. Bobby Duck, Johnny Hale, Chad Duncan, Buddy Bishop, Chad Hubanks, Will Valance and Mick Smalley. The seven men walked up on the stage. He said, "I understand you men have been jumping out of airplanes. You are out of uniform." He began handing them airborne wings. Attached to the wings were small replicas of the quads. He shook each of their hands as he handed them the medals. He had the seven men do an about face to face the other men. He walked back over to the microphone and said, "Follow me!" The men in the audience and the others on the stage said in unison "All the way." The general then excused the seven men from the stage. He asked, "Will Chaplain Noe please come up here now?" The general stepped back from the microphone and Chaplain Jimmy Noe approached. He said, "Let us pray." The men took off their hats and bowed their heads. "Lord, we come to you today to ask for your divine guidance for these men here today. They leave the safety and comfort of their homes to defend us against our enemies. Please watch over them and if it is Your will, please let them all return safe to us. We ask this in Your name. Amen." All the men followed with ""men." Sergeant First Class Kroeker called them to attention again, then dismissed them. They all began walking out of the hangar. The plane wasn't quite loaded yet. The army band began playing. It was the theme song to the movie The Magnificent Seven. As the men stood waiting to board the airplane, Bobby and Johnny noticed the congressman talking to the plane's crew. They watched as the congressman shook their hands. " few minutes later they began getting on the plane.

CHAPTER 5

It finally started raining as promised by the weatherman. The men finished boarding. The aircraft was full of men and equipment. Johnny said, "I hope this bird can take off with this load." The plane's ramps closed up. The big engines started winding up. Soon the big bird was airborne. Bobby said to Johnny "Aren't they the same guys we flew with to the Philippines?" Johnny looked and said, "It sure is." This was going to be a long flight. The men did their best to get comfortable. Most of the men tried to sleep. Johnny dozed off. When he woke he looked and saw Bobby talking to a couple of guys from the airplane crew. He made his way over to them. When he got there Bobby introduced Johnny to them. He said, "This is Jim and Marty. This one is Billy Gregory." Johnny said jokingly "Any kin to Congressman Jack Gregory?" Billy said, "He's my uncle." Bobby said, "Get this, the pilot's name is Billy Gregory." Billy said, "He's my cousin, the congressman's son." Johnny said, "Both of you are Billy Gregory. I don't get it." Billy said, "My grandpa is Billy Joe, my dad is Billy Dean, I'm Billy Wayne and my cousin is Billy Jack." Johnny laughed and said, "Cool, but I bet it gets crazy at your house on the holidays." Billy said, "You've got that right." Bobby said, "We've got a plan. We stop in Paris for fuel. It usually takes about two hours, not long enough to do anything. Billy here has worked it so we can be there six hours." Johnny asked, "How are you going to do that?" Billy said, "My cousin is going to have a hydraulic pump replaced." Bobby said, "That will give us time to see some of Paris." Johnny said, "Cool, I always wanted to see that tower." Bobby said, "You've got it ol' buddy."

The men continued to talk for hours, mostly about racing. Almost everyone else was asleep. They grabbed a sandwich, chips and cold drink. One of the airmen asked if they wanted to play some cards. They played nickel and dime poker for the next couple of hours. They were still several hours away from Paris. Bobby was losing and decided to take a nap. Soon the card game broke up and Johnny drifted back to sleep. About thirty minutes from Pairs the airmen started waking the soldiers up. Bobby and Johnny began spreading the word about the six hour layover. The plane landed and all the men got off. First Lieutenant Wooley told all of the men to be back in five and a half hours. If anyone didn't make it back in time they would be left behind and in big trouble. They wandered off in small groups. The seven pros, First Lieutenant Wooley, Sergeant First Class Kroeker, Staff Sergeant Ketcher and Specialist Money pooled their money and rented a stretch limo. Specialist Money said, "This is my first time in a limo. I thought my only limo ride would be on the way to the cemetery." They all laughed. Paris was beautiful. The temperature was in the low seventies. There was very low humidity. People were everywhere. The driver, who spoke broken English, asked their destination. The men wanted to eat lunch at an outdoor café. He took them to one on the way to see the famous Eiffel Tower. Bobby and Chad Duncan made a pack that someday they would bring Charlotte and Jill there. Soon the limo parked and they walked a short distance to a café. They were having trouble ordering until a beautiful young woman who spoke both English and French helped them out. They thanked her. Staff Sergeant Ketcher said, "How are we going to pay for this? We don't have any French money." The woman again offered to help. She said, "Let me pay for it and you can pay me in American money." She added "I'm going to Los Angeles in a week and I can use your dollars then." The men agreed. Each of them gave her twenty dollars, which more than covered their meal. Johnny asked her name. She said, "I'm Angelic. I'm a clothing designer." Johnny was shot down when he found out she was married. Buddy asked her for a favor. She said, "Sure, what do you want?" He said, "I want to buy some wine to take with us. Can you help me out?" She told him of a store two blocks away and they would take the American dollars. She asked them why they were in Paris. Johnny just said, "We are on our way to the Middle East to fight terrorists." "Bless you" she said. "My brother was killed by a terrorist bomb in Israel. They have to be stopped." She added "I must go now, good luck to you all." She left. The men were enjoying their wine and lunch. Soon a man appeared carrying a package. He asked, "Which one of you is Buddy?" Buddy raised his hand. The man said, "My wife asked me to give this to you." Buddy took the box and opened it up. It was a case of fine French wine. There was an envelope inside. It contained all their money and a note. It read "Thank you, Thank you all' and she had signed it. Buddy told her husband "Thank you." He said, "No, thank you. God bless American." He then turned and walked off. The men were speechless. Then Specialist Money said, "I wished I would have asked her about the wine." They all laughed. Soon it was time to get back to the plane. Buddy opened one of the bottles. The limo had glasses. He poured everyone some. It wasn't Bud Light but it was good. The limo got them back in plenty of time. They boarded and prepared to take off again. Buddy offered the airmen a bottle of wine. They gladly accepted. Several other men did the same. Once they were in the air again Buddy opened another bottle and passed it around to his brothers. They all toasted Angelic. When they finished, one by one they drifted off to sleep.

Several hours later they awoke to the sound of landing gear doors opening and the landing gear being lowered. They were beginning their descent to an undisclosed United States airbase in Turkey. Nobody knew where their forward base was from there. It was early in the afternoon and it was hot. Dry and hot. The tarmac made it even hotter. There were lots of planes there. This was a huge base. " couple of buses pulled up, the men grabbed their personal gear and loaded onto them. They were driven to some buildings a quarter mile away. First Lieutenant Wooley was talking to some other officers when the men were unloading. He soon came over to them. He said, "The trucks will be here first thing in the morning to pick us up. If you are hungry there is a mess hall open twenty-four hours over there." He pointed to a big, brown building. "Inside there are bunks and showers if you want to get cleaned up. The only entertainment is a movie house not far from here. They even have hot buttered popcorn. Next door to the movie house is a chapel. The barracks are air conditioned. Enjoy them, they will be the last for awhile." Very informal but informative. He showed signs of jet lag. In fact, they all did. The men went into the cool barracks. Each found a bunk to put their gear on. Some headed directly to the mess hall while others opted for a shower first.

The showers seemed to revitalize them. When they finished they headed over to the mess hall. There were men there from all over the world. The mess hall was like the one at Fort Hood, only bigger. Officers and enlisted men ate together. Bobby and the others never let that stop them from eating with whoever they wanted to anyway. They had broken bread with generals to privates. They did respect rank. They were often saluted at Fort Hood. It was hard for them to adjust to it. Anyway, they all got something to eat. The food was good. They sat down at a table near some Australian airmen. Bobby was fascinated by their accents. When the airmen left Bobby and the others tried to emulate them. Bobby said, "Good day, you all." Buddy said, "That's all we need, an Australian Okie." They all laughed. Johnny asked, "Hey, you guys want to go see the movie after a while?" They all said it sounded like fun. After they ate the men went over to the movie house. They got there early and got good seats. It's a good thing they did because the place was packed. It was dark and cool and it allowed the men a place to go to forget about everything else. Instead of rifles the men carried popcorn and sodas. The movie was one they all had seen before. That didn't matter anyway. It was Star Wars. " futuristic battle between good and evil. Bobby thought, how appropriate. The men really enjoyed the movie. When it was over they walked over to the runway. It was dark now and really starting to cool off. " number of fighter jets were taking off to patrol the northern no fly zone. Their afterburners and their thunderous noise were cool to watch. Chad Hubanks said, "Now that's power." No one could argue with that. It was getting late. Even though they slept a lot on the plane they were all tired. Back to the cool barracks and into bed.

The next morning the men were up early. First Lieutenant Wooley had been in contact with the colonel. Captain Davis, Staff Sergeant Gollihare and Staff Sergeant Tisdale, along with drivers and escorts would be arriving anytime. First Lieutenant Wooley told the men to go eat breakfast and to meet him at storage area where the equipment was located. So they did. Mick asked First Lieutenant Wooley how far away the camp was. He told him he thought between a three and four hour drive. After the men ate they grabbed their gear. They reported to the staging area where the equipment was kept. Besides the quad riders, there were ten other men, supply clerks, cooks and mechanics, but they were all airborne trained, capable soldiers all of them. They showed up about the same time the trucks pulled in. First Lieutenant Wooley met with Captain Davis. They walked over to the men. Captain Davis said, "Welcome to Turkey. We've got a problem. Trucks are

124

in short supply here. We need supplies real bad and we need you and your quads just as bad. Trouble is, we don't have enough trucks to do both. What we want you to do is ride your quads from here to our base. Bobby said, "It sounds like fun. Let's get these trucks loaded and get out of here." Captain Davis smiled and said, "You heard him, let's get rolling." They loaded up ten trucks with supplies. It didn't take any time with everyone pitching in. Captain Davis said, "That's the fastest we ever loaded out that many trucks." The soldiers checked out their quads, filled them with fuel, suited up and were ready to go. Thirty quads were ready to go also. The men boarded their quads and moved out. Captain Davis led the way in his Humvee, followed by the quads, then the ten trucks, two more Humvees and an escort of Turkish soldiers in two more Humvees. The whole thing stretched out for a half mile, drawing looks from everyone they passed. The asphalt road soon turned into a dirt road, dry and dusty. The quads spread out even more to try and keep from eating so much dust. They stopped every hour for water and fuel if needed. The heat and dust were wearing the men out. During their third break Captain Davis walked back to check on the men on the ATV's. He said, "" half hour more and we will be at Camp Q." Bobby, still upbeat, said, "Sir, the force is with you." The others laughed, remembering the movie they watched the night before. Johnny said, "Quad riders, let's roll." They finished the last half hour ride and drew a crowd as they pulled into the camp. Bobby, Johnny and the rest of the pros rode wheelies into camp. The soldiers cheered them on.

CHAPTER 6

Captain Davis came over and talked to First Lieutenant Wooley. He told him where his men could billet. He told him when he was settled for he, Sergeant First Class Kroeker, Bobby, Johnny and the others to join him at a briefing with Colonel Hill. The quad riders knocked the dust off themselves and got a drink of water. Sergeant First Class Kroeker billeted the soldiers, including the seven pros. Then First Lieutenant Wooley, Sergeant First Class Kroeker and the seven went to the briefing. Colonel Hill met them at the entrance of the tent. He said, "Man, am I glad you guys are here." He was happy as a boy on the last day of school. "Find a seat and I'll let you know what's going on. They were joined by other officers. Colonel Hill walked to the front of the room. Colonel Hill said, "For the benefit of our newcomers I'm going to start from the top. We have been in operation now for a little over two weeks. This is our A.O. (area of operations)." He points to a map. The area is fifty miles long and fifty miles wide. Our base here is just inside the Iraqi border. The Turkish border is half mile west of here. Our forward base is right in the middle. As you can tell, this area is the roughest along the border. There are very few roads in this area, that's why the need for our quads. We can cover lots of ground in a hurry. We are very lucky to have seven of the best riders in American, that means the world. I have served with these men before. They may be young, but they perform any task given them with positive professionalism. I've never seen any group of men that work so well with each other. Their primary tasks are to train the others. Their secondary task will be to lead assaults if needed. Hopefully they won't. We are here to observe and report. We also supply the Kurds with weapons and training. Major Haitham Krais is in charge of the Kurds. We now have about two-hundred fifty Americans in our American operations. We have twice that many Kurds helping us and in training.

126

We operate fifty observation posts. They are staggered about every mile or so. Each operation is manned by two U.S. soldiers and 3 Kurds, so that at any given time we have two-hundred fifty men operating these positions. Each team stays in position for two weeks then they are due to rotate out. Some can be reached with our dune buggies. We have about two dozen of these. They can carry a team in and a team out. We also use them as much as possible for resupply. For the other observation posts we use the quads to rotate men in and out. Some areas have their own quads, others we go in and get them. We have two ways of resupply. We move their supplies up by parachute to a drop zone a half mile from the forward camp. This is the preferred method. It's less likely our camp will be discovered. If we have to we can go in on the quads. The observation posts are due to start rotating. We will drop fresh troops in tonight. First Lieutenant Wooley, you and your men will go in tomorrow night. Get familiar with the maps and codes. You will be replacing Captain Randolf and his team. They will be trained on the new quads by our instructors. We can no longer expect more men. Special operations is spread real thin. We have a team ready to help if one of the camps comes under heavy attack. We also have air cover if needed. As soon as all the politics get settled an invasion force will be brought in with all of our heavy stuff. Then we'll stop Saddam for good, possibly avoiding nuclear war. Well, that's pretty much it in a nutshell. Oh yes, you were issued chemical suits. Keep them with you at all times. That's all I've got. Go get some chow." First Sergeant Holliman called the men to attention and then dismissed them. As the men were walking out Bobby turned to Johnny and said, "Man, that was a mouthful." Johnny said, "It sounds like it could get a little hairy around here." Bobby said, "Yeah, we'd better be on our toes." Johnny said, "Or they are going to get stepped on." They went to eat. They sure were glad to have a mess tent instead of MRE's. The menu was limited, but overall the food was good. They had access to a satellite phone. They had to sign up for it and were limited to one five minute call every two weeks. Buddy said, "You know, we may be here for awhile." Chad Duncan said, "I don't even want to think about that." The mail would run as often as possible. Bobby asked, "Where did the colonel say the men went to board the plane for a parachute drop?" It seemed to him that the airbase would be too far to go. He no sooner got it out of his mouth when a transport plane flew over. It was low and had its landing gear down. "Well" he said, "That answers that question." There was a landing strip less than a half mile away. They kept flights to a minimum to try to avoid detection. The instructors walked the base to get an idea of the facilities.

In the maintenance area they had no power tools. If a mechanic was needed they could go to the airbase. They did have a gasoline powered welder. " bunker had been dug for the ammunition. It was located in the middle of the camp to prevent sabotage. There were always at least two guards on it. The quad trainers were issued 9mm pistols. They were told to keep them with them at all times. All the tents were the same color as the surrounding terrain. The camp was fairly large, several tents for sleeping quarters, a mess tent, headquarters tent, communications tent, maintenance tent, a tent for showers and a supply tent. There were five trailers for water, ten trucks, four Humvees, about a dozen dune buggies, about the same for motorcycles, and of course the quads. There were sixty of them in camp now. All of this surrounded by barbed wire with claymore mines strung out all along the perimeter. There was also a fuel dump. Most of that was in a bunker also. This would be home for sometime. Outside the wire was a target range to train the Kurds. " helicopter landing zone was marked off. The seven men walked all over the camp, visiting with the men, some they had served with before. They drifted by the motor pool. Master Sergeant Miller was there. He had his men cleaning the air filters on the quads they had brought in. He told Bobby "The filters aren't too bad but it's better safe than sorry." Bobby agreed. He asked him "What do you think of the new quads?" Master Sergeant Miller said, "They seem to be good solid machines. The Honda and Polaris people did a good job." About that time Major Dobson walked in. He said, "We've had a faux routed to us. It seems Lonnie Eubanks is concerned about the valves loosening up on us. He suggests we look at some of the motors." Johnny asked, "Did he say why?" Major Dobson said, "Lonnie said these are high performance motors with close tolerances. They are well built with high compression pistons. With that much power he was afraid the valves might need adjustment." Master Sergeant Miller said, "I trust Lonnie. If he has a concern maybe we should check out a few of the motors." Buddy asked, "Can we help?" Master Sergeant Miller said, "Sure. The tools are here, help yourselves." All the men were pretty good mechanics. They've all had to work on their own quads. Each one of them grabbed a quad and began tearing into them. Two hours later they were finished. Only one of the seven was loose and it just barely was about a thousandth out. Nothing to worry about. They did, however, notice some of the rear brake pads were wearing down. Master Sergeant Miller had his men check and replace some of them. He thanked the seven for their help. They told him anytime. Bobby said, "Well, I'd better write a letter and let my folks know I made it here and everything's okay." Chad said, "I was just thinking the same thing." They all agreed, so they went to their tent to write letters home. The replacement troops were gearing up to go make a night jump. They would be isolated for two weeks. They had just finished their last hot meal. MRE's for two weeks. No one complained though. They were all eager to get involved. They would take off as soon as it got dark. They would be met with quads and dune buggies to take them to their post, or at least close to them. The men going tonight would replace the operations that didn't have quads. They all would have to be ferried. The troops they replaced would be brought back to the landing zone. They would stay there until the following night. That's when the other quads would go up to replace the other observation posts. Those men would pick up the men on foot and bring them down to the trucks. They had it all figured out. Both operations would take all night. The quad trainers had nothing to do but wait. They did go out and find a good training area a couple of miles from camp on the Turkish side of the border. That night the transfers went without a hitch. Everyone monitored the communications. The next morning First Lieutenant Wooley gave his men a briefing. When he finished they got busy doing weapons checks and equipment checks. The instructors helped with their quad checks. They then kicked back and waited for dark. Actually they pulled out before dark. They moved to a staging area five miles away to wait until dark. As soon as it got dark they moved out. Some of the teams would take most of the night. First Lieutenant Wooley and eight others made their way to the forward base. Captain Randolf sure was glad to see them. He gave First Lieutenant Wooley a quick briefing. Captain Randolf and his team were already loaded so they began their trip to rally point. They were some of the first ones to arrive. He had men double up on the quads. They began the five mile trek to the waiting trucks. By three o'clock in the morning all the quads had checked in. Captain Randolf came out with the last group. The quads started drifting into camp and soon the trucks rolled in led by Captain Randolf on his quad. Colonel Hill called for a briefing from Captain Randolf for all the officers including the warrant officers. Colonel Hill wanted to know if any changes needed to be made in the rotation process. No one said anything. Finally Bobby raised his hand. He stood and said, "Sir, I was thinking, instead of using two nights to make this transfer we only use one. Forget the airdrop of the men. Have the trucks move them as far as possible then double up on the quads. Have the quads drop them off on their way to their observation posts. The replaced quad then recovers the others and brings them straight back to the trucks, lowering the risk of parachuting at night and not having men hide for a full day." Colonel Hill said, "Thank you Bobby. Major Dobson and I came up with the same idea. We will use the plane to only drop supplies from now on." He continued "When we first set this up we overlooked the obvious. I just want to add one more thing. I want to send more quads along to act as escort with the support quads doubled up. They aren't as effective. We need to protect them. Bobby, you and your men will select the support riders." Bobby said, "Yes, sir. Will that selection include us?" Colonel Hill said, "You guys are the best but I will leave that up to you." He then turned to Captain Randolf and asked, "Were there any other problems that haven't been reported?" Captain Randolf said, "One sir, we had trouble communicating with the Kurds but I think we have that resolved now. We use interpreters on the radio. The only problem there is the Kurds don't know our code system." Colonel Hill said, "We'll get right on that. Thank you for pointing that out. This has been an educational meeting. If at any time you think we have a problem, please let me know. That's the only way we can correct them. That's all for now." The men left. Captain Randolf and his men got some food and a shower. Later that afternoon they started their training on the new quads.

Over the next week and a half the training went well. Everyone got a chance to call home. Bobby called his dad, mom and Jill. Everything was going well for them. Jill had started school and was working with Sandy at her store. She decided to stay there until Bobby's return. He said he would call again in two weeks.

The operations were reporting more and more troop movements. Colonel Hill decided he should take a look with First Lieutenant Wooley personally and see for himself. One of the dune buggies was broken down, so Master Sergeant Miller went with Colonel Hill and Captain Davis to have a look at it. Early that night they made arrangements to go to the forward camp.

CHAPTER 7

Right after dark the three men were joined by Staff Sergeant Ketcher. They headed to the forward camp. They were met by Staff Sergeant Culp and Staff Sergeant Prince. The men made their way to the forward camp. Only two other American soldiers had remained in the camp, Sergeant First Class Kroeker and Specialist Wolfe. Sergeant First Class Kroeker welcomed the men to the camp. Colonel Hill asked, "Where are the rest of the men?" Sergeant First Class Kroeker said, "Sir, First Lieutenant Wooley would be back before dawn. He and the others are on a supply run." The Colonel said, "Fine. What can you tell me about what's going on?" Sergeant First Class Kroeker said, "Well, several of our outposts on the northern end of our American operation are reporting increased sightings of large military convoys including T-72 tanks." Colonel Hill said, "Boy, ol' Saddam is getting nervous about all the news reports. Well, I guess the old SOB should be nervous." He asked, "How many men do you have here?" "Besides the four of us, we have about two dozen Kurds," he answered. The colonel said, "Good. It's getting late, we might as well turn in. I'll talk with First Lieutenant Wooley when he returns in the morning." Sergeant First Class Kroeker showed the men where to bed down. Four Kurdsmen remained on guard. Specialist Wolfe and another Kurdsman remained on station in the communication tent. At about 0300 in the morning things started happening. One by one the sentries were being taken out. As the last one hit the ground, Specialist Wolfe heard a groan as the last one fell. He grabbed his rifle and headed for the entrance of the tent. Just as he was stepping outside the lights went out. The Kurd that was with him had sold them out. Twenty Iraqi soldiers made their way into the camp. They captured the entire camp without firing a shot. Colonel Hill and the others didn't have a chance. All the American soldiers were tied and gaged. They were led away. The Iraqi soldiers rounded up the frightened Kurdish soldiers. They then mowed them down with automatic gun fire. They left Specialist Wolfe there assuming he was dead. At least two observation posts heard the shots. They tried to contact the camp with no success. They then contacted Camp Q putting them on alert. Meanwhile, First Lieutenant Wooley, Sergeant Firey and Sergeant McFarlane were near the camp returning from their mission. From the south also nearing the camp was Specialist Martin, Specialist Baiers and Specialist Allen. The three of them split up for their approach to the camp. Specialist Martin spotted the Iraqi soldiers. He called it in to First Lieutenant Wooley. He told him to trail them and keep reporting their position. Major Dobson, monitoring the radio transmissions, said there was an assault force on their way, estimated time of arrival one hour. They would not be on stealth mode. Captain Randolf led the force. But Bobby and his group led the way on their quads. First Lieutenant Wooley pulled into the camp cautiously. His men covered him. What he saw made him ill. Bodies laid everywhere. The Kurdsman had been gunned down. But no American bodies. He then heard a groan. It was Specialist Wolfe who had a gash on the back of his head. He came to. First Lieutenant Wooley went to him. He asked, "Are you all right?" Specialist Wolfe answered, "I have a bad headache, sir, but I guess I'm okay." First Lieutenant Wooley asked him, "What happened, Jamie?" Specialist Wolfe said, "I heard a noise then the lights went out." The others joined their lieutenant and began checking for survivors. Sergeant McFarlane began first aid on Specialist Wolfe. First Lieutenant Wooley called into Major Dobson. He reported, "Sir, all of the Kurdsmen at the base had been killed, Specialist Wolfe is injured. The rest have been abducted. Specialist Martin has spotted the Iraqis and is trailing them." Major Dobson said, "You men hold tight. Captain Randolf is on his way. He should be there soon. " strike force is also on the way from the airbase. Some will come here, others will be there to secure your base." Soon quad motors could be heard. Captain Randolf and his men weren't sparing any horses getting there. " few minutes later the seven pros came flying in. Bobby said, "The rest of the force will be here in a few minutes." First Lieutenant Wooley said, "Fine, you guys spread out for cover fire." The seven scattered over the small camp. Captain Randolf and twenty two other quads pulled in. Before First Lieutenant Wooley could check in with Captain Randolf, Specialist Martin called in. "Sir, they have stopped about five miles from our camp almost straight east. They have joined with other

Iraqi soldiers. There are about forty of them. I don't expect them to stay long." Captain Randolf called Bobby and his men over. He said, "I've got a mission for you guys. I want you guys to pick three men that can keep up with you and go to this point." He pointed to a place on the map. "We think Colonel Hill and the others are being held here," He pointed to another area of the map, "remain there for further orders. If they move our men before we get there, you guys will attack. Specialist Martin said there was a force of forty men. We will catch up as soon as we can. Make sure you monitor your radios. Things might get hairy." Bobby said, "You got it." He hollered at Sergeant Stockstill, Specialist Mangrum and Specialist Money to join them. They gassed up and took off. They ran at full throttle for two and a half miles covering the ground in just a few minutes. They then went on whisper mode for another two miles to the point the captain had told them to go to. Johnny radioed in to the captain. "Captain Randolf, we are on station. Specialist Martin contacted them." He said, "There are more troops in the area." He continued, "There are about twenty troops hidden below a ridge and above the valley that leads to the camp." Captain Randolf said, "They must think we will try a rescue and that's an ambush." Chad called, "Captain, I think we can get above them." Captain Randolf said, "Good, go for it. Call us when you're in position. We are on our way. Don't do anything until we get there. We will coordinate our attack." Specialist Martin called back in. "" helicopter just landed in the enemy camp." Captain Randolf said, "What now? Keep me posted on what they're up to. We are on the move, we will be there shortly." Major Dobson called, "Captain Davis, you are going to attempt a rescue and fight a superior force. Do you want to wait on the assault force?" Captain Randolf answered, "They may have more men but they aren't a superior force. Keep those helicopters out of the area, sir." Major Dobson replied, "Okay, but if you need back up they are in the neighborhood."

Captain Randolf and his force reached the area. They could hear the helicopter take off. Specialist Martin called in, "The copter took off, sir. I'm off my quad and have moved in for a closer look. Our men are being held on the west side of the camp in a tent. We can get to them from behind the tent. First Lieutenant Wooley said he could take three men in to rescue and protect the prisoners. Captain Randolf said, "Get to it. We attack in ten minutes." He radioed the ten men on the ridge. "Ten minutes, open up." Johnny responded, "Yes, sir." Captain Davis split his attack force in two groups. One group would come in from the south, the other from the southwest. They would hit the camp and join forces. Everything was ready.

He signalled the men on the ridge. They opened fire with their rockets and machine guns, completely wiping out the ambush force in seconds. Captain Randolf's attack force at the same time hit the camp. They were lightening fast taking out everything in sight. Also, at the same time, First Lieutenant Wooley and his men came in, took out the guards, got the prisoners out and backed into rocks where they supported Captain Randolf on his right flank. On their first pass they took out half the camp garrison. The rest of the Iraqis took up defensive positions to their rear. They were preparing another run when the ten men from the ridge came thundering in. They took out the remaining Iraqi troops before they could readjust their positions. Then it was over. In less than five minutes they had rescued their friends and killed sixty enemy soldiers. Not one American soldier got killed. Two were wounded but only superficial wounds. Specialist Hughes and Staff Sergeant Royce were the injured men.

Captain Randolf ordered his men to check the area. First Lieutenant Wooley came out with the captured soldiers. Captain Randolf said, "Hey, where's the colonel and Captain Davis?" Master Sergeant Miller said, "They took them in the helicopter. They are coming back for us in a little while." Captain Randolf asked, "Do you know where they took them?" "Yes, sir," he said, "They are in a village twenty miles from here." Captain Randolf said, "Show me on the map." Master Sergeant Miller said, "Not now, sir. We need to make this camp look normal for the returning copter." Captain Randolf ordered his men to get their quads out of sight and make the camp look good. The men did as he asked. He ordered some of his men to put on enemy uniforms. " few minutes later they could hear the helicopter coming. He told his men to get out of sight. The helicopter, not expecting trouble, came right in. As soon as it touched down, Captain Randolf's men took out the crew. Captain Randolf called in to Major Dobson and told him of the mission's success and failures. He requested resupply so he could go get Colonel Hill and Captain Davis.

Major Dobson said something had come up. He would accompany the resupply copter. Captain Randolf had Sergeant First Class Kroeker put out sentries and told his men that Major Dobson was bringing them supplies and fuel. An hour later the helicopter landed. Captain Randolf quickly ordered his men to refuel and rearm their machines. Major Dobson had three men with him and introduced them to Captain Randolf and First Lieutenant Wooley. He said, "Gentlemen, this is Mark Schneider. He is an American working for the Homas. These two men are CI". Captain Randolf said, "I know Gary and Kevin Smith. We've met. Sir, what does this have to do with a rescue mission?" Major Dobson said, "Nothing and everything. The village they took them to is a suspected chemical manufacturing plant. When you attempt your rescue we need you to get proof of the chemicals and then blow the place up. We have incendiary explosives so it will burn the stuff and not spread it. Can you and your men handle it?" Captain Randolf said, "Yes sir, consider it done." "How?" he asked. "Trickery sir, and special ops, sir." Major Dobson said, "I have a couple of more things for you. Our forward camp is being moved to alternate site B. Also, Major Krais wants to be involved in the rescue mission at the village. He's looking for some payback. Some of his men are from that village. They may be able to help you." One of the CI" men handed the captain a small pack. He tells the captain, "There are cameras in here. Get us some pictures if you can." Captain Randolf asked the Major, "Where is Major Krais and how many men does he have?" Major Dobson says, "He and his men are in a dozen of our dune buggies. They will meet you three miles from the village in this old river bed. He has close to fifty men with him. Some of them are ours." Captain Randolf said, "Good. Now Mr. Schneider, what kind and how much chemical agent are we talking about?" Mark said, "We believe he has both Sarin and VX stored there and it is believed to be between thirty to forty metric tons of the stuff." Captain Randolf said, "That SOB Saddam. Does Major Krais and his men have NBC protective equipment?" Major Dobson said, "They sure do, they even have extras if you need them. We also have about a dozen suits on our chopper." "Great," said Captain Randolf. "I think we need them. The guys we rescued don't have one." He continued, "I have two wounded men, sir. Can you take them with you sir?" Major Dobson said, "Of course. Get them on the chopper." Captain Randolf said, "Staff Sergeant Ketcher, get our wounded on the helicopter and get those extra chem suits for us." Staff Sergeant Ketcher didn't say a word but did as he was ordered. Major Dobson and the others started boarding the helicopter. As he was getting in he asked if there was anything else. Captain Randolf asked, "What kind of support can we expect?" Major Dobson said,

"The Air Force is standing by to offer anything you need." The helicopter fired up. As it was lifting off Major Dobson saluted Captain Randolf. Captain Randolf returned the salute.

CHAPTER 8

Captain Randolf got together with First Lieutenant Wooley, the seven pros, Sergeant First Class Kroeker and Master Sergeant Miller to work out the plan. The radio on the enemy helicopter started blaring. Staff Sergeant Ketcher got on it. He spoke perfect Iraqi. When he got done talking, Captain Randolf called him over. He asked, "What was that all about?" Staff Sergeant Ketcher said, "The helicopter was due back. They were calling on its status." Captain Randolf asked, "Well, what did you tell them?" Staff Sergeant Ketcher replied, "I told them we were having trouble with the transmission and would be back in two or three hours. They said we were always having trouble. That was it, sir." Captain Randolf asked him, "Where did you learn to speak their language?" He answered, "I had a friend in school that was from here. I helped him with English and he taught me their language." Captain Randolf said, "Well, Ill be, thanks. You're dismissed." Staff Sergeant Ketcher turned and walked away. Captain Randolf said, "That gives me an idea." He yelled at his men. "Can any of you guys fly a helicopter?" "Yes sir," came a reply. It was Sergeant Higgonbotham. He came walking up. "I used to fly Black Hawks, sir." Captain Randolf asked, "Do you think you can fly this helicopter?" He replied, "Yes sir, it was a piece of cake." Captain Randolf said, "Go check it out and let me know if there are any problems." The Sergeant replied, "Yes sir." First Lieutenant Wooley asked, "What do you have in mind?" Captain Randolf said, "We need to move soon. What I have in mind is to use the helicopter as a diversion and to get men inside to rescue Colonel Hill and Captain Davis. We have a twofold mission. Rescue and destroy a chemical supply depot. Both are very dangerous. Make sure everyone has on their chem suits. I have no idea how many enemy soldiers are garrisoned there. We are to meet with Major Krais. He has a better knowledge of the layout. We will finalize plans with him. But for now we need to get to him." He looked at Bobby, "You and the nine men that were with you on the ridge will lead the way. We have seventeen miles to the rally point. The terrain is mostly open with scattered boulders and deep ravines. We will avoid all roads. Check your maps, gear and communications. We move out in ten minutes. Bobby, you and the rest here will move out in five. That's all I have. Good luck, gentlemen." The meeting broke up and they began their final checks. Captain Randolf got with Sergeant Higgonbotham, Staff Sergeant Ketcher and Master Sergeant Miller. He told them to stay put in the helicopter until he called. Sergeant Higgonbotham and Staff Sergeant Ketcher's main function was to cover and help Master Sergeant Miller plant the charges. Captain Randolf gave them the cameras. He told them, we need pictures, lots of pictures." Master Sergeant Miller asked, "What about the colonel and the captain?" Captain Randolf said, "If everything went right, First Lieutenant Wooley would be in charge of the rescue. I'll let you men know more when I know more." The seven pros and the other three took off. Will led and Chad brought up the rear. They stuck close to the rocks. Will said, "Let's roll." " voice came over the radio. It was Sergeant First Class Kroeker. He said, "May the force be with you." Occasionally they would have to pop out in the open to avoid the crevasses. The men were making good time. They had gotten about half way to their rally point when Will popped over a hill. There parked was an armor column. It was too late, he had been spotted. He told the others to stay put, he would try to lead them away. Bobby said, "We are brothers and we stick together." He told Sergeant Stockstill, Specialist Mangrum and Specialist Money to stay put and lead the rest of the team to the rally point. He said, "We'll join up with you guys in a little bit. We're going to play a little while." Bobby, Mick, Chad Duncan, Chad Hubanks, Buddy and Johnny joined their friend. The Iraqis started shooting. The seven got away from the small arms fire. The enemy soldiers gave chase. Soon they were all out of sight. Sergeant Stockstill called into the captain and told him the situation. He said, "If anyone could outrun an armor column, it would be those seven men. You other three are our eyes and ears now. Keep going." Johnny said to Bobby on the radio, "Hey, this kind of reminds you of Little Sahara (a sand dune park in Western Oklahoma), doesn't it?" Bobby said, "Yeah, but there they don't have a hundred

138

men in tanks and stuff trying to shoot you." Johnny said, "Good point. We are far enough out now, let's lose these clowns." The seven men split off from each other still maintaining the same general direction. The enemy soldiers split off, too. Bobby and Johnny were still fairly close to each other. The gap between the seven men widened. " few minutes later Bobby and Johnny were facing a deep ravine, twenty feet across and a half mile long. They stopped to see if they could climb in and out of it. "No way," Johnny said. Bobby said, "We'd better do something, they're getting closer." Johnny said, "Follow me." He had spotted a rock that was a natural ramp. He got a good run, ramped off the rock and flew across the ravine. Bobby said, "I'm there, man." He hit the ramp and yelled, "Oh craaaaaap!" He made the jump fine. They sped off on the other side and the ravine stopped the enemy cold. They began closing back to their friends. Everyone had lost the enemy but two. " truck with a machine gun was closing on Chad Hubanks and Buddy. They yelled for help. Bobby and Johnny got there first. They swung in behind the truck. Both of them fired missiles taking out the truck and killing its occupants. They knew that would bring in the rest of the enemy force. The four of them took off. Soon Chad Duncan, Will and Mick joined them. They split out to the south to rejoin the others. Will said, "Well now, that was exciting." Chad Hubanks said, "Too exciting, I think I wet myself." They all laughed. They sped off avoiding any hidden hills.

By the time they rejoined the others, they had hooked up with Major Krais and his men. They reported to Captain Randolf. "Welcome back," he said. "Did you guys have fun playing with the enemy forces?" Bobby said, "Yeah, but they didn't play fair so we had to shoot some of them." Captain Randolf laughed. He said, "Come with me, we're figuring out what to do." All of the officers huddled up the rest of men, refueled the quads, drank some water and relaxed. They kept a close eye out, though. If the enemy caught them here, they'd be dead meat. Major Krais drew a rough sketch of the village and the military post on the ground. He used a rifle cleaning rod to draw with and then to point things out. He said the military post covered about ten acres and was completely surrounded by chain link fence with barbed wire. It only garrisoned about seventy five to eighty men. But there was another base ten miles to the south that had over two hundred men.

He pointed out the four corners. "Here are guard towers. Each of them has an unobstructed view of two of the other towers. The long building on the south was a warehouse and loading docks. On the east fence is the main gate. Building number one is the chemical labs., number two headquarters and number three barracks. This little building in the northeast corner is where they keep prisoners. The village is on the west." Captain Randolf said, "Thank you, sir. It's going to be dark in a couple of hours. That's when we hit them. Major Krais, you and your men will take out the barracks with your TOW missiles on your vehicles. You can then cover the main compound with your fifty calibre machine guns. I will split my men into two teams. My team, Alpha, will take out the main gate and the two guard towers on the east side. Once we are in, some of my men will get the prisoners, the rest of us will assist Master Sergeant Miller with destroying the chemicals. First Lieutenant Wooley will bring a team in from the southwest. He will take out the southwest tower, the lab and headquarters. Staff Sergeant Culp and Specialist Martin and Sergeant Firey will try to get the communications with their rockets. Major Krais, instruct your gunners to be careful with their shooting once we hit the gate. The whole thing will kick off 30 seconds after the helicopter touches down. Hopefully all eyes will be focused on them. Do you have any questions?" Bobby asked, "Where do you want us?" The captain said, "You guys are with me inside the compound. You will be raising as much hell as you can." Bobby said, "Cool, sir, we're there." "Any more questions?" asked the captain. Bobby said, "Sir, just one more. What do we do when we're finished?" Embarrassed, Captain Randolf said, "Oh yes, we will rally a mile east of the camp and make our way back home. Thanks, Bobby."

The captain called Major Dobson to let him know of the plan and their exit route. Then he called the helicopter and informed them of the plan. It was an hour and a half before dark. The teams were chosen and told what to do. They worked their way into position. The major positioned his men a quarter mile away. After they fired their TOWs they would move in closer. Both " and B quad teams got within a hundred and fifty yards. They didn't dare try to get any closer on their quads. In fact, the last seventy five yards they pushed their quads.

At last it was almost dark. They could hear the helicopter coming. It would be completely dark by the time they landed. Everyone put on their night vision goggles and turned on their infrared sighting systems. Once inside the compound the goggles would come off. The helicopter landed. Just as planned, thirty seconds later TOW missile rounds slammed into the barracks and it exploded like a balloon popping. Total devastation. Three seconds later they took out the communications tower. Captain Randolf and his men hit the front gate. " couple of missiles from Sergeant Wright took care of that killing all the guards. Specialist Bookout took out the northeast tower. Staff Sergeant Fomby took out the southeast tower. The rest of Alpha team entered the compound.

Staff Sergeant Royce, Specialist Upton, Sergeant Shipman and Specialist Allen took out the guards and rescued Colonel Hill and Captain Davis. Master Sergeant Miller, Staff Sergeant Ketcher, Sergeant Higgonbotham made their way to the chemical warehouse. They put down several guards but were inside setting charges and taking pictures. First Lieutenant Wooley and his men were hitting the southwest corner. Specialist Mangrum took out the tower. First Lieutenant Wooley and Staff Sergeant Prince hit the lab with rocket and machine gunfire, others hit the headquarters building. Fifty calibre machine gunfire took out the last tower. Bobby, Johnny, Mick, Chad Duncan, Buddy, Will, and Chad Hubanks were raising cane in the compound along with the others. The enemy soldiers were falling all around them. The charges were set. The three men made their way out of the warehouse. Several enemy soldiers began firing at them. Captain Randolf and Staff Sergeant Culp shut them down. Bobby saw an enemy officer try to hide behind a truck. He got off his quad and pulled his pistol. He told Johnny to cover him. Bobby walked up behind the officer who was clutching a briefcase. Johnny yelled, "Look out." An enemy soldier popped up behind Bobby. Johnny mowed him down. Bobby had turned to see. When he turned back around the officer had seen him and was attempting to pull his pistol. Bobby fired first, hitting the officer in the head. He grabbed the briefcase and tied it to his quad. Soon the order came to pull out. Within a minute everyone was out, guns and rockets still flying. They all beat a path to the rally point.

Six men had been wounded, one serious, Specialist Taylor. He had lost a lot of blood but was stable. Captain Randolf shook hands with Colonel Hill and Captain Davis and welcomed them back. He turned to Master Sergeant Miller and asked, "How long before it blows?" He didn't answer.

He held up one hand and looked at his watch. He dropped his arm and said, "Now!" " gigantic fireball erupted. The warehouse and everything in it was consumed by fire. Johnny said, "Thank God, at least ol' Saddam won't be able to use that stuff on anyone." Colonel Hill said, "Let's roll." The Magnificent Seven took the point. They rode all night. An armor column threatened them, but a couple of A-10's changed their minds for them. At dawn the next morning the men pulled into Camp Q. They were all worn smooth out. The camp erupted into cheers.

CHAPTER 9

Bobby said, "I never thought this hot dusty camp could look so good." After the congratulations petered out, Colonel Hill called all the men together that had been in on the mission. He said, "Men, first of all, thanks for saving my sorry butt. You performed magnificently. You put down some bad guys and destroyed some nasty stuff destined for who knows where. You men are all tops in my book. I know this isn't much but I've arranged to spend a couple of days at the airbase, air conditioning and a USO show. I wish it could be more but we still have lots of work to do around here. We pull out in the morning. That's right, I'm going too. For now relax, shower, eat and get some rest. I'll see you in the morning. Dismissed."

The men all cheered the colonel. Buddy said, "I don't know what to do first, eat, shower and sleep, or the other way around." Chad Duncan said, "Shower first, okay?' They all laughed. Bobby remembered the briefcase. He took it off his quad and took it to Major Dobson. He said, "Major, I found this on a dead Iraqi officer. Well, at least he was dead when I took it." Major Dobson said, "Thanks. I'll get Major Krais to interpret it when he wakes up after while. Now, go get a shower, please." He smiled at Bobby. Bobby wasn't sure he had enough strength to take a shower. He did though and felt better. He hooked up with his friends at the mess tent. They ate but right after they were so tired they couldn't tell you what they ate. Somehow they all found a bunk to lay down in. It was good and dark when Bobby was awakened. It was First Sergeant Holliman. He said, "Sir, the colonel needs to see you now." Bobby sat up, put his boots on. He grabbed his hat and shirt and followed First Sergeant Holliman to the headquarters tent. First Sergeant Holliman said, Sir, Bobby is here." Colonel Hill stood up and said, "Come on in Bobby and have a seat." The colonel's eyes were sunken back into his head. He was clearly running on nerves alone. Bobby said, "Excuse me, sir, but you need some sleep." The colonel said, "You're telling me. Thanks for your concern. I have only a few questions for you then you can go back to bed." He picked up the briefcase. "Where did you get this?" Bobby said, "I told Major Dobson. I was near the chemical storage warehouse. I spotted this officer clutching this briefcase and trying to hide between a loading dock and a truck tire. I went up behind him. He spotted me and tried to pull his pistol while still holding onto this thing. I shot him first. I thought the briefcase might be important, so I grabbed it and tied it to my quad. When we got in this morning I gave it to Major Dobson." Colonel Hill said, "Good report. Do you have any idea what's inside?" Bobby said, "No, I didn't even open it." Colonel Hill said, "Well, that answers my next question." Bobby asked, "Sir, what's so important about this briefcase?" Colonel Hill said, "What I'm about to tell you must stay in this room. Don't tell anyone. I know I can trust you." Bobby looked puzzled and said, "Of course, sir." Colonel Hill continued, "Only you, myself, Major Dobson and Major Krais know we have this. It belonged to a senior shipping officer in Saddam's military. It contains locations of every chemical manufacturing and storage facility in Northern Iraq. We must assume they don't know we have it. It lists the chemicals they have and how much they have of it. There is also a list of materials that would be used in nuclear explosives and where they are kept. If valid, this information would put a halt to all of the foot dragging by Congress and our allies. We will finally be able to go in and take this crazy man and his regime down. This briefcase and its contents will be on the President's desk by tomorrow morning Washington time." Bobby said, "This is some heavy stuff." Colonel Hill said, "You're right, this is some heavy stuff. I'm waiting for the CI" boys and their escort to get here. You can go back to bed. I'm still going with you guys in the morning. I don't want anyone to suspect anything. If I didn't go, everyone would know something was up. I can count on you, can't I?" Bobby stood and said, "Yes sir." He saluted the colonel, the colonel saluted him back and said, "Go on, get back to bed."

Bobby went back to bed but couldn't sleep. He lay there for an hour mulling over what had happened to him in the last year. It started out normal enough. He had a job, started school, did some racing on the weekends. Then Colonel Hill came into his life. It started out doing what he liked, riding quads. He met a wonderful girl. Now he was shooting and being shot at. He figured someone had to do what he was doing. What made him think he was any better than anyone else. Besides, he was good at it. He knew he owed a lot to his friends. He would never forget them. He looked at his watch, another hour before sun up. He decided to go run. He got ready and was about to leave when he thought, better grab my pistol or they won't let me out of the gate. He picked it up and stuck it in his pocket. He had run abut a mile when he spotted movement up ahead. He stopped and ducked in behind a tree. Who was that, he thought? He decided to sneak up to see what was going on. He saw one of the Kurds standing near a big rock. He watched for a few minutes. " second man showed up. He had a bag with him. The two talked for a minute, the second man handed the first one the bag. Bobby thought his boss would like to meet these two men. He pulled out his gun and stepped out from behind the rock and said, "Stop. Put your hands up." The first man now with the bag put his hands up. The other man went for his gun. Bobby shot him but it didn't kill him. Bobby disarmed him, then motioned for the other man to lay down. He did and Bobby took the bag from him.

" couple of minutes later a Humvee pulled up. Sergeant Kevin Lowry was one of the soldiers to arrive first. He asked, "What's going on here, sir?" Bobby said, "I don't really know, let's get these two guys back to base. Maybe we can get some answers."

They loaded the two men into the Humvee then drove back to camp. It was just breaking daylight. The whole camp heard the shot. They went on full alert. The Humvee drove through the gate and straight to headquarters. " medic was called to attend the wounded man. Colonel Hill, Major Dobson, Captain Davis, Captain Randolf and Major Krais were waiting. The colonel said, "Report Sergeant." Bobby stepped out with the bag. "Maybe I should tell you, sir." The colonel said, "Okay, I'm listening." Before he could say a word Specialist Wolfe was standing nearby, saw the wounded man. He said, "Colonel, this man was from our forward camp. He was the one that hit me." Major Krais was taking it all in. Bobby said, "Sir, the wounded man gave this bag to the other man." Major Krais said, "This other man is my clerk." Bobby handed the bag to the colonel. He opened the bag. He said "It's dirty laundry." He pulled the clothes out. "Wait a minute, he said. "We have a bomb. Everyone get back." Colonel Hill carried the bag right out the front gate. Then he disarmed it. He came back in, madder than a rabid dog. His face was beet red with anger. He looked at the Kurdish soldier like he would like to tear him apart. He calmed down quickly. He said, "Captain Davis, have the camp stand down." He said, "Yes sir." Colonel Hill said, "Captain Randolf, get your men ready to leave for the airbase." Captain Randolf said, "Yes sir." The colonel then said, "Major Dobson, Major Krais, take the piece of crap man here and find out what you can." They, along with two guards, took the man into the headquarters tent. Colonel Hill had calmed down. He turned to Bobby and said, "You, in my tent." Bobby and the colonel walked in. The colonel sat down. He said, "Boy, I could use a drink." Bobby jumped up and ran out of the tent. The colonel didn't even try to stop him. Bobby went to Buddy and said, "I need a bottle of wine." Buddy got it and asked, "What's going on?" Bobby said, "I'll tell you later." He left with the wine, walked into Colonel Hill's tent, opened the bottle and handed it to him. Colonel Hill took the bottle and took a big drink. He said, "Now, that's good wine." I'm not even going to ask you what happened yet. We'll talk about it on the way to the airbase. You and your friends will ride with me in my Humvee and with Captain Randolf in the other one." He took another drink. He added, "And if you can get another bottle of this wine I'll share it with you. Now go get ready, we leave in thirty minutes." Bobby just got up and walked out. He went back to his tent and started getting dressed to go and packed his bag. As he was changing his friends surrounded him. Johnny said, "Well?" Bobby said, "Oh, it was nothing. I'll tell you guys all about it on the way to the airbase, we leave in thirty minutes. Buddy, the colonel said thanks for the wine. He asked if you would bring another bottle." Buddy said, "I'm taking two." Johnny said, "I think we all could use a drink." Bobby finished getting ready and grabbed a sandwich out of the mess tent. Soon they were headed to the airbase.

The young men were excited about the break. Colonel Hill seemed to be rejuvenated in their presence. The ride in was informal to say the least. They were having fun. When the men got close Colonel Hill's radio came alive. He answered it. When he finished talking on the radio, he said, "Well, if it ain't one thing, it's another." He had his driver pull over. Next he had all the trucks empty out. He had something to say. "Men, we are just a little over a mile and a half from the airbase. It seems the whole world wants to know about our secret base and our activities. It's very important to not release any information that would compromise our mission. If someone asks the location of the base, just say it's classified or refer them to me. Do not tell them anything of our recent activities. We know it happened, the Iraqis know it happened but they aren't saying anything either. If Saddam makes up a lie about his activities at that base and accuses us of something, let him. We know better and when the time is right the rest of the world will know. They, the press, must have picked up our injured men that were brought here. They are on a fishing trip. Don't let them trick you. When we arrive at the base, I will talk to the press. The rest of you avoid them. If you are approached by them be friendly and courteous but don't tell them anything. It will drive them nuts. Now, get back on the trucks , we're going in." He turned to Bobby, "I want you guys to stay with me while I talk to the press. Besides CNN, the Times and US" Today, there are a couple of ATV magazines here. They know about our quads and they want to talk to you guys about their performance. I want you guys to talk abut the way the quads handle. If they ask about its armament just tell them they are armed, nothing specific. Okay?" All seven men said, "Yes sir." They loaded up and drove into the base. At the parking area the press was waiting. Colonel Hill told Captain Randolf to get the men on the buses and take them to the barracks. Colonel Hill and the seven approached the reporters. He was polite to them. They asked him what his mission is. He told them we are here on a joint training mission and specifics were classified. That pretty much ended that.

Most of the reporters just backed off except for the ATV magazine reporters. Colonel Hill said, "I've got seven of the finest men here teaching my men how to ride. Honda and Polaris have developed some very fine machines for us. They have a lot of special features that you won't find on other ATV's. The basic design, though I'm told, will be out on the market soon." One reporter asked, "How do they handle?" Johnny said, "Like a dream. They are well balanced, have good speed throughout the gears and have plenty of power." The reporter asked, "You are Johnny Hale, aren't' you?" Johnny said, "Yes sir." He started pointing at the others. "This is Bobby Duck, Will Valance, Mick Smalley, Buddy Bishop, Chad Duncan and Chad Hubanks. They are all good riders and teachers." He was asked, "How are the soldiers doing on the quads?" Johnny's reply was, "We have shown them a few things that we've learned and they are doing great." The men were asked to pose for a picture. Johnny said sure. The seven grabbed Colonel Hill and had three or four pictures taken. Then Colonel Hill said, " We are awfully tired, we need to go." So they left. The men boarded a waiting bus. Colonel Hill just said, "Thanks guys, good job. I'm going to take a shower and get some sleep. I'll hook up with you guys later."

The bus pulled up to the barracks. They all went in to drop their stuff off. Colonel Hill got undressed and headed for the shower. The seven headed for the mess hall. They ate their fill. Buddy said, "There's a new movie on, we can catch the early show." They all agreed to go. When they got there they had about a half hour before the doors opened. Will said, "I'm going next door to the chapel." The rest went with him. When they got inside they discovered several men from their unit. They found an empty pew, all seven knelt and began to pray. They prayed for themselves, the other men and for the families of men they had killed in battle. They even prayed for Saddam, that he would realize his unrighteous path that he was on. After awhile they started drifting out, not saying a word to each other.

They got in line for the movie. It was a classic they all had seen before, Forest Gump with Tom Hanks. They watched the movie and ate their popcorn. After the movie ended Bobby said, "I'm tired. I think I'll shower and get some sack time." They all agreed. Someone asked him about the incident that morning. He told them what happened. Chad Duncan said, "Thanks." That made Bobby feel good.

The men got back to the cool barracks, showered and slept twelve hours until the next morning. The colonel slept longer than that. He had been totally drained. The next morning they went to breakfast. They were starting to feel better. Colonel Hill and Captain Randolf joined them. Colonel Hill said, "I've been in contact with Major Dobson. It seems they were made to do what they did. Some of Saddam's men had taken their families captive. They feared for their lives. Fortunately, they didn't disclose the true location of Camp Q. They probably both will be shot. Unfortunately for them it was damn if you do and damn if you don't. The man with the bomb was going to put it in the ammo dump. He was scheduled to go on guard duty there. That sure would have ruined our day. Thank you, Bobby. You saved us all." They all clapped for him. Bobby said, " I didn't do anything you guys wouldn't do if you had been there. God just picked on me to be there." Will said, "Yeah, we might have done the same thing but we didn't, you did." Captain Randolf said, "Thank God you were there." Buddy said, ""men to that, brother." They all laughed. The Colonel said, "Captain Randolf and I have a meeting after we eat. I've made arrangements for tonight's USO Show. We've all got good seats." Johnny said, "Who's the main act." Colonel Hill said, "It's one of your fellow Okies, a country music singer named Vince Gill." Chad Duncan said, "Country music?" Bobby said, "Hey, this guy is good, you'll like him." The men finished eating and parted company from the colonel and captain. Bobby said, "I sure would like to call home." Johnny said, "I think we all would. A young Air Force guy overheard them. He said, "You can, they've set up phones next door for us to use." They all headed next door.

There was a long line for the phones but they patiently waited for their turns. They were limited to ten minutes each. Bobby called and got a hold of his mother, Sandy. She was excited to hear form her son. She asked so many questions, Bobby had a hard time answering them. He asked about his dad and about Jill. She told him they were both fine. Jill was doing well in school and was working out real good in the shop. Soon their time was up. They told each other that they missed them and loved them. After he hung up it was all he could do to force the lump down and out of his throat. The rest of them had mixed feelings about the phone calls home, also. They were glad they called but all were a bit homesick. They decided to go check out the club. The whole team was there. Sergeant Stockstill said to them as they walked in, "Come in guys, I'll buy you a beer." Chad Hubanks said, "That's what I'm talking about." The place was packed, not a chair to be found. Will said, "Did you guys know about the phones to call home?" " dozen chairs freed up. Chad Duncan said, "Smart thinkin' ol' buddy." They sat and talked to their friends.

Captain Randolf and Captain Davis walked in. They sat down and ordered a beer. Bobby asked Captain Davis, "What was it like being a prisoner?" Captain Davis thought for a moment. Then he said, "Frankly, it scared the shit out of me. I just knew that I was going to be beaten and tortured. We would have too if you great guys hadn't showed up. Bartender, I want to buy these men a beer." Johnny said, "Way to go, Bobby. I knew you'd get us a beer." Captain Davis said, "Aw, you guys are crazy." Johnny said, "Hey, just kidding. We're all glad that we could save your sorry butt."

They all laughed. Mick asked, "What was the big powwow about?" Captain Randolf said, "You know I can't tell you guys. However, changes are coming. Colonel Hill is still there getting more details. He's the one to tell you, not us."

The men blew off the lack of information. They figured they'd find out when the time came. They hung around the club for the rest of the afternoon. Bobby said, "I'm hungry, let's go eat and get ready for the show."

That night at the show the colonel was right. They had good seats, VIP seats. They all enjoyed the show, even Chad Duncan. By the end of the show he was singing right along with Vince. Bobby laughed, "Charlotte would be proud of you." Buddy said, "I could talk to Vince and see if he needs a backup." Chad turned red and the rest of them laughed, even Colonel Hill.

Colonel Hill enjoyed their company. Their youthful exuberance seemed to make everyone feel better. He thought these guys are good, but don't feel the need to flaunt it. They were just being themselves. The rest of his men couldn't act that way around him.

The next morning after a nice shower and breakfast, they all loaded up for the trip back to Camp Q. Colonel Hill wasn't looking forward to telling some of them the news he had. When they pulled into the camp, he called for an officers' meeting. Once they were inside and seated, he said, "I've been in contact with General Johnson. We have trouble brewing. Not here but in Afghanistan. It seems there are at least two large groups of al-Qaida in Northern Pakistan and are preparing to attack Afghanistan. We have airplanes and satellite coverage. Somehow they have been able to circumvent all of our surveillance. It is suspected they may come across the border in the very rugged terrain in the north. We've been asked to help out with planting surveillance markers like they use on the border between Mexico and the U.S. Ground forces could do it but it would take weeks. We will also operate ops like they use here. We will take the entire quad force except five. The following quad riders are First Lieutenant Wooley, Staff Sergeant Butch Culp, Staff Sergeant Rick Prince, Staff Sergeant James Fomby and Staff Sergeant Bill Royce. They will stay behind to teach the Kurds how to ride. Nothing fancy, just the basics for transportation. Besides the quad force, the following staff will go. Myself, Staff Sergeant Ketcher, Master Sergeant Miller and two of his men. The balance of our force here will remain here. The mission is still the same. Man the op's and supply and train the Kurdsmen. There has been one change here. All base security will be run by U.S. soldiers. No offense Major Krais, but in light of the past events, we feel this is a must, at least for now." Major Krais said, "I fully understand, Colonel Hill. I assure you if it was my decision to make, I would do the same. Most of my men are very trustworthy patriots, but I can't say that about all of them." Colonel Hill continued, "Thank you, Major. I hoped you would see it that way. Major Dobson will be in charge. Captain Davis will supervise the training. We will leave in the morning and hopefully we will return in a few days. Major Dobson, I want you to get the quad riders from our force that still man observation posts to be replaced by morning." Major Dobson said, "Consider it done, sir." Colonel Hill said, "Well, that's about all I have. Captain Randolf, get your men and machines ready. They will have to ride them to the airbase."

After the meeting Bobby said, "Boy, now this is going to be a sight. Over fifty quads running down the road." Johnny said, "Yeah, we better get packed."

The next morning the men and quads were ready. The convoy consisted of one truck, two Humvees and fifty three quads. They made it to the airbase in just over three hours. They drove the quads right out to two waiting C-130's.

CHAPTER 10

The planes took off. Bobby said, "Here we go on another adventure." Mick said, "I've been wanting to get a crack at ol' bin Laden. I wish we could get bin Laden and Saddam in our sights just once. Maybe we could put a stop to all of this." Chad said, "I just want to come out of this in one piece." Buddy said, "Don't worry, Chad, you're too ugly to get hurt. Besides, I've got your back."

By late that evening they were landing in Afghanistan. They were fed and went right into a briefing. Things were moving fast. A sense of urgency prevailed. Maps and assignments were issued. Some of the men were taught how to set up the surveillance devices. The briefing was complete, covering most possible scenarios. They would have plenty of backup if they came under fire. Things ended up later that evening. They would be trucked to their AO in the morning. I think what bothered the men was Colonel Hill wasn't calling the shots. At one point Bobby and his friends were going to be split up. Captain Randolf went to bat for them. The seven were kept together as an assault force. The fifty three man team would be spread out over twenty miles. There would be backup in the air and by air. Duration of being on station hadn't been defined. Everyone was of the opinion the attack would be in the next few days, but nobody knew for sure. The next day the entire force moved up in the hills, dropping off teams at the appropriate locations. The assault force, consisting of fifteen men, picked a spot half way across their line. The going was slow even on quads. Trails were few and far between. The attack team studied the map. They figured it would take at least twenty minutes if not longer to respond to the outer edges of their sector. They were issued cold weather gear but really didn't understand why until the sun went down. By early in the afternoon everything was set. All they had to do now was wait. It got cold sitting there, bone chilling cold. At observation posts there were two men assigned, one man had to be awake at all times. They stayed in small tents, not the two man pup tents. They were big enough for the sensor monitors and an infrared scanner. The scanner was programmable. It could rotate three hundred sixty degrees or one hundred eighty degree sweeps at varying speeds. If something was detected it could lock on. The only problem was the terrain. The machine couldn't see through the large rocks that were everywhere. It was strictly line of sight, it could scan both vertically and horizontally, it could detect body heat inside of buildings. It did a pretty job. That's why they had the motion detectors planted. If something tripped the motion detectors a radio signal would be activated. Each signal was unique allowing the men monitoring them to pin point locations. There was no real good intelligence from the detectors. It couldn't tell who, what or how many moving objects there were. If the detector was close the men would try to get a visual. The operations were scattered a mile apart. That meant the teams had a half mile either way to cover. If the detector was on the outer edge they would have to rely on others to check it out either by roving patrols or the fly boys, helicopters or planes. The tents the men stayed in were equipped with small propane heaters; the men had enough propane to last two nights. Three nights if they were conservative. The monitors and radios were battery operated. They had a three day supply of batteries with them. The men had water and food (MRE's). The tents were canvas with a liner that wouldn't allow light to escape. " tent that lit up could be seen for miles in the dark especially since they were perched up on high points. If the men left the tents at night they first had to shut down all lights before they exited or entered the tents. It would be possible for a small number of men, one, two or maybe even three, to get through the area. Not a thousand like they said could be coming.

Three days and three nights went by. Colonel Hill had managed to get hold of a helicopter. He wanted to take care of his men. He managed to deliver some hot food to them along with other supplies. On the fourth day a strong weather front moved in. Lots of rain and up in the hills it was a cold rain. It virtually shut down the patrols. The attack group with the seven pros in it spent their time reading, writing letters or playing cards. Everyone was nervous about the weather. They were placed on high alert. For good reason, too. The terrorist force decided to use the weather to make their move. Instead of coming through the hills they used a series of roads and rails just to the south. They were mobile. They had trucks and jeep-like vehicles. They even had some artillery. The area they came through was controlled by the Afghan Army. The advance force took out several defensive positions. Everyone was alerted.. Troops and equipment were rushed to the area. The weather was fighting them. The terrorist force had moved to within two miles of a large town in the north before our forces could attack them. " squadron of Apache helicopters hit them, stopping them cold. The battle was on. The fire fight was intense. Within minutes armored vehicles arrived. They joined in the fight. The terrorist assault was stopped. They began trying to escape. The rain finally stopped and the sun was starting to come up. Other forces blocked their retreat on the roads, forcing the enemy forces to abandon their vehicles. They began scattering out. " large number of them were headed for the hills. The quad force had abandoned their observation posts, joined forces and prepared to attack. All fifty three quads joined up at the base of the hills. At least one hundred fifty enemy soldiers were pinched between the armored assault force and Colonel Hill's quad force. They were headed right for them. The enemy figured their only chance was to make it to the hills. The radio was blaring the enemy force was now a half mile away. More helicopters were on their way. When the enemy closed to within three hundred yards the quad force opened up with their rockets. They dropped about half the enemy. Still they advanced. They began taking fire from the enemy, still out of range of their 9mm machine guns. But a few of the quads fired them anyway. They closed to within one hundred and fifty yards. Then Colonel Hill's helicopter popped up. It was armed with a Vulcan (a multi barrel machine gun). It opened up. That stopped the enemy force. They began surrendering. Some still tried to escape. The quads quickly ran them down and they too surrendered. Mick said, "I wonder if bin Laden was in this group?" Bobby said, "I don't know. But if he's still alive you can bet he planned this attack." The quads split into five ten-man teams. One team took charge of the prisoners. They disarmed them and held them. The other four teams patrolled up and down the base of the hills. They captured at least twenty more enemy soldiers. Others decided to keep fighting. Bad mistake. Somehow a jeep like vehicle had escaped. It had a fifty calibre machine gun mounted on it. It opened up on one of the quad patrols injuring two men. Bobby and his patrol was nearby. They

154

managed to get in behind the vehicle. Bobby, Johnny and Chad Duncan fired rockets almost at the same time. The vehicle and its occupants were destroyed. " helicopter was nearby. It landed and evacuated the two injured soldiers. It was Sergeant Wright and Specialist Bookout. The medic on the chopper radioed and said both of them would be okay. The quad force spent the rest of the day, along with other forces, searching for the escaping enemy. The quad force had no more encounters. The sky was filled with helicopters and planes. More men were rushed to the area. The dead and wounded enemy soldiers were recovered. Throughout the day more of the enemy was captured or killed. They estimated the enemy force was twelve hundred strong. Almost half of them had been killed, another four hundred captured. They figured about two hundred of them managed to escape, most made it back to Pakistan. The Pakistani Army tried to capture them and did get a group of about fifty. The threat was over for now. They knew that there still remained large numbers of al-Qaida forces scattered around. They continued the cat and mouse tactics. An assault of that size wouldn't be tried again for awhile. The enemy force had killed or wounded about fifty of the friendly forces. The American casualties included the two quad guys and a Black Hawk helicopter had been shot down killing one and injuring five others.

Early the next morning the quad force was relieved by a company of British troops. They were sent to a rear area base. All the men began wondering what was next. The men spent the next two days in the rear area camp. They got hot food and showers. Some of them visited Sergeant Wright and Specialist Bookout at the hospital before they were flown out. Both men would fully recover from their injuries. The would be taken to a hospital ship and would be better stabilized before going home.

Some of the quads had been damaged. Master Sergeant Miller and his men got busy repairing them. Bobby and his friends offered to help. Master Sergeant Miller said, "Thanks guys, you did your part. Now let us do ours." Bobby laughed, "Just offering, Sarge. If you need us we're here." Master Sergeant Miller said, "You guys get out of here before I throw you out." He smiled and winked at Bobby.

Colonel Hill got called away to another briefing. He was gone for hours. That meant only one thing. Things were fixing to happen. The men speculated on their fate. Buddy said, "Maybe we are going to fight terrorists in Hawaii." Chad Duncan said, "No, we will probably go to Iceland or maybe even the North Pole." Specialist Upton, Sergeant Shipman and Specialist Money were sitting near the seven. Specialist Money asked, "Do you guys joke about everything?" Bobby asked, "What do you want us to do? Sure, we have fun. The things we do here are serious enough. I've seen more death than I ever wanted to see. This is stuff you see on TV news. We know what's at stake. Other peoples' lives depend on what we do. People that can't defend themselves. Our joking around lets us forget about all of this. I would go nuts if all I did was think about all of this." Johnny said, "He speaks for all of us, when it comes down to it." Will said, "All of this fighting will stay with us forever. We get serious. We worry about you, about our families, our country and each other. So cut us some slack, okay?" Sergeant Shipman said, "He didn't mean anything about it. He's young like you guys. I know you guys could walk away anytime you want to. I'm personally glad you guys are here. I'm sure a lot of us who are in this room wouldn't be here if it weren't for you guys." Colonel Hill had walked in and caught most of the conversation. "You got that right," he said. Sergeant Shipman stood and called the room to attention. Colonel Hill said, "Sit down, take a load off. You men deserve it." He said, "Well, we're leaving. We are going to be part of a large multi unit assault force. It's all Bobby's fault." They all looked at Bobby. "When you guys hit the chemical storage and rescued Captain Davis and myself, Bobby took a briefcase from a gentleman. That briefcase listed locations all over Northern Iraq that is either storage facilities or manufacturing locations of some of the deadliest chemicals known to man. We also have locations on a couple of labs that are working on nukes. We are going to help destroy these places. Details aren't worked out yet. We will return to Camp Q in the morning. As soon as I know more, you will too. Now I have a surprise for you. Staff Sergeant Ketcher started bringing in some cold beer. Even the colonel had a beer with his men. They spent the rest of the evening talking.

The next morning they loaded up on the C-130's and headed back to Camp Q.

CHAPTER 11

They landed at the airbase. In the week that they had been gone the airbase had grown. More planes had arrived and many more men. They didn't stay at the airbase. They went straight back to Camp Q. They were glad to see their friends. They had heard about their battle. First Lieutenant Wooley told Bobby and his friends that things were about the same. They heard rumors about something big coming up. Bobby said, "It's not rumors. Things are going to happen. We are going to be right in the big middle of it." He wouldn't say what it was. The orders finally came down. All of the officers got together to do the planning. Colonel Hill said, "We have two missions and they will be done at the same time. There is a chemical storage facility much like the one we took out before. It's about seventy miles from here. Major Krais will work out our route. I will lead the attack. We will be taking seventy five percent of our quad force along with two dozen dune buggies. The Air Force is bombing most of the sites. This location is right in the middle of a village. They didn't want to take any chances on civilian casualties. The rest of our quad force will go part way with us. Then they will split off for their own target, a nuclear bomb making facility. They won't actually attack the facility; they will take out three SAM sites so our Air force can take it out. We have a time line to follow. All of the attacks will take place all at once. Captain Randolf will lead the smaller group. The following men will be in his command, Staff Sergeant Fomby, Sergeant Grigsby, Sergeant Shipman, Sergeant Lowry, Sergeant Stockstill, Sergeant Higgonbothom, Specialist Money, Warrant Officer Duck, Warrant Officer Hale, Warrant Officer Samlley, Warrant Officer Duncan, Warrant Officer Hubanks and Warrant Officer Vallance. If all goes well we will rendezvous and all be back in time for breakfast. Be aware there are enemy patrols everywhere. It's going to be very difficult to cross that much ground without being discovered. We take off at dark. We will only go as far as the edge of the mountains. We will lay up tomorrow then move out to our targets. You have four hours to gas up and get your gear together. We will have other units in the area. If you get in trouble we will do all we can to get help to you. Any questions?" Buddy said, "Just one, sir. I have two bottles of wine left. Will you join us for drinks when we're finished?" The colonel laughed and said, "You betcha, Buddy." Buddy said, "Cool." Everyone laughed. The colonel said, "Well, let's roll." Johnny said, "Hey, that's my line." Bobby said, "Come on, idiot, let's get ready." They walked out.

They spent the next two hours getting ready, checking everything twice. They were about as ready as they could be. They grabbed something to eat and studied the maps and codes. They also studied satellite photos of the SAM sites and the surrounding terrain. They waited for time to pull out. Bobby spent this time writing Jill a letter. He wrote to her that he couldn't wait to see her. She should practice holding her breath because of the kisses he would be giving her. Well, it was time to go. He put a quick finish on the letter and stuck it in the outgoing mailbag. He had closed the letter with a simple I love you

The force prepared to move out. There was a quick radio check. Colonel Hill, standing in the lead dune buggy, looked at Bobby and said, "Will The Magnificent Seven please lead us out?" Bobby looked over at Johnny, nodded his head at him. Johnny said, "Let's roll." They took off. As they headed out the seven men pulled wheelies out of the gate. The rest of the convoy followed. They used their night vision and infrared to guide them to the other side of the mountains. They arrived way before sun up. They found places to hide and settled in for the wait. Bobby and Johnny looked out over what lay before them. Soon the sun came up over the mountains behind them. It lit up the desert. Guards were posted; the rest of the men tried to get some sleep. It got hot. Bobby drifted off to sleep. He began dreaming of home. He was swimming in the pool. His dad was charcoalling steaks. Jill came out to join him in the pool. She looked great in her swim suit. She jumped in the pool. They swam and kissed. He was awakened by the sound of motors. It was an Iraqi patrol. Everyone was nervous. The patrol passed within a quarter mile of their position. When they passed they all breathed a sigh of relief. Bobby decided to stay awake. It would be dark in a couple of hours anyway. He opened an MRE. He forced most of it down and drank some water. He checked his quad and filled the gas tank. He told the others to do the same. Will said, "We already have, brother." Bobby said, "Sorry, dude." Will just said, "Cool." They shook hands. Sergeant Shipman walked up. "The captain wants to see us." They all made their way over to a secluded spot the captain picked out. Once they were all together he started, "I think you guys are the best in this unit. Not just because of your riding skills, you're all team players. When we leave out Will, Mick, Bobby and Johnny will lead. Chad Duncan, Buddy and Chad Hubanks will bring up the rear. We will keep it tight. No matter what, we stay together. It will take all of us working together to make this work. We go in as one and we all come back" We pull out in thirty minutes, check your gas." Bobby and Will just looked at each other and smiled.

Soon the attack force moved out. About an hour later Captain Randolf and his men peeled off from the main body. With the quads on whisper mode they made good time. Will opened his microphone on the radio. He said, "Hold up. I'm getting a heat signal on my scope." The team stopped. Captain Randolf took Sergeant Stockstill with him on foot to take a closer look. They found an enemy patrol camped out. " quick look at the map showed they had to pass here or go out of their way an hour. " quick decision to take out the patrol, two vehicles and eight men. He had the seven pro riders mount their quads in case they were needed. The captain and the rest of his men moved in on foot. Within a few minutes all eight enemy soldiers were dead. Not a shot had been fired. They placed the bodies inside the vehicles and pushed them into a nearby ravine. Soon they were moving again. Finally they reached the SAM sites. They scanned the area for sensors. The nuclear facility was a half mile away. No roads led to this place. Everything had been brought in by helicopter. No patrols in the area, they didn't want to attract any attention.

At the same time Colonel Hill's force was getting into position. His plan " was to have some of Major Krais' men put on Iraqi uniforms. They would stroll right up to the main gate, take out the guards, allowing a team of demolition experts to move in and place the charges. Then it was get out of there, no muss, no fuss. If plan " didn't work plan B would be used. An all out assault with the quads hitting the main gate and blowing up everything. They got into position. Plan " seemed to be working. The guards were taken out. The demolition team moved in but they were discovered and an alarm was sounded. The quads hit the gate followed by three buggies with fifty calibres. Rockets were fired into all the buildings, enemy soldiers came running out. The quads opened up on their 9mm machine guns. The demolition team got in and laid down the charges. Outside, the fire fight continued. " rocket from a hand held launcher hit, knocking two riders off their quads. They were slightly injured. They turned their quads back over and surprisingly started. The demolition team made it out of the storage area. They all backed out of the compound. The demolition team loaded up on dune buggies. They headed out of the village. One of the buggies got hit with rocket fire killing all four men. They were Kurds. "Damn," the colonel said. First Lieutenant Wooley took out the man on the launcher. They headed south out of the village and then would turn back to the northeast.

At the same time Captain Randolf's team took out the SAM sites. They hightailed it out of there. " couple of minutes later two F-15's fired missiles into the nuclear facility. Captain Randolf contacted Colonel Hill and said, "Alpha, this is Bravo. Mission a success. Fifteen in and fifteen out." Colonel Hill responded, "Bravo, this is Alpha. Same here. Four Kurd's down. Rendezvous point Echo." Both teams were on their way out. They were about an hour away when they heard a call for help. An F-15 had been hit and was going down. The two men on board ejected. They were about five miles away. Everyone knew enemy troops would close in on them. Captain Randolf didn't hesitate. He peeled off with his team and headed for the downed airmen. Captain Randolf contacted the airmen and said, "Hold on, help is ten out." The quad riders were off the whisper mode. Will was the best cross country rider and led the way. Captain Randolf contacted Colonel Hill. He said, "Sir, we won't make the rendezvous. Suggest you go on without them. We will try to hook up at point Mike. We expect unfriendly guest." Colonel Hill said, "Watch yourselves. Keep me informed." The quad team reached the airmen. One of them had a broken ankle. They loaded them behind Chad Hubanks and Buddy. They started to move out. Will and Mick led the way, Bobby and Johnny moved to the rear. Buddy and Chad Hubanks moved to the middle. Captain Randolf plotted a route. They took off. Five minutes later they were discovered. " half dozen jeep like vehicles opened fire on them. The quads did some fancy riding to avoid the fast moving vehicles. The quads were moving fast but the enemy was gaining. The quads decided to fight. One by one some of the quads dropped off behind rocks. The rest kept going. When the enemy got close the quads popped out taking out four of the vehicles with missile fire. The other two turned tail and drove away. The quads rejoined their team. " few minutes later they ran into more trouble. This time it was T-72 tanks. Captain Randolf radioed for help. The quads made a hard right turn to avoid the tanks. What they didn't know, they were headed into a box canyon. The tanks gave chase. Their radio came to life. Help was on the way. The canyon was three miles long. The quad team covered that three miles in a hurry. The quads were out of rockets. They lined up at the end of the canyon. When the tanks arrived maybe they could ride past them. There were three tanks. Captain Randolf radioed, "Situation critical, where's the help?" " voice came back, "Thirty seconds from your position." The enemy tanks rolled in. Chad and Buddy got the airmen hidden behind some rocks then rejoined their unit. The pilot recalled later, he had never seen such bravery. The fifteen quads all lined up ready to do battle with three tanks. The tanks rolled within a hundred yards then they stopped. Captain Randolf said, "Get ready boys, here we go on my command." Then the tank hatches opened up. The enemy soldiers got out with their hands raised. Bobby said, "Hey, they are surrendering to us." Johnny said, " Well, wouldn't you if you faced us." About that time two A-10's flew over. They looked up behind them on the ridge. About a dozen dune buggies had lined up with TOW missiles. It was a British outfit. They were responding to the downed airmen and were close enough to help. Buddy asked, "Well, what do we do with these prisoners?" Captain Randolf said, "I don't know." " few minutes later a couple of trucks from the British unit showed up to take them. " Black Hawk helicopter flew in, landed and picked up the airmen. The pilot told the quad force thanks. The British commander said, "You chaps better get a move on. There's still plenty of enemy around. The quad force pulled out and headed for the rally point to hook up with Colonel Hill. After they were clear of the area, the A-10's came in and destroyed the three enemy tanks. The quads went back on whisper mode. They rode the last twenty miles with no more conflicts. Buddy said, "I've never been so scared in all my life." Bobby said, "You, I'm going to have to change my drawers." Sergeant Stockstill said, "Don't think you guys are alone, my quad seat has a permanent crease in it now." Captain Randolf called into the colonel and gave him a situation report. It was just breaking dawn when the fifteen quads rejoined the others. They all took a break, got something to eat and refueled. Colonel Hill contacted headquarters. When he was finished giving his report he called in his men. He said, "Men, I've just been in contact with headquarters command. The mission was a success. They tell me ol' Saddam is one pissed off S.O.B." The men cheered. "Now let's get out of here, we've still got thirty five miles to go. We're not going to wait for dark. More enemy troops are on their way." Captain Randolf's team took the point.

By early afternoon they rolled into Camp Q. Everyone parked and got out. Colonel Hill called a quick meeting. He said, "I want everyone to do a weapons check and get something hot to eat. Officers meeting in one hour. Bobby said, "I don't know about you guys, but it's like my dad used to say, "I'm so hungry my stomach thinks my throat's cut.'" Johnny said, "Good saying, corny but good." Will said, "Yeah, dudes, let's chow." Chad Hubanks said, "I'm with ya'." They all went and ate. Buddy asked, "I wonder how long they are going to keep us here?" "That's the sixty four dollar question," Chad Duncan said, then continued, "I don't know about you guys but I'm about worn out." Bobby said, "We all are, man. Maybe we will get some news in the meeting." After they ate they walked over to the headquarters tent. Everyone else was already there. They were just talking amongst themselves. Colonel Hill stood up. "Well, let's get this meeting going. First of all our mission was a success, we did suffer four casualties, though. We lost four of Major Krais' men. It was unfortunate and it could have been any of us. You plan and then all you can do is hope for the best. I don't believe if we had done anything different it would have mattered. Major Krais, would you offer our condolences to the families?" Major Krais said, "Thank you, sir, I will." The Colonel continued, "Because of what we have done, I believe Saddam will get more aggressive in his actions. So does high command. I want everyone to be alert. Congress is finally ready to act. We can expect massive troop movement from all of the coalition forces. The President feels that he has the support he needs to launch an all out attack on Iraq. He believes the majority of the Iraqi people are tired of Saddam and his bully tactics. There is no love for this man or his regime. For the most part the Iraqis are poor and uneducated. They have the same dream as all of us. They want to do better for themselves and their families. Anyway, enough politics. We've been ordered to maintain our current status until sufficient coalition forces arrive. When that happens we will then turn over total control to Major Krais and his men. U.S. forces here will be pulled to the rear where we will operate more as a covert unit. That's all I have for you. See to your men." They all got up and started to walk out. Colonel Hill said, "Will the quad instructors please stay behind for a minute." The seven men sat back down. The colonel waited for the room to clear, only Major Dobson remained. The colonel said, "I know all of this is more than you bargained for. You're ready to get back home. I don't blame you. Believe me if I felt we could do without you, I would send you home. You men have done so much and have been vital to the success we have had. Bobby, I'm putting you in for the Silver Star, the rest of you, the Bronze Star. Your country is proud of you." He opens the drawer on his desk and pulls out seven magazines. He said, "Do you remember when we got our pictures taken for the ATV magazine?" They all nodded yes. "Well, several other magazines picked up on them." He put the magazines on the table for them to look at. "Several reporters are doing stories on you seven. The country is hungry for heroes. Guess what, you're them. People back in the states know more about you than you do. Our public relations people are busy putting together a schedule of public appearances for you. You are scheduled to leave here in two weeks. By that time we should have enough forces here to pull us all out of this camp. Major Krais has doubled his force and our men have done a good job training them. You guys will do great. You're smart, good looking, well, you're smart anyway." They all laughed. "You will be kept real busy. Our enlistment numbers are already up from young men reading about you. " boost in morale is what our county needs with us fixing to go to war. We must have your permission to continue. What do you say?" Johnny said, "Well, if it's for the good of the country, of course." They all laughed. Bobby asked, "Sir, what about the rest of the quad team?" The colonel said, "Don't worry about them. You guys have done an excellent job training them. I would stack them up to any unit in the Army." They all agreed to do it. Buddy asked, "What do we do for the next two weeks?" Colonel Hill answered, "The Kurds are having a hard time on the quads. Master Sergeant Miller tells me they are real rough on them. I will assign an interpreter to you so you can teach them a few things." Chad Duncan said, "Sounds good." Colonel Hill said, "Great, now go get some rest. You'll start tomorrow." They stood up, saluted the Colonel and left.

It all hadn't soaked in yet as they walked into the team tent. They were met by several members of the quad force. Sergeant Stockstill said, "Can we have your autographs?" Bobby said, "Aw now, come on guys." They laughed and joked around for a few minutes. Sergeant First Class Kroeker said, "Seriously, you guys deserve it, if anybody does." Chad Duncan said, "I just wish it was all of us going." Mick said, "Yeah, we are all a team." The Sergeant First Class Kroeker followed up, "Well, remember wherever you go the force is with you." They all laughed again. Soon the joking petered out and they all got some sleep.

CHAPTER 12

The next morning brought hope for the seven men. They had mixed feelings of leaving the unit. The thing that got them over it was the fact that they too would soon be pulled off the front area. Major Krais was busy making his force stronger every day. After breakfast they went to the motor pool. Ten Kurd soldiers stood by their quads along with the interpreter, who turned out to be Specialist Money. Bobby said, "Luke, I didn't know you spoke their language." Specialist Money said, "Yeah, I speak four languages." Johnny said, "Well, let's get loaded up and see what we've got." They fired up the quads and headed out the gate for a test ride. They headed out over some flats to see how well they handled speed. The Kurdsmen were terrible. Most of them had never driven anything before.

Over the next three days they worked hard to improve, which was very hard because of the language barrier. "At the end of the third day, they could all do high speed runs and turns without falling off. They got them to having fun which helped them to relax. When they came in at the end of the day, they did some high speed passes in front of their friends. They got all kinds of cheers. The next three days they worked on climbing skills. The men worked hard. They struggled but were making progress. They had made it through the week.

Major Krais was preparing to take his force up in the hills for more training. They would be gone four days. That left only a small force at the camp. Major Krais took almost four hundred men with him including twenty five special Observation posts men for training. They left behind the fifty three man quad team, fifty Kurds including the ten that were training on the quads, and about seventy five garrison troops which included cooks, mechanics, clerks, and other assorted troops. Captain Davis had gone along

165

with Major Krais. There were still the fifty observation posts with about one hundred and fifty men and the forward base camp with fifteen men. Everything was running fine, though.

That night two quad patrols would be sent out. Captain Randolf would take fifteen men and patrol to the north. Bobby and his team would patrol to the south. The first half of the night went without incident. Then they got a message.

It was Staff Sergeant Ketcher. He said, "We've lost contact with one of our observation posts. We want your team to check it out. They may just be having radio problems. Use extreme caution." Bobby said, "We're on it. We'll let you know what we find." They were about six miles southeast of the camp. Moving slow, all of a sudden the infrared scanner went wild. He had the team back off and move to higher ground. " group of five to seven enemy soldiers were moving down the trail past them. Johnny said, "Let's take them." Bobby said, "No, look. There are more coming." They were scattered all up and down the trail moving in small groups. There were hundreds of them. Buddy said, "What are we going to do?" Bobby said, "We've got to notify the colonel." He called in, Staff Sergeant Ketcher was on the other end. Bobby said, "Get the colonel." The colonel got on the radio. "What's going on up there, Bobby?" Bobby said, "Sir, hundreds of enemy soldiers are making their way toward you in small groups. They are armed mostly with small arms and RPG's. They will be there before dawn." The colonel asked, "Are you safe?" Bobby answered, "Yes sir, we are above them. They don't know we are here." The colonel said, "Good, stay put. We'll get things ready here. Pick up any escapees."

The colonel put the base on full alert and contacted the airbase. They expected to be attacked by dawn. Captain Randolf intercepted the radio conversation. He said, "Colonel, we are four miles out, returning to base." The colonel said, "Your quads will be better off out in the open. Be advised I'm sending First Lieutenant Wooley and the rest of the quad force out to meet you. I want you to lay out there about a mile and wait for my call." Captain Randolf said, "I understand, sir." Meanwhile Bobby was surveying the terrain around them. The enemy troops were making their way through high rock passages. Just below them was a small canyon with high sides all the way around. Bobby told the others he had an idea. He told them they could capture a lot of enemy troops. Johnny said, "Are you crazy?"

Bobby said, "Maybe, but listen. The enemy is coming in small groups. We can hide in the rocks, jump them as they come through, disarm them and funnel them into this canyon. We will have the Kurds guard them and keep them quiet." They decided to try it. By the time they got set up about two hundred and fifty enemy soldiers had already passed. They were ready. " group of five approached. Bobby and the others stepped out and surprised the enemy troops. They had no time to react. Specialist Money told them to put their weapons down, be quiet and go into the canyon where the Kurd soldiers were waiting. It worked. They kept it up time and time again. Finally there were no more enemy soldiers moving down the trail. When they had finished they had captured about one hundred and fifty enemy soldiers.

The rest of the enemy kept going and got set to attack Camp Q. The camp was ready. At dawn they attacked. They had to cross two hundred yards of open ground. They began firing at the camp. Colonel Hill and his men returned fire. The enemy soldiers advanced. They were yelling and screaming, firing wildly at the camp. Two Apache helicopters popped up. They opened up with their Vulcan machine guns and rockets. The enemy soldiers began falling. They soon turned tail and headed back for the safety of the rocks. Then Captain Randolf and the quad force moved in. They took down many more. Some managed to get back to the rocks. Others dropped their weapons and gave up. About thirty men had made it to the rocks and began to try to get away, about forty had surrendered. The rest lay dead or wounded. It was a bloody mess. Wounded men lay moaning or screaming in agony. Not one U.S. soldier had ben killed, three were wounded by stray bullets, only one of them seriously. Captain Randolf took charge of the prisoners. Others began checking on and disarming the wounded. Over a hundred were dead and eighty wounded. Medics were called in.

As the thirty men made their escape, Bobby and his team captured the others. They now had one hundred eighty prisoners. They held them there until the colonel called. It was two hours later. The colonel had been busy. He had Staff Sergeant Ketcher call. He asked Bobby, "What is your status?" Bobby replied, "Eighteen out, eighteen okay. We have prisoners." Staff Sergeant Ketcher said, "Well, bring them on in," figuring at the most thirty prisoners. Bobby laughed in the microphone. "Sorry but we need help." Staff Sergeant Ketcher, getting a little put out said, "We're kind of busy around here. How may prisoners do you have?" Bobby replied, "At last count about one hundred eighty." Staff Sergeant Ketcher said, "Say again. I thought you said one eight zero, confirm." Bobby said, "Correct, one eight zero, that's a one hundred eighty, isn't is?" The radio went silent. A minute later Colonel Hill got on the radio, "Bobby, hold on, we've got men coming to help you. Give us your location. I can't wait to hear the story. You guys are amazing." Colonel Hill sent thirty men from the quad force to help Bobby's team bring in the prisoners. Three hours later they arrived with the prisoners. Some of the men had abandoned their quads. They left two men behind to guard the machines. When they arrived several trucks had arrived to carry off the dead, wounded and the other prisoners. Some of the trucks carried soldiers to reinforce the camp. The attack was over, though. The whole force was tired. They all had seen a lot of mindless death, all in Saddam's name. Later that afternoon Major Krais showed up with his force. Everyone felt better. The op had been taken out. They moved it and re-established the outpost. There were no other signs of the enemy.

That evening when everything settled down, Colonel Hill called in the seven quad pros. They walked into the colonel's office. He asked them to sit down. "I've seen a lot of good men come and go. But you seven are something else. There's not another group of men I know that would have done what you men did today. We had overwhelming fire power and that's · true enough. But you guys capturing that many men save lives, ours and theirs. You guys truly are magnificent. We've got to get you guys out of here. You're making the rest of us look bad." He smiled. Johnny said, "Sir, we haven't done anything that anyone else wouldn't have done in our place." The colonel said, "No one else would have even thought of trying that. Who's idea was that anyway?" They all looked at Bobby. The colonel said, "I should have known. How did you figure that out?" Bobby said, "I don't know. It just sort of came to me. It took all of us to pull it off, though. I know my friends here are smart and if they didn't think it would work, they would have told me." Chad Duncan said, "No, we wouldn't, we're just as crazy as you are. That's why we work so well with each other." Johnny said, "Yeah, we're all idiots. If we had given it much thought we never would have tried. We would have waited on help to arrive, letting them go right on by us." Buddy said, "We knew we had to do something. When Bobby laid it out for us it all made sense at the time." Chad Hubanks said,

"Together we are good, separate we would be like anyone else." Mick said, "He's right, colonel. It's like magic." The colonel said, "Incredible! Well, like I said, we've got to get you out of here. Pack your bags, you're pulling out tomorrow. You'll spend two days at the airbase and will be on a flight to Fort Hood. The quad force and myself will escort you to the airbase. I need to make arrangements to pull the rest of the men back next week. Now go pack. We pull out after breakfast. Before they could salute him, he saluted them. They left to go pack.

They all had a hard time sleeping that night. They had made good friends. In some strange way they felt like they were abandoning them. They next morning they ate breakfast with their friends. Then they grabbed their gear and put it into the back of one of the trucks. They prepared to climb into the back of the truck. Captain Randolf said, "What are you doing?" That's not how you got here." They walked around the side of the truck. There were all fifty three quads lined up. Not only that, but almost the entire camp was standing in formation at attention. First Sergeant Holliman yelled, "Present Arms." Almost six hundred men saluted them. The seven walked to the front of the formation, lined up, snapped to attention and returned the salute. First Sergeant Holliman yelled, "Order Arms." The seven put on their riding gear then mounted their quads. The rest of the quad force mounted theirs. Bobby looked over at Johnny. Johnny smiled and said, "Let's roll." Cheers went up from the crowd of men. All seven wheelied out of the front gate. Bobby had goose bumps.

The ride into the airbase seemed like nothing. When they reached the base they used a side gate to enter to try to avoid reporters and photographers. It didn't work. They were met by a horde of each. They spent the next two hours answering questions and getting their pictures taken. The post commander finally was able to free the men. Bobby said, "I think I would almost prefer having the enemy shooting at me. At least I could shoot back."

That night there was another USO show. It was another country music star from Oklahoma. It was Garth Brooks. Chad Duncan said, "I'm kinda getting used to country music." They all laughed. Johnny said, "He lives in my home town." Colonel Hill said, "Well, maybe we can go talk to him after the show." Johnny said, "That's for important people, not us." The colonel laughed.

The show Garth Brooks put on was great. He sang all of his hits. About half way through the show, he began to talk about the seven men. "We have some men here with us tonight that are celebrities in their own right. I've heard stories about them and I would like to honor them." His band started playing the theme song to the movie The Magnificent Seven. The spotlight remained on Garth as he stepped off the stage to shake their hands. It embarrassed the seven men. But they were honored at the same time. The seven men stood up to shake hands. The crowd cheered them. As Garth was shaking their hands they introduced themselves. Johnny was the last. When Garth got to him, Colonel Hill said, "This young man is from the town you live in." Garth said, "You're from Owasso?" Johnny said, "I sure am, I'm Johnny Hale." Garth said, "I love it there. Go Rams." He talked to Johnny for a minute. He said, "So you guys ride ATV's? I'd like to ride one." Johnny said, "We have fifty three of them at the motor pool." Garth said, "Great, they are having a little get together after the concert, maybe you guys can come. We'll slip off and go for a ride." Johnny said, "You got it." The music was ending and Garth returned to the stage. He finished his concert.

The seven men along with Colonel Hill, Captain Randolf and First Lieutenant Wooley went to the party. It was put on by the base commander, Air Force General Scott Lewison. When the ten men arrived at the party they were met by the deputy post commander, Colonel Duane Whittman. There were a lot of people there. Officers and everyone connected with the show. There was plenty of food and drink. Most of the people there made it a point to meet the seven men. When they first arrived they felt uncomfortable but soon relaxed. They told and listened to soldiers' stories. The men were actually having fun.

Soon Garth approached Johnny. They shook hands. Garth said, "Hey, are you guys about ready to get out of here. I want to check out your machines." They all left and headed over to the motor pool. They checked out eight quads. They went over the basics with the star. He caught on fast. Soon all eight men were riding. Colonel Hill, Captain Randolf and First Lieutenant Wooley stood and watched. They just putted around. Garth asked, "how fast will they go?" Bobby and Chad Duncan throttled down, brought up a couple of wheelies and took off. Garth said, "That's too fast for me." They rode for about twenty minutes. Garth's manager showed up. He said,

170

"The plane is ready." Garth thanked the men. He told Johnny, "Look me up when you get home." Then he got in the Humvee and left. After they put the quads up, Colonel Hill said, "How about a drink?" He had taken a couple of bottles of wine from the party. The men sat down and passed the bottles around. Colonel Hill said, "We sure are going to miss you guys around here." Captain Randolf added, "Yeah, things won't be quite the same." Bobby said, "Well, if you need us you know where to find us." They talked for what seemed like hours. Colonel Hill said, "Well, I'm going to bed." The rest of them joined him. On the way back to the barracks they all whistled the Army song.

The next morning the entire quad unit met and had breakfast. They all said their good byes. After that they parted company. The quad team had briefings to go to. Bobby and the others had some out processing to do. They had to get medically checked out. Especially since they had been exposed to possible chemical contamination. They all checked out fine. They made a trip over to the post JAG officer to review their new contract doing interviews for newspapers, magazines and television shows. They were assured of some time off to spend with their families. It was October now. They were assured by March, April at the latest, they would be done. They had a heavy schedule planned for them. They would be given three days when they got home to visit family and friends. Everything looked okay. They signed and headed to the plane. It was a C-5 Galaxy. It had just brought in another load of supplies and men. They would be taking their quads with them. As they approached the plane they saw an awesome site. The entire quad unit was lined up to see the plane off. The seven men felt proud that they could be a part of such a unit. They waved goodbye and boarded the plane. As the plane taxied the quad formed an honor guard until they reached the runway. Johnny said to himself may the force be with you.

CHAPTER 13

The plane took off. No one said anything for a long time. Then Johnny broke the silence. "Well, we made it, we're going home." Bobby said, "Yeah, I hope they make it home too." Chad Duncan added, "You gotta admire those guys." Buddy said, "I'll never forget them." Will said, "No way will I ever forget them. If I have kids some day I will tell them what we saw. If they don't cry, I'll beat them." Buddy said, "I wish there was a way to do away with war." Chad Hubanks said, "There will always be war as long as men like Saddam comes to power." Bobby said, "Yeah, it's been that way since the beginning of time. Even the Bible has lots of stories of war and of evil, power hungry men." Johnny said, "You read the Bible?" They all laughed. Bobby said, "No, my mom used to read it to me. But I'll tell you what. I'm gonna start." Johnny said, "Me too." Buddy said, "I'm not what you call a religious man, but I do believe in God and His goodness and mercy." Mick said, "I grew up going to church and when I got older I drifted away. Now maybe it's time to go back." Will said, "I used to go to church and sang in the choir. My voice changed and they asked me to sing solo." Chad Duncan said, "Yeah, so low they couldn't hear you." They all laughed again.

Their next stop was Germany. " public relations officer came and got them. They would be there in three hours. His name was Captain Gary Purceful. He was a nice enough guy. He took them to get haircuts and new uniforms. They also got some food and had a beer. He said, "I've been assigned to you guys. If there is anything you want or need, I can get it for you. There will be two of us going with you, myself and Staff Sergeant Bob Sullivan. He will join us at the plane. Do you have any questions for me?" Chad asked, "When do we get home?" The captain said, "We will be at Fort

Hood tomorrow morning." Bobby asked, "Do we have time to call home?" The captain answered, "Sure, you all can. I'll take you over to the phones." The airbase they were at was large, there was a lot of activity. Planes were coming and going, all filled with soldiers and equipment. They were going to Bosnia, Turkey, Kuwait, Afghanistan and many other places. Bobby thought, I'm no hero, these men and women are the heroes. He told the captain his thoughts. The captain said, "You know Bobby, you're right. They deserve the best, don't you think so?" Bobby said, "Of course I do." The captain said, "Well, a big part of that is having the people at home supporting them, giving them inspiration to do their best. You know, we are spread pretty thin. We need more men. That's where you guys come in. You guys are the inspiration needed for the support." Bobby said, "I think you underestimate the American people." The captain said, "Let me ask you a question. You are a quad racer. Are there others that inspired you to be a racer? Someone that you wanted to be like or even better than them?" Bobby said, "Oh yeah, there are a lot of great riders that I admired." The other men just listened, not saying a word. The captain continued, "When you were riding with your quad team, don't you think those men looked up to you and wanted to be as good as you are?" The light went on. Bobby said, "I guess I understand. I wanted to be a famous rider. I just didn't think it would happen this way." Johnny finally spoke up, "Bobby, you'd better take what you can get." The others laughed.

They arrived at the phones. All the men called home. " few minutes later they all returned. Chad said, "No one was at home." They all said the same thing. Bobby said, "Well, I guess when I walk in the front door they will be surprised." The captain said, "Well, it's time to get to the plane." Soon they were back in the air. They met Staff Sergeant Sullivan. He had a surprise for them. Snacks, beer and wine. Chad asked, "Do all the returning troops get this?" Staff Sergeant Sullivan said "Well, not exactly, but we try to take care of them. Captain Purceful wasn't sure if Bobby and the others were convinced of their importance. He continued talking to them. "You know, the people at home are scared. Fear can be your friend or your enemy. When you face your fear like you men did on the battlefield time and time again, it was a good thing. People at home will learn how you faced your fear. Maybe they will too." Bobby said, "Okay, you've got me convinced. I still have fear. I'm comfortable on the seat of a quad, but I'm scared to death I'll screw up in front of the reporters and the cameras." The captain said, "That's why Staff Sergeant Sullivan and I are here. You helped others learn how to become better riders, we will help you handle the press if you need us. From what I've seen of you guys, my job is going to be easy. Probably easier than you teaching others to ride." Bobby and the others had a beer and kicked back for a little sleep. They slept all night. They were awakened as Staff Sergeant Sullivan said, "We are about an hour from Fort Hood. I thought you might want to freshen up and have some breakfast." Buddy said, "I'm starving, what do you have?" Johnny said, "You're always hungry. Does it matter what it is?" The men all laughed, even Buddy. " little later the landing gear door opened and the gear dropped. Soon they were on the ground. The plane rolled to a stop and the rear door opened. The sun was bright as the men walked out into the open, they shielded their eyes.

What they saw was awe inspiring. There were hundreds of people. They were reminded of their return trip from the Phillippines, except this time it was for just seven of them. Bobby said, "Well, let's get to it." He looked over at Johnny, smiled, and said, "Let's roll."

The Army band was playing. " full battalion was on hand as an honor guard. The press stayed away for now. The men made their way to the stage. They walked in a line. When they all got on the stage, they snapped to attention, did a left face and saluted the dignitaries and brass. The officers on stage snapped to and returned the salute. Then the seven men did an about face. The crowd cheered them. That's when they all saw their families. All of them. General Johnson approached the microphone. "Honored guests, ladies and gentlemen, welcome to Fort Hood. My name is Major General Robert Johnson. I'm commander of Special Forces. I'm also the commander of these seven men we are here to honor. About eight months ago I had a crazy idea to start up a small elite quad force. That's when I brought in two men. Colonel Don Hill, who was away and Lieutenant Colonel Mike Purcell. They are the ones that gave life to my idea. Lieutenant Colonel Mike Purcell went out and got the finest machines possible for our men. Honda and Polaris stepped up to the challenge, quickly developing and producing quality tools for our men. Colonel Hill knew we needed someone to train our men. These seven men were the result. They were asked and stepped up to the challenge. Within two months they transformed

174

twenty four special operations soldiers into a force to be dealt with. Towards the end of the training a couple of situations arose that required our quad force. We asked these seven men to lend a hand on the missions. They stepped up to the challenge. As a result, maybe thousands of lives may have been saved. We thanked them and they went home. Two and a half months later we received a whole new batch of high tech ATV's. We also doubled the size of our quad unit. We once again called on these men to train our troops. Well, one thing led to another. These seven men became more involved. They have been on several dangerous missions. Their accomplishments have been amazing. One example before I shut up, on their last mission they were on a routine patrol. They discovered a large enemy force, over four hundred men. These men, with the help of the others on the eighteen man patrol captured one hundred eighty enemy soldiers, earning them all the Silver Star that I would like to present to them now." The crowd went wild. The general walked over to the men. He began presenting them their medals. The cameras started clicking. He asked the men if they and their families would join him for a barbecue later. Of course they couldn't refuse. Other officials on the stage welcomed them back and congratulated them. The Army band struck up the theme for the unit, The Magnificent Seven.

After the ceremony the families came up to them. They hugged and kissed. Chad found Charlotte and Bobby found Jill. Chad Hubanks even found his girl Brigette. All the while photographers took pictures. Not one reporter interrupted them, at the request of the Army. They all were promised interviews after they had spent three days with their families. Vans were waiting to take the families away. Places had been made to accommodate the families.

CHAPTER 14

It was around noon when the seven men and their families reached guest housing. The housing was a permanent thing at Fort Hood. For temporary visitors that only spend a few days at the Fort. All of the larger bases had them, kind of like a hotel. The rooms were modestly furnished. They were scheduled to be at the general's barbecue at three o'clock p.m. It was Thursday, they didn't have to report back until 0800 Monday.

Since Bobby found Jill in the crowd she hasn't left his side. Bobby's mother, Sandy, said, "We are all so proud of you, all of you. Your pictures have been in every major magazine and newspaper. Jill and I have been busy gathering articles about you guys." Bobby's face got red from embarrassment. He said, "Well, I guess you're really going to be busy for awhile. We are going to be spending the next few months travelling around the country giving interviews, going on talk shows and putting on shows." Jill said, "That sounds exciting. Will you get any time off?" Bobby said with a smile, "They promised us we would but we haven't seen our schedule yet. I figure we will be real busy for a month and then things will slow down quite a bit, especially with other things fixing to happen." Bobby's dad said, "It's going to get real hairy, isn't it?" Bobby said, "Yeah, dad, it is. I saw a lot of troop movement. That battalion they used for our honor guard today I heard was leaving in two weeks. That's a tank battalion." Sandy said, "Well, I'm just glad you're home and in one piece." Bobby replied, "Thanks, Mom. I guess I'm glad too." Jill said, "You guess, what does that mean?" Bobby said, "You know, I missed all of you so much. I don't know if I can explain it." Bobby's dad said, "I know what he's talking about. He feels guilty for coming home and the rest of the unit he served in is still over there. I understand, son." Bobby said, "Thanks, dad. I knew you would understand. One good thing though, they are being pulled off the front line." Sandy tried to change the subject. She said, "You look thin, have you ben eating?" Bobby saw what his mother was doing. "Mom, I've always been thin. But actually I have been eating well except when we had to eat MRE's. I have missed your cooking though." He thought he had better throw that in. Sandy said, "Jill is a good cook. She really helps out around the house." Bobby looked at Jill and said, "I'll bet she's good at a lot of things." He tried to embarrass her. It didn't work. Jill said, "Well, if you're lucky you may get to find out." It backfired on him. His face turned red. Bobby said, "Well, I need a shower." He looked at Jill and smiled. "" cold shower." He finally got to her. Her face turned red. He laughed as he walked towards the bathroom. She said, "You got me." They all got ready to go to the party.

All seven men and their families loaded up and drove over to the barbe- cue. They were all greeted by the general and his wife. Introductions were made. The general asked, "Would you seven men please do me a favor?" Bobby answered for the whole group. "What do you want us to do, sir?" The general said, "Those two teenaged boys over there are dying to meet you and get your autographs." Bobby smiled and said, "Not a problem." The seven men walked over and introduced themselves. The boys' eyes lit up. Each man took his turn and shook their hands. The younger boy said, "Would you sign our T-shirts that say 'An Army of One'?" They handed them a marker. The boys were clearly excited. When the seven men fin- ished the boys thanked them. They went over to show their father. The general looked up at Bobby and the others and mouthed the words "Thank you'. Bobby just grinned. The seven men rejoined their families. They had already begun fixing plates of food. The setting was very informal. The food was set up buffet style. They sat down at a real long table. As they ate several people came by and welcomed the seven men back. All seven men sat together since the party was in their honor. They all sat and talked and were having a good time. Captain Purceful came by. He asked, "I was won- dering if you all have made plans?" Everyone said, "We're just playing it by ear." Then he asked, "How would all of you like to go to a football game Saturday?" Buddy said, "What football game and where's it at?" Captain Purceful said, "It's a college game between Texas and Oklahoma." Bobby looked over at his dad, his eyes lit up. He had always wanted to go to that game. Bobby said, "That game is always sold out. Where did you get the seats for this many people and where are they?" Captain Purceful said, "Well, we are a television sponsor for the game. As part of the deal we've got over fifty seats set aside for us. I happened to get my hands on them. I can get more. The seats are between the forty and fifty yard lines about eight rows up." Bobby said, "I'm game, what about the rest of you?" They all agreed to go. To them it sounded like fun. Captain Purceful said, "The Army will foot the bill for the hotel rooms, reservations have already been made. There's only one little catch." Bobby thought, oh boy, here it comes. The captain continued, "They want you seven to act as honor guard for the flag." Bobby looked at his friends. They all smiled and nodded their heads. Bobby said, "We can do that." The captain said, "Great, Ill set everything up. You can use the Army vans for transportation." Jill asked Bobby, "My dad would love to go to that game. Do you think my parents could come? It would be a good time for our parents to meet." Bobby said, "I'll go ask. Be right back." He went and found Captain Purceful and asked him about Jill's parents. The captain knew it was important for Bobby. He said, "Sure, what's two more people? I can make the reservations for them but they will have to pay for the room." Bobby said, "Cool. Thanks a lot." He told Jill what the captain said. She said, "My dad will be so happy." She pulled out her cell phone and called her parents.

After they finished eating the general had arranged for a band. It was a country band. Charlotte said to Chad, "You probably won't like this." Chad said, "I'm getting to where I like country music." He told her about the USO shows. She was impressed. The party lasted till about 1800 hours (6 p.m.). Everyone had a good time. The family members got to know each other. Jill tried to teach Bobby the two step. The general even danced with Bobby's mom.

After the party they all went back to their rooms. Bobby's parents decided to go for a walk. They were joined by Chad Duncan's parents. Bobby still had his truck there on base. He and Jill decided to go for a drive. They drove out to the lake where they had met. They got as close as they could to the bluff overlooking the lake. Jill grabbed a couple of blankets. Bobby had stopped and bought a bottle of wine. They walked to the bluff. It was a cool but clear October evening. The moon was full. Jill spread one of the blankets on the ground. They sat down. Bobby poured them a glass of wine. The lake was beautiful. It was like glass and the moon reflected off of it.

178

They huddled up under the second blanket and drank the wine. Bobby looked at Jill. She looked back into his eyes. They were clear and blue. They kissed and hugged each other. Bobby said, "Jill, I've seen a lot in the last couple of months. I've faced death more than once. There has not been a day go by I haven't thought about you. I know we haven't known each other very long. I know there is a lot you don't know about me. What I do know about you, I love. You're caring, funny, we like to do the same things. I feel like I want you in my life from now on. Oh shoot, I am trying to ask you to marry me." She answered, "It's true, we haven't known each other very long. The first time I met you, I knew there was something wonderfully special about you. I feel as though I've known you all my life. There's a lot of maybes and unanswered questions. I feel like that is all small potatoes. I love you very much. Yes, I'll be your wife, if you promise one thing. If you find you don't love me anymore, tell me." He said, "I love you now and forever." They kissed, they held each other and they talked for hours. They both wanted to make love but didn't. Their relationship wasn't going to be sexually oriented. They talked about children. Both wanted kids. They talked about their future, both near and in the distance. They both enjoyed just talking to each other, rare in the fast paced world we live in. They both expressed their fears. Bobby had put away his Army pay for the most part. They would use some of that to buy rings. They decided to wait to set a date after the first of the year, when hopefully things would start to settle down. They were both passionate about how they felt about each other, but wouldn't let passion consume them. They hoped friends and family wouldn't try to pressure them into a quick marriage. The conversation was serious, the text was serious, but both did it with usual light hearted antics. It was getting late and they knew they would have a full day on Friday. So they loaded up and drove back to the base.

The next morning they got up. All the families were to meet for breakfast before heading to Dallas. Jill's parents also met them. Bobby and Jill introduced them to everyone. Bobby looked at Jill, she smiled and nodded. Bobby stood up. "Everyone, I have, I mean we have an announcement to make. I have asked Jill to marry me and she said...." Before he could finish, she stood up and said, "Yes." Everyone clapped and the congratulations began. Bobby's parents and Jill's parents seemed genuinely happy for them. Chad Duncan asked, "Well, have you set a date?" Bobby said, "No, we have decided to wait until after the first of the year." Both sets of parents seemed to be pleased at his answer.

Breakfast was over. They loaded up and headed north to Dallas. In the van, the trip was filled with all sorts of questions. Bobby and Jill answered each one. By the time they reached Dallas everything was cool, to put it in Bobby's terms. Everyone was genuinely happy for the two of them.

When they got to Dallas they all checked into the hotel. The men and women decided to split up for the afternoon. The women all went shopping. The men decided to go check out Commerce Street. Later they all met back at the hotel for a late night supper. That night everyone discussed the day's events. The men had chosen sides for the game the next day. They had a lot of fun picking at each other about who was going to win. The women talked about the day's purchases. Captain Purceful had come by to drop off uniforms and a schedule for where the seven needed to be and at what time.

The next morning the seven men put on their Class " uniforms. They looked sharp and went to the stadium. They also took a change of clothes with them. Their families would come later.

At the stadium they practised on the flag ceremony. Staff Sergeant Sullivan and Captain Purceful were there to assist. While they were practising their moves some of the players from both teams showed up for warm up drills. Captain Purceful let it slip who the seven men were. It was hard to tell who was more excited to meet, the quad riders meeting the players, or the players meeting the quad riders. All of them exchanged autographs. Bobby got autographs from players from both teams. Some for his dad and some for Jill's dad. The stadium started to fill. Soon it was show time. Before the seven men came out on the field, they were introduced as the honor guard. The tens of thousands of people cheered them as they walked out with the flags. The seven men felt extremely proud to be the honor guard. They marched out to the center of the field and the National Anthem was played. At the conclusion the men wheeled around and marched off the field. The crowd cheered them and the flag as they departed.

Soon the game was on. It was almost the end of the first quarter before they rejoined their families. They said they had been signing autographs. It's not very often at a football game that the honor guard gets asked for autographs.

The game was a good one as usual. The men were enjoying every minute

180

of it. The women could have cared less but they were polite and yelled when everyone else did. Bobby's mom, Sandy, at the end of the game asked, "Who won?" His dad just looked at her. They all laughed. She could care less about the game. She just came to watch her son and have a good time. Jill's mom confessed later she didn't know who won either.

After the game all the parents wanted to go eat. The younger people decided to let them go and they would come later. The seven men, Charlotte, Jill and Brigette decided to take in the state fair. They all had a ball. They played games, did the rides and ate corn dogs. Jill told Bobby about some rings she had found. Bobby said, "Why didn't you buy them. I trust your judgement." She said, "That's what your mom said so I bought them." Bobby said, "I'll pay her back. Do you have them with you?" She said, "Yes, they're here in my purse." She got them out and showed them to him. He took the engagement ring right there in the midway. He got down on one knee and placed it on her finger. Everyone around them began to clap for them.

The next morning was Sunday. Everyone got up for breakfast. They checked out of the hotel and headed back to Fort Hood. They arrived in time for the church service. They all went and listened to Chaplin Noe. The place was packed with men and families. The men would be shipping out in a couple of days. Chaplin Noe prayed for their safe return. So did Bobby and his friends.

That afternoon the seven men took their families to the airport. There were a lot of hugs, handshakes and tears. After they dropped them off, they returned the vans to the motor pool, all except one that they kept. Buddy said, "I could use a drink." The rest of them agreed. They drove over to Pete's. They each had a couple of drinks. They weren't in a party mood, though. They knew that starting tomorrow they would be busy.

They went back to the family guest quarters. They had a message for them. It listed the next day's events. Starting with a breakfast briefing at 0800.

CHAPTER 15

This morning the men got up early. They decided to try and get in the right frame of mind. They found a unit they could do physical training with. It was a cool morning. The physical training started with a series of stretching exercises. They worked out for half an hour then went on a five mile run. It was a tough run. None of them had run much in days. When they finished they cleaned up and packed. Their schedule called for a flight to California Lake in the afternoon. It was 0745, time to meet the captain for the breakfast briefing.

The men met at the Officer's Club in a room off by itself. As they walked in the captain greeted them. He asked that they take a seat at the table. He said, "Someone will be here to take your order in a minute." He continued, "I hope you had a good time in Dallas and the game." They all answered positively. He said, "Good. Now we need to get down to business. We have scheduled a press conference at 10:00." "waiter came in. He took the breakfast orders. The captain again spoke. "Here's what is going to happen. We will go over to your old training room. The reporters will be seated there. Also your ATV's will be on display. You will enter the room and walk up and sit down at a small stage. You'll walk up and sit down at a table that is covered. On the front of the table will be a banner that says "An Army of One". The reporters have been given bios of you. Oh yes, before you sit down I want you, from left to right, introduce yourselves. After you say your name please sit down." Their breakfast was served and they started eating. The captain never skipped a beat. "The reporters will call you by name. They will ask you questions, some personal, some about you in the Army. You can answer questions about missions. Don't give dates or locations. That's important, okay? After the interview they may want pictures.

We will go to lunch. You guys are free to go anywhere for lunch. I'll bring the press here. After lunch we will do some action shots. This evening we will load onto a C-130. Our destination is California. We will spend a solid week, maybe longer, out there. Any questions?" Bobby said, "Yes, would you pass the pepper?" It stunned the captain for a moment. He smiled and they laughed.

It was time for the press conference. The men walked into the room and lined up behind the chairs. From left to right, Chad Hubanks, Buddy Bishop, Chad Duncan, Bobby Duck, Johnny Hale, Will Valance and Mick Smiley. They were ready. The reporters asked one man one question and so on. The first asked Chad Hubanks, "How does it feel to be home?" Chad said, "It's all better here at home in the US"." Next, "Buddy, how did you guys get the name Magnificent Seven?" He answered, "When we started teaching with eight men. Harvey Light was our eighth. He got hurt and couldn't ride anymore. We were sitting with some of the other guys and one of them said there was eight, now there is seven. Another man said, yeah, the Magnificent Seven. It was on from there." Captain Purceful was thinking, so far so good. The next question was for Chad Duncan. "Chad, can you tell us how you got here?" He said, "Yes sir. Colonel Don Hill recruited us. He told us the unit was being started. They needed someone to teach his men how to ride. He told us we were needed. We've talked and we all feel the same way. The way we see it, it's the least we could do for our country. We couldn't pass it on to someone else." The reporters loved his answer. Next was Bobby's turn. He was asked, "How does it feel to be a hero?" Bobby thought for a second, "I don't think of myself as a hero anymore than the rest of the men and women that serve our country. I guess we've done some good, but not any more than any one of them wouldn't do in our place." Johnny was asked about his rank as a Warrant Officer. "How did you men get the rank of Warrant Officer and has it caused any hard feelings against you since you have only been in the Army a few months?" Johnny said, "Sir, when the Army contracted us to teach, they gave us this rank. It was to separate us from our students. Our contract was for only two to three months. After our second mission the President gave us this rank permanently, as a token of his appreciation. No one has shown any bad feelings toward us or our rank. The men we have served with are professionals and they don't get into petty jealously. They respect us and we respect them." Mick was next.

He was asked, "Mick, can you tell us what you did to earn your Silver Star?" Mick said, "Sir, I'll try. We were on patrol and spotted a large enemy force headed toward our camp. We called in and warned them. The enemy force was large but they were moving in small groups to try and avoid detection. Bobby actually had the idea. We just all participated. Anyway, we managed to capture one hundred and eighty enemy soldiers with an eighteen man patrol." Captain Purceful had said no numbers but he let that one slide. Now it was Will's turn. "Will, you're one of the top racers in the country. Your race quad must be fast. How would you rate the Army's quads?" Will said, "Sir, Lieutenant Colonel Purcell and his team, along with Honda and Polaris, have developed two of the finest machines I have ridden. They are fast and well balanced for handling. I rate them excellent." They all had gotten through the first round of questions. Captain Purceful was very pleased. The question and answer session continued for the next two hours. Finally they concluded with some pictures. They took a lot of pictures, individual pictures and group pictures on and off their machines. It was 1300 hours before they broke for lunch. An hour later they were back taking more pictures, this time action shots. The seven men thought at least they were getting to ride some.

Late that afternoon the men boarded the airplane bound for California. The week they were supposed to spend there stretched into three weeks. They were filming commercials for the Army. The commercial turned out great. They were filmed partly on location in the desert. It showed the men riding their quads hard in the dunes. Each man had a segment. At the end of each individual segment, it showed a close up of that man. He would simply say, "I am an Army of One." Then there was a shot of all seven men jumping off a dune. At the end it showed all seven men on their quads and they said in unison, "We are an Army of One." The men had fun doing the filming.

Every once in awhile, they would feel guilty about leaving their friends behind. Captain Purceful knew this. He managed to get updates on the unit's activity for them. They had been used as spotters for the Air force. " squad sized patrol would be parachuted into an area then ride their quads to the target area and give target locations. Then they would ride out of the area to be picked up by large helicopters. They were dangerous missions but had become pretty routine. The buildup of men and equipment kept increasing.

Saddam spent most of his time down in one of his holes, like the snake he is, willing to sacrifice his people for his personal glory. He has no concept of the value of life. He's just concerned with his own.

Anyway, the seven men worked until almost Thanksgiving. Then they got a break. They were going home for almost a week. Then it was on to New York for a date with talk show host David Letterman. The men said their goodbyes and headed home.

Bobby and Johnny were on the same flight. They were met at the airport by their families. Bobby told Johnny, "Maybe we can get together one day and just ride for fun." Johnny said, "Cool, give me a call." Jill was there, she looked great. They hugged and kissed. He hugged his mom and dad. On the way home he asked Jill, "Well, do you feel the same?" She said, "No, I love you more each time I see you." They both smiled at each other. Over the next several days they visited with families and friends, two grand-mothers, a grandfather, assorted aunts, uncles, cousins, and kids of cousins. Also, both of Bobby's sisters and his brother-in-law.

Jill said she missed her parents, so Bobby sent tickets to her parents and her brother. Her brother's name was Bill. He was her twin brother. Her family stayed through Thanksgiving but left early the next morning. Bobby said he thought he gained five pounds from so much eating.

The next day was beautiful. They all went riding, Bobby, his dad, Jill, Johnny and some of their friends. They had a ball. The weather was cool and crisp but the sun was out and it felt good. Bobby said to Jill, "We are going to New York next week. Would you like to meet me there?" Jill said, "Sure, that sounds like fun." She would be off from school for another few days. She had considered going home for an extended visit but New York with Bobby was a better offer. They called Chad and Charlotte to see if she could come too. Chad said, "We had the same idea and were going to call you."

The following Monday morning Bobby, Jill and Johnny boarded a flight to Dallas. There the seven men met with the captain. They loaded onto a cargo plane again. Jill and Charlotte flew commercial.

In New York the men had some press interviews again. Their big inter-view would come on the Letterman show the next day. Captain Purceful arranged for the seven, Jill and Charlotte a tour of the city. They were amazed at the shear number of people in the city. Up until now Dallas was the biggest place they had been. They enjoyed meeting people and seeing the sights. They were proud when they saw the Statue of Liberty. They were angered when they saw the place where the Twin Towers once stood.

The next day they went to the Ed Sullivan Theater to do their thing on the Letterman show. Letterman did a bit on them telling the folks about their heroes. Then he said, "Bring 'em out." Six of them marched out to meet him. He looked and said, "I thought there were seven of you." Then Buddy rode his quad out on the stage. He said, "Sorry I'm late guys. I got caught in traffic," The audience loved it. Letterman asked a series of questions. The men answered each one, questions like what did you do before you became heroes? They all told him what they did. Then he asked a question none of them had thought about. "Are any of you planning on staying in the "Army?" Johnny answered, "We are just contract help." Bobby added, "I don't know if the Army wants to keep us around. We are an awful lot of trouble." A few minutes later the show was over.

That night after dinner Bobby and Jill were talking. He said, "You know I've been thinking about one of Letterman's questions." Jill said, "I know, the one abut staying in the Army. Bobby, I love you. I want you to do what makes you happy. I will go anywhere as long as we can have our time together." Bobby said, "I love you, too. I don't even know if the Army wants me. If they do offer, I want to be involved with the quads. We will just wait and see. I won't do anything until we talk." She said, "Fair enough."

The next day Charlotte and Jill flew home. The seven men switched to a bus and a truck to haul their quads. They spent the next three weeks on the road. They travelled up and down the East Coast. They never stayed more than a day in any one spot. They would set up a display at a military base or a high school. Sometimes it would be a shopping mall. The shopping malls were the worst. They were crowded with Christmas shoppers. Everywhere they went the people were friendly and supportive. They answered the same questions over and over. Finally they were in Atlanta, which was their last stop before they could go home for the holidays. They would be off until the third of January, then they would meet in Dallas again to continue their tour.

The men were tired, they needed a break. Bobby said, "I'm worn smooth out. I'll betcha though any of the old unit would trade places with us in a heartbeat." They all agreed. They decided to send the unit a card and a care package of a case of bourbon. They all chipped in. Captain Purceful said he would make sure they get it by Christmas.

CHAPTER 16

Bobby got home two days before Christmas. Jill was in Texas visiting her folks. She would be back the day after. He spent the next two days just resting, not doing much of anything. He had a good talk with his dad. He said, "Dad, I've been thinking about the future. I know Jill will support me because we've talked some." His dad just listened to his son. "I've been thinking of staying in the Army if they let me keep working with the quads. If not, I'm going back to school and continue that way. What do you think?" Bobby's dad thought for a minute then said, "Well son, I know you will do well in whatever you do. I think it's important to do what makes you happy. You must consider Jill since you are going to marry her. You have done well for yourself in the Army. But remember you love to race. You haven't done much of that lately. You've had tons of offers from people who want to sponsor your racing. If you stay in the Army, I think your racing days will be over. You may be sent all over the world. Jill might be behind you now but what about later on, especially when you start having kids? You know there are a lot of ways to serve your country. This is a decision you'll have to make for yourself. Whatever you decide, I will back you." Bobby said, "Thanks, dad, I don't know if the Army will even make me an offer. I just keep seeing men and women going into harm's way. I keep asking myself what can I do? You know, dad, we owe them so much." Bobby's dad said, "You're right, we do. The best thing we can do is show them respect and gratitude. Never forget what they do for us. We work for an airline. The terrorists have knocked us out of the sky. That would be terrible if our country would let a handful of terrorists destroy an entire industry. We must not let this happen. What would happen if terrorists infected a few cows or even chickens with bio virus? Would we stop eating beef or chicken? Some would, I'm sure. They would say "I'm scared for my family'. What I'm trying to get at is, we are American. We must not let terrorism ruin our lives. Our military is doing their part. We at home must do ours. We must all stand together and say "Hey, give it your best shot. We'll kick your butt'." Then he said, "I'll get off my soap box now." Bobby said, "You're right dad, we do live in the greatest nation. I've seen it all across the country." Bobby's dad said, "Son, I'm very proud of you and what you've done. With your acts of bravery you have saved many lives. Now we'd better get ready. We've got to go to grandma's. I'd hate to see the headlines tomorrow, 'Hero is beaten by grannie's broom'." Bobby laughed. The rest of the night went well. All the relatives were there. Everyone wanted to know what Bobby was doing. They were all happy and proud of him.

The next morning was Christmas. Bobby got up first thing and called Jill. They both said they missed each other. She told him her flight number for the next day. They talked for awhile and then hung up. He told his mom, "I sure do miss her." Sandy said, "She's a wonderful girl and I should count my blessings." That afternoon before dinner they all prayed for world peace.

The next day Bobby went to pick Jill up at the airport. They spent the next few days together. They decided on a wedding date. They told everyone that they would announce the date New Year's Eve. Bobby's mom was going to have a party in his honor.

That night she had it all spread out. Their house was packed with friends and family. About five minutes before midnight Bobby said, "Jill and I have set a date. May first." One of his friends said, "Hey, don't we have a race that weekend?" They all laughed and rang in the New Year. Three days later Bobby was back in Dallas. Buddy said, "Let's roll."

CHAPTER 17

They loaded on an airplane. It was back to New York. Captain Purceful said he had some news. He said, "First, we are going to turn you guys loose the first of February." They all cheered. "Second, Colonel Hill and his men will be home by the end of January. I've made arrangements for us to be there." More good news, they cheered again. "Third, we are going in after Saddam by the end of the week." The mood changed. Buddy said, "I hope this thing doesn't last long." Chad Duncan said, ""men brother, but it has to be done." Will asked, "Has the quad unit's mission changed?" Captain Purceful said, "No, as a matter of fact, with our armor moving in they are in a standby mode." Bobby said, "Thank God for that." The captain said, "Well, let's get to our mission. We are going back to New York for a spot on the show 20/20. After that we go to Chicago, then across the Midwest, the Plains and end at Fort Hood. Any questions? No, Buddy, I don't have any pepper." They all smiled. Johnny said, "Well, it wouldn't hurt my feelings if the war ends before we do February first." Mick said, "Mine either brother." Captain Purceful said, "I know you guys are close to the quad unit. This plane is equipped with Sat Com. Why don't we give them a call. It's a secure line." That brought their spirits back up. They called and Staff Sergeant Ketcher answered the phone. They put it on a speaker phone so they all could talk and listen. Bobby said, "Hey dude, what's up?" Staff Sergeant Ketcher said "Bobby, is that you?" He sounded excited to hear from them. Johnny said, "Yeah man, it's all of us. We wanted to check on you guys to see how everything's going." Staff Sergeant Ketcher said, "Everything was good until last night. We had two men injured. Colonel Hill is over at the hospital now. Staff Sergeant Fomby and Sergeant Wright were injured when they hit a land mine." Mick asked, "Are they okay?" Staff Sergeant Ketcher said, "Yeah, I heard that the quads flipped when they hit the mine. Staff Sergeant Fomby has a concussion and a broken collar bone. Sergeant Wright got some shrapnel in his upper thigh. They'll both be okay." Bobby asked, "Has anyone else been hurt?" Staff Sergeant Ketcher said, "No, it's really been pretty calm around here since you guys pulled out." Chad Duncan said, "Hey, we hear you guys are coming home soon." Staff Sergeant Ketcher said, "That's what we hear too. Soon they won't need us. We hear rumors of other places. Not until we get rested up first." Will said, "Hey, we'll meet you at Fort Hood for a drink." Staff Sergeant Ketcher said, "You've got a date. The guys here sure liked the bourbon you sent. Well hey, listen, Top wants me for something. I'll tell everyone you called." They hung up the phones. They were feeling much better about the situation for their unit. Captain Purceful said, "It sounds like they are alright. Anybody hungry?" They all said yes.

" couple of hours later they landed in New York. The men would get a briefing on the news show. The taping would begin the next day. It was cold in New York. The city had just gotten a wet blanket of snow.

The next day they started the interview. Several questions would be asked, they would edit it all later. They started out with an introduction of who they were and what they were. "Folks, here with us tonight is a group of men. There are seven of them. They are called The Magnificent Seven. They are connected by one thing. Riding and racing ATV's. These men were hired by the U.S. Army to teach special forces soldiers how to ride. ATV's were specially built for them by Honda and Polaris. You won't find these machines at your dealership. These guys were contracted for a period of two to three months. They got permission to train with the special forces troops. They thought it would be fun and help them in determining how to help them on the ATV's. While nearing the end of training things changed. Tonight we hear their story." The seven men are seated at a table. "Bobby, what made you want to continue with the special forces unit? You were under no obligation." Bobby said, "We got into the Army under special circumstances. When that first mission came down our unit was just supposed to be observers. Things happened that changed all of that. The next mission was a must for us. They needed our help. We couldn't turn them down. Our country needed us." "Buddy, after you left you came back. Why?" Buddy said, "The Army got new quads and more riders. We were asked to help teach the new riders on the more powerful machines. I knew if my friends came back, I would too. After all, you can't have a Magnificent Six. It just doesn't sound right." "Johnny, how did you end up in the Middle East?" "The unit had been split, some of the new riders were sent. We went over to teach them." The questions went on and on. There was file footage of the men in training. Questions were asked about patriotism, the machines and others in the unit. They worked all day on the interview. When they were finished, they were complimented by the entire staff of the show. One executive said, "You guys truly are magnificent. You make me proud to be an American. Thank you."

The next morning it was off to Chicago. They loaded onto the bus. They visited several towns and cities in the Midwest and the Plains. Time passed quickly. Things began winding down. Soon they were entering Fort Hood. Their friends were due to land the next day. Captain Purceful had one more meeting with the men. "Tomorrow will be your last day with us. After that you will be on your own. I must tell you, my time with you has reinforced my faith in our country. If ever you need my help, please don't hesitate to call me. I've been given my next assignment. " crew from 20/20 will be here filming your unit's return. They will include the footage with your story, so behave yourselves.

The next day the quad unit returned home. They looked tired but excited to be home. They didn't have as much fanfare as Bobby and the others. It wasn't their way. Most just wanted to be home with families. General Johnson did give a brief speech welcoming them back. He also praised the way they did their job. All of American is behind them. He thanked them for making the unit a success. Colonel Hill approached the microphone. He said, "Men, it has been both an honor and a privilege to have served with you. I would be honored even more if you would join me in a group photo." He added, "Would the seven men responsible for the success of our mission please join us. The entire unit was photographed by the base photographer. After that they started going to their families. Bobby and his friends watched as they were reunited. Staff Sergeant Ketcher walked by. He said, "Pete's 1900 hours." They knew what he meant. The seven men spent the rest of the afternoon driving around Fort Hood. They talked about what they had been through together. They relived the high points. They went by their old training site. Bobby said, "I'll never forget this place." Will said, "I'll never forget all of these guys." Buddy said, "I'll never forget you guys." Chad Hubanks said, "I'll never forget MRE's." They all laughed. Will said, "I'm hungry. Let's eat." They all went and had a steak.

They got over to Pete's about 1900 hours. When they walked in they were surprised. The entire quad unit was there. They figured ten or fifteen guys would be there, not the entire unit. "As they walked in First Sergeant Holliman yelled, "Attention." They all saluted the seven men. Captain Randolf said, "You think we would let you go without saying goodbye? We all owe you our lives." For the first time the seven men were speechless. Specialist Money said, "What's the matter, cat got your tongue?" They all laughed. Bobby said, "Man is this a surprise. I can't believe it, you guys spend months from your families, when you get back you come here." Staff Sergeant Culp said, "Who do you think sent us." They laughed again. Colonel Hill said, "We are a strong unit. I would put us up against any other unit. We wouldn't be here if it weren't for you guys. You seven are one of us and always will be." Johnny said, "Sir, we all feel the same way. When we left the unit in Turkey it felt like we had just cut off an arm." Colonel Hill said, "When we sent you home, it wasn't because we wanted to. You guys were needed here at home. We need public support. You guys helped provide it." Staff Sergeant Ketcher raised his glass. He said, "To The Seven." The rest of the room raised their glasses. They said in unison, "To The Seven." The jukebox played their song. Bobby, Johnny, Mick, Will, Chad, Buddy and Chad raised their glasses and said, "An Army of One." The soldiers did the same. They spent the rest of the night visiting with their friends. The next morning Staff Sergeant Sullivan came to take them to the airport. The men got into the van. Johnny was the last. He took one more look around. Then he jumped in the van, looked at his friends and smiled. He said, "Let's roll."

EPILOGUE

This book is fiction but it could be true. Everyday, all over the world, men and women are ready to put their lives on the line for you and me. Most don't have exciting jobs, but each one of them is important. In a lot of places in my book our heroes are having a meal. Well, some guy is back there cooking it for them. Some other guy is pulling guard duty while they sleep. Someone else is driving that tanker truck bringing them fuel for their ATV's. They all are volunteers. No one makes them do it. So the next time you see someone in a uniform, go up and shake their hand or pat them on the back. Believe me, that goes a long way. I served during the Gulf War in 1991. My job wasn't glamorous. I drove a forklift and worked in a warehouse. If I didn't do my job though, the guys on the front line might not get the spare parts or ammunition they needed. My daughter served too, as a cook in a hospital unit. The doctors and nurses couldn't do their job if they didn't have anything to eat. The patients couldn't survive on tender loving care alone. It takes a total force to win.

I hope you enjoyed my book. Our country loves heroes, from Sergeant York to Lieutenant Audey Murphy. It's good to have someone to look up to. I tried to show the courage and ingenuity of the American fighting man. Maybe you can take a piece of this courage with you in your lives. Courage to invest in a new business. Or maybe the courage to do something about the way others do things that aren't right. We are a strong people with hopes and dreams. Do something to help others reach their dreams and goals.

Thank you
Eddy Duck

ISBN 1553953135-4

9 781553 953135